Mum & Dad

JOANNA TROLLOPE

Mum & Dad

MACMILLAN

First published 2020 by Macmillan
an imprint of Pan Macmillan
The Smithson, 6 Briset Street, London EC1M 5NR
Associated companies throughout the world
www.panmacmillan.com

ISBN 978-1-5290-0338-3

1 3 5 7 9 8 6 4 2

A CIP catalogue record for this book is available from the British Library.

Typeset in Legacy by Palimpsest Book Production Ltd, Falkirk, Stirlingshire
Printed and bound by CPI Group (UK) Ltd, Croydon, CR0 4YY

Visit **www.panmacmillan.com** to read more about all our books
and to buy them. You will also find features, author interviews and
news of any author events, and you can sign up for e-newsletters
so that you're always first to hear about our new releases.

For the Arbuthnot family

CHAPTER ONE

This was Monica's favourite time of day, these early mornings – dawns, really, and surprisingly dark, even in southern Spain – when nobody except the village cockerels appeared to be up. The cockerels started an hour before she did, and the villagers took no notice of them, but Monica heard them with pleasure. They were a sort of signal to take her morning cup of tea, made with leaves sent from England, out onto the terrace and stand there, sipping, while the light slowly brightened below her to reveal the Rock of Gibraltar, like a great war horse plunging towards Africa, thirty kilometres away. It was miraculous, that moment. Every morning, without fail, through autumn mists and spring downpours, the rearing Rock and the cascading mountainsides down to it gave Monica a feeling of exultation that no place or landscape had ever given her in her life before. Not even the magnificence of the West Highlands, where she'd started life, sixty-eight years before. Life in Spain, and accommodating herself to her husband's stubbornness, hadn't exactly been easy, but this morning ritual of tea on the terrace while watching the day steal up on the night was one of the day's unlooked-for bonuses.

The terrace, of course, once it was fully light, revealed its perpetual neediness. Some plants – the disappointingly scentless plumbago, for example – seemed to have no trouble in thriving, tumbling over walls in extravagant abundance, dense pale blue flowerheads mingling with the deep, almost violet blue of the convolvulus, which grew everywhere, in profusion, if she didn't keep a sharp eye on it. But some bougainvilleas behaved, Monica thought, extremely neurotically, perpetually and fretfully shedding papery leaves and petals onto the terrace that she had to remind Pilar to sweep up. Pilar considered outdoors as another planet, a planet ruled by men with all their attendant idiosyncrasies, and properly inhabited by animals and machinery and weather. Outdoors was nothing to do with her. She said as much to Monica, volubly and constantly, banging her broom about the terrace. 'Why are you English so obsessed with stupid *flowers*? Can you *eat* them?'

Pilar had worked for Monica since 1994, when she had been a nineteen-year-old from the village with parents who could neither read nor write. Her father, who was still alive, kept rabbits for the table in a ruined shed, fattening them with bread and water in the dark. Monica had protested both to Pilar and to her father about the cruelty of keeping rabbits in such dreadful conditions, and the old man had stared at her, shaking his head, as if confronting someone certifiably insane. Monica had rounded on Pilar.

'The way you treat animals is a disgrace to humanity. It really is. Those poor, poor rabbits. Don't you understand?'

Pilar leaned on the mop she was using to wash the kitchen floor.

'You think it's cruel? If you want to see real cruelty, you

should go to North Africa, to the Rif Mountains. Those donkeys can hardly *move*, for their burdens!' She brandished the mop. 'Go and water your silly flowers.'

Sometimes, Monica thought she had had quite enough of Pilar. Just as she thought she had had quite enough of Gus, too. At twenty-three she'd had every sympathy with Gus's rage and despair at his own father's obtuse intractability and the consequent terrible quarrels that resulted in their abandoning England for Spain in 1993, old Gus bellowing that Spain, in all its post-Franco confusion, was welcome to his useless, disloyal eldest son. Old Gus would have been a figure of fun if he hadn't been so powerful and if her Gus hadn't craved his father's approval and affection so pitifully. It was old Gus who named the Spanish vineyard in the end too, the vineyard they'd had to sell everything in England to start, despite her objections.

'Don't you see?' she'd said pleadingly to Gus. 'Don't you see what he's doing? He's suggested Beacham's Bodega as a joke, a contemptuous joke. As if running a bodega is all you're fit for. As if we weren't having to leave two of our children at school in England—'

'Paid for by my father.'

'But I don't *want* him to!'

Gus looked away from her.

He said, quietly, 'All the same.'

'Do you even know what a bodega is?'

'No.'

'It's just a shop. A little shop, selling groceries and wine. It's a belittling name for a proper vineyard like you're planning. Can't you see that?'

Gus squinted past her.

3

'All the same,' he repeated, 'it alliterates. The Spanish can at least manage the initials.'

'Gus,' Monica said despairingly, 'why won't you admit the absolutely obvious?'

He had looked at her for the first time in that conversation. Still handsome Gus then, blond and blue-eyed with rolled-up shirtsleeves and bare feet in cotton espadrilles.

'Because,' he said, 'I actually think Beacham's Bodega is a very good name.'

And that was that. Sebastian and Katie stayed – miserably, in Katie's case – at their English schools and the rocky, unpromising stretch of virgin land just west of one of the famous pueblos blancos became their vineyard. Gus had done his homework, she had to give him that. The soil of the vineyard was almost identical to the soil of the Rioja region. There were two rivers nearby which cooled and watered the air and the earth. There were also crucial warm winds blowing up from Africa, but cooler winds at night, which would encourage the grapes Gus was planning on planting to develop the thick skins so beneficial to red wine.

He bought hundreds of Tempranillo vines, all of which had to be planted in the newly cleared, newly turned earth, five feet apart and positioned to shoot vertically. Along with four men hired from the village, Gus worked doggedly all the daylight hours, only stopping when Monica, adding the task of project managing the building of their future house to the business of being Gus's wife and the mother of three children, demanded he give his attention to some essential decision about construction.

'I don't care where the bathrooms are,' Gus said. 'You mind

about that far more than I do. You decide what you want and that's fine by me.'

'I want you to focus,' Monica said. 'It'll be your house as much as mine. I want you to be part of it.'

He was dusty and sweaty from planting. He had a ragged blue bandana tied around his throat, above a faded T-shirt. He'd leaned forward and kissed her.

'As long as you're in it, any house is fine by me.'

So she had designed the house – long and low to take advantage of the view – with occasional input from Jake, her youngest child. She had been thankful, on a daily basis, for this village girl called Pilar, who managed to clean their small village house, and rough launder their clothes, and who often arrived in the mornings with a basket of vegetables from her father's *huerta*, outside the village.

'A *huerta*?' Monica asked in her careful new Spanish.

'He goes there every day,' Pilar said, her arms full of sheets she'd dried on the bushes outside, 'to get away from my mum. All the men do. It's the only time they aren't nagged.'

'But I thought,' Monica said, 'that this was a society famous for machismo.'

'It is,' Pilar replied. She dumped the sheets on the table and began, rapidly, to fold them. She didn't look at Monica. 'Things go wrong for men . . .' She sucked her teeth. 'Wham, their women suffer.'

'But—'

'You have to accept,' Pilar said, still folding, 'you come from one culture. Here is another. Different. You want to live here? You accept.'

Over the years, Monica thought now, she'd got less good at accepting. At the beginning, she'd given way to Gus's determination, bent to submit to Pilar, worried endlessly about the children, how their parents' abrupt change of lifestyle was affecting them – had never stopped worrying, in fact, however good their Spanish was now, especially Jake's. For goodness' sake, Sebastian was forty-three and married with sons of his own. Katie – Monica felt the pang of remorseful anguish that she experienced every time she thought of Katie – was forty-one and had been living with Nic for almost twenty years now, and was the mother of three daughters. And Jake, darling, easy, sunny Jake, had finally married his Bella after all those years of living together because of Mouse, who was eighteen months old and whom Monica saw most days on FaceTime, putting bubbles on her head in the bath or drinking noisily from her sippy cup. Six grandchildren in England, even if Gibraltar airport was only just over an hour away. Six grandchildren, never mind three children and their three partners. Thank goodness, at least, that old Gus was finally dead and that her own parents, who had been admirably self-sufficient all their lives, had managed their final years in the same spirit of competence. 'You would hardly believe,' Monica's brother wrote to her after their father's death, 'the order in which he left their affairs. All I've had to do is follow his precise instructions. I don't know about you, but I'm left with the feeling that they chose to be strangers to everyone except each other, even their children. What do you want me to do with your share of the money from selling the house?'

'I propose,' Monica said to Gus, 'giving it to the children.'

He was hunched over his computer. The office, despite the occasional presence of a secretary who drove all the way from

Ronda, was crammed and chaotic, and had never moved from the tiny room next to the fermentation tanks. Gus was absolutely insistent on bioculture, on the organic nature of everything in the vineyard – when the grapes had been harvested in September, the vines were left to rot and then Grazalema sheep were turned out to finish the job – but that meticulousness didn't extend to his surroundings. Monica stood, as she often stood, leaning against the outer doorframe of the office.

'What?' Gus said, not turning round.

'I propose dividing the proceeds of my share of my parents' house between the children,' Monica said patiently.

Gus raised his head. On the wall above his computer hung his first award, the best newcomer Tempranillo for the Denomination of Origin in the province of Málaga for 2009. It was framed in corks, arranged like regimented teeth; Spanish corks which had to be dampened before they were wedged into the necks of bottles which were also made in Spain, even if of Italian design.

'Why don't you,' Gus said, as a statement, staring up at the corks.

'Don't you have a comment? Or even an opinion?'

'In a good year,' Gus said, 'every hectare here produces five thousand bottles.'

Monica stared at the back of his head. The blond hair had faded to the colour of dead leaves and there was a small but definite bald patch at the crown.

'Do you mean that we are in a sufficiently secure financial position ourselves that we can at last be generous to our children?'

'Something like that.'

'Then why don't you say so? And turn round to look at me when you do?'

Slowly, Gus turned round to face her, in his swivel chair. 'That better?'

'Honestly,' Monica said, 'you are a piece of work. You really are. Don't you *care* about the children?'

'Very much.'

'Then why—'

'Stop it,' Gus said suddenly. '*Stop* it. *Enough.* I'd react more strongly if I didn't feel such an absolutely fucking *useless* father to those poor children. That's all.'

Then he swivelled the chair sharply back again and bent towards his computer screen.

Monica mouthed 'Wow' to herself. For a long moment she stared at Gus's hunched back and then she crept away, across the yard to the house she had designed to be some kind of fanciful symbol of family life and which had become, in fact, the default dwelling of two people who had tried all their lives to make something positive out of rejection.

Well, she thought now, nursing her tea and watching the astounding view gradually reveal itself, things could only get better. That had been a low moment, possibly the lowest. But it was ten years ago, ten years in which the two youngest grandchildren had been born, other awards had been won, Gus had started keeping bees in the vineyard, running geese through to eat the pernicious snails, using the sediment from the wine vats as compost to feed the earth. And she had started a business, a specialist grocery shop attached to the vineyard. She'd called it Rico, and Pilar's sister Carmen ran it for her, as manager. She stocked English foods for homesick expats there, as well as their own wines, displayed in an

imported English bookcase, the bottles interspersed with
teapots and milk jugs, and beside it, a refrigerated glass case
of made-up dishes, stuffed red peppers, aubergines fried with
the vineyard's honey, spinach croquettes, which Carmen's
friends and nieces cooked in a tiny kitchen behind the shop.
The friends and nieces were a perpetual chattering procession
of women, so Monica paid Carmen for a set number of hours'
work each week, and left Carmen to sort out who should be
paid how much. The shop made a small profit about which
Gus seldom enquired, which Monica used to buy air tickets
back to England to see her grandchildren. Gus seldom came.

'If they want to see me,' he said, as if the onus only went
in one direction, 'they know where to find me. I'm always
here.'

He always was. Sometimes, Monica tried to summon up
the Gus she had met at twenty-three, the diffident, sad, lost
Gus whose existence was clouded at best and almost obliterated at worst by an impossibly demanding father. Gus had
been an unquestioned basket case, a wounded animal in need
of rescue, a misunderstood, unappreciated lovely boy, just
begging to be saved and valued. She remembered very clearly,
and now with some regret, that feeling of rapture at finding
in Gus a cause and a purpose for the rest of her life. Her
brother had only alluded to it once, remarking mildly that
the saving of Gus appeared to have taken hold of Monica
with the fervour of a religious conversion, and she had
rounded on him with such ferocity that he had never gone
near the subject again. In fact, Alasdair hardly mentioned
Gus and relations between the two were only sustained by
Monica being the sister of one and the wife of the other.
When Katie, in a mood Monica guiltily interpreted as

defiance, took her three girls up to Scotland to stay with Alasdair and Elaine, Monica knew that her silence on the subject spoke volumes. She was silent because, in truth, she did not know how to express the reality of what she felt, without shame. It was dreadful, it really was, to resent your own daughter behaving like a proper niece. Especially when that daughter had been miserable at her English school, and Monica, obeying the social conventions of her class and time, had known that all too well, and still persisted in the separation.

She could hear Pilar now, in the kitchen behind her, talking to the dogs. They were Gus's dogs, technically; English Labradors who were severely tested by the heat. When Gus was invited to go shooting on the coast, he loaded the dogs into his battered shooting brake and returned with reports of how much they had been commended for their retrieval skills, but for most of the year, it seemed to Monica, they lay gasping in patches of shade, pink tongues lolling. Pilar affected to despise them, but they loved her, thumping their tails in welcome when she arrived, circling round her while she unloaded her basket and put on the sleeveless flowered overall that was her uniform for housework. She talked to them as if they were children, half scolding, half encouraging, and sometimes, if her father had killed a rabbit, she slipped them something raw and red from a much worn supermarket bag.

'You want more tea?' Pilar said from the kitchen doorway.

Monica turned. 'Don't worry. I'll make it.'

Pilar held out a hand. 'Give.'

'Really, I—'

'I need distraction,' Pilar said. She snapped her fingers.

'Give. I had a row with Carmen this morning. You know what? She's giving her children *cereal* again this morning. I said to her, "Excuse me, is that what we had for breakfast when we were children?" I tell you, we had bread our mother had baked and olive oil. And now what? Now it is all sugar, sugar, sugar. The supermarkets are stuffed with sugar. Cereals are all sugar. No wonder Carmen's children are too fat. That boy of hers! He can't run because of his thighs.'

Monica held her cup out. 'Thank you, Pilar.'

'And you are too thin.'

'And the dogs are also too fat.'

Pilar took the cup. 'In winter, they get thin again. With working.'

'Have you heard Mr Gus this morning?'

'No,' Pilar said. 'I wake him soon. I take his coffee.'

'I'll do it.'

Pilar eyed her. 'OK.'

'It's Tuesday morning,' Monica said unnecessarily. 'He needs to get going.'

Pilar took the cup back into the dimness of the kitchen.

'I make his coffee then you take it.'

Monica waited where she was. Pilar had made no comment when Gus had left the marital bedroom and moved to sleep in the room Monica had allotted for Sebastian's use when he came out to Spain. He'd come a lot at the beginning, helping Gus with the planting, explaining seriously to his mother how the vines, for the first year, simply had to be cut down to the base to allow the roots to strengthen, but his own life had gradually taken over and absorbed him, and now he and Anna and the boys almost never came. The reason, he said frequently to his mother, was his business, the office-cleaning business he had started with a school friend, and now ran himself with Anna meticulously doing the books. It meant, Sebastian said often, that they couldn't really get away, because of Profclean, which always needed attention, it seemed, especially with regard to staffing problems. Gus had assumed that Sebastian would be named Augustus, the fifth Augustus Beacham, but Monica, full of righteous indignation at Gus's treatment by his own father, had demurred.

'I'm sorry, but I can't. I can't bear his name to be perpetuated.'

'But it's my name too.'

'I know. I know. It isn't logical. It isn't logical in the least, but I feel it really intensely, I feel that I just couldn't bear our baby to be burdened with his name.'

Gus, fresh from another berating from his father, had held her shoulders in genuine bewilderment.

'What then?'

'Sebastian,' she said in joyous relief.

'Sebastian? What has Sebastian got to do with anything?'

'It's the Greek translation of Augustus, which means emperor. I mean, it meant emperor for the Romans.'

'Golly,' Gus said admiringly.

'Yes.'

'Well, yes. I mean, fine. Sebastian.'

'Can we call him that?'

They looked down at the baby, lying neatly on his side in his hospital crib.

'Yes,' Gus said. He bent over his son. 'Hello, Sebastian.'

Sebastian and Anna didn't know, officially, that his parents no longer shared a room. Nor did Katie, although Monica suspected that she'd guessed. As Jake and Bella must have, too. If it mattered. Did it matter? Wasn't it historically the case, anyway, to sleep – and, she mentally emphasized, sleep – separately? Surely this fashion for togetherness was contemporary and very much to do with sex? Monica looked up at the sky. It was blue and clear and fathomless. Sex. The mere idea of it was now as distant to her as the moon.

Pilar came out with Monica's tea. It wouldn't taste quite as it did when Monica made it herself. She had taught Pilar about boiling water and loose leaves and a teapot but all the same, Pilar's tea tasted odd. Not unpleasant, just odd. Different.

'Thank you, Pilar.'

'Now I make Mr Gus's coffee.'

'Is Carmen in the shop today?'

'No,' Pilar said, 'is Pepie.'

'Pepie?'

'My niece Pepie. Married to José Manuel who is *enólogo* to Mr Gus.'

'Ah. Of course. I'd forgotten.'

'You don't forget José Manuel.'

'Of course I don't. I'd forgotten he was married to Pepie, that's all.'

'How do you say *enólogo*? Winemaker?'

'Yes. Winemaker.'

'Drink your tea.'

Monica turned away. The sun was high already and the descending slopes below her looked completely exposed to the heat, vulnerable somehow, despite their antiquity, the fact that for millennia they'd known nothing else. She drank her tea rapidly. The time, the landscape had lost its privacy, its exclusivity. It belonged to the whole world now and her brief possession of the day was over.

—

Pilar had made Gus's coffee as he now liked it, strong and Arabic, with an almost gritty texture. Sometimes she added cardamom pods, just two or three. He loved that. He loved anything Moorish anyway, anything that was redolent of Andalucía's past, of those long centuries before the Catholics reconquered the south and uprooted all the mulberry trees the Moors had relied on for their silk trade, and replaced them with cork oaks. The cork oak forests were everywhere now, interspersed with the yellowish green of Aleppo pines and, higher up the mountains, the darker Spanish firs.

When they first came to Spain in 1993, Gus had been wildly enthusiastic about the culture, about the fact that this had been an area of huge importance to the Romans – 'What else did the Romans do, but plant vines?' – and that the then Prime Minister, Felipe González, was from Seville and was determined to put Andalucía on the map. He had taken advantage of the Olympic Games being held in Barcelona in the same year – 1992 – that Madrid was European City of Culture, and he had created Expo '92 in Seville which had attracted over 40 million visitors and celebrated the 500th anniversary of Christopher Columbus's first voyage to the New World, in 1492. Spain, Gus said excitedly to Monica, was the land of opportunity. Cheap and full of possibility. He'd taken her hand and pulled her into a crowd in Seville, a dancing crowd full of girls in ruffled dresses. He'd danced himself, in fact he'd have danced all night if she hadn't run out of breath and energy, slumping against a wall, laughing and helpless. It had been like courting again, like those first exciting, tentative dates, before parenthood, before the full realization bore down upon her of what it was like to live with someone who only ever wanted the one thing he couldn't have.

She paused outside his bedroom door. Sebastian's door, really, even if Gus had colonized the room, getting men from the vineyard in to move the old wardrobe Monica had bought in Sotogrande. Left to himself, Gus would probably never open the shutters to see the view, never straighten his bedclothes or pick up socks from the floor. It wasn't that he was spoiled, Monica told herself, it was more that he simply did not see untidiness, could not perceive the value of homemaking.

She knocked. There was, as usual, no reply. She turned the handle and pushed the door open. A line of sunlight as precise as a stripe of yellow paint lay across the tiled floor from a gap in the shutters. Yesterday's shirt lay in the stripe, as did yesterday's socks and the boxer shorts Sebastian and Anna sent every Christmas from an old-fashioned shirtmaker in Jermyn Street. Monica was dismayed to realize that her first instinct was to pick up Gus's laundry, open the shutters, sort the room.

Gus wasn't in the bed. The sheets looked as if they had been dragged to one side, as if a weight had pulled them. Monica put the coffee cup down precariously among the piled paper beside Gus's bed and put her hand on the crumpled pillow. It was cold. A sudden fear clutched her throat, at the same moment that she saw him, on the floor, on the far side of the bed, slumped on his side.

She hurried round and knelt by him. His eyes were open and his mouth was working, working, but no sound came out of it.

'Gus?' Monica said. Her voice sounded high and frightened, as if coming from far away. 'Gus?'

She put a hand on him. He was breathing but clammy cold. His eyelids dropped briefly shut, as if in relief.

'Can you speak? Can you tell me . . .'

She noticed tears on his face, tears pouring out of his eyes, saliva pooling below his mouth onto the tiles.

'Oh my God, Gus,' she said. 'I think – I think you've had a stroke.'

She raised her head. The children flashed through her mind, name after name as if on ticker tape.

'Pilar!' Monica yelled at the top of her voice. 'Pilar! Come quickly!'

CHAPTER TWO

'He's in hospital,' Katie said to her brother Sebastian on the telephone. 'There's a new hospital in Ronda. He's there.'

Sebastian said, 'I remember an old cottage hospital in Estepona.'

'Well, there's this new one. And it's wonderful, Mum says. It's where all the expats go to have their vision lasered.'

'Poor old Dad.'

'I know. And poor Mum.'

Sebastian sucked his teeth.

'I wish I could go out there.'

Katie said shortly, 'Jake has.'

'What? Jake's gone *already*?'

'Yup.'

'But Dad only had the stroke two days ago.'

'Jake went today. Bella and Mouse are going at the weekend.'

'Did – did Mum ask him to?'

Katie looked at her screen. A letter she was drafting had been interrupted by an incoming email. It was an email from the head of her office, the man who had founded her legal firm, and therefore required attention.

'I don't think so,' she said to her brother, her eyes on her screen. 'I think it was Jake's own idea.'

'I am not suggesting,' Katie's boss had written, 'that anything too drastic is desirable in your client's case. But I think you should advise doing nothing. Absolutely nothing. That might frustrate the other side into making some useful errors.'

'Can you go?' Sebastian asked.

Katie sighed. She had spoken to her mother for over an hour that morning.

'Of course I'm going, Seb. As soon as I can. Dad's had a *stroke*.'

'Yes. Well.'

'I think Mum feels suddenly very alone there, in Spain. I got the strong impression that if she could persuade him to come back to England, she would.'

'He'd hate that.'

'I'm not talking about him. I'm talking about *her*. I think she'd like him to be ill in his own language. *Her* own language.'

Sebastian cleared his throat.

'If you asked Dad about the future, he always said it was there. Firmly there.'

'It's different when you're ill.'

'Is it?'

'I think,' Katie said, 'that when something really bad happens, like a stroke when you are seventy-three, you just need to be where everything is familiar.'

'Dad didn't like English familiar. In fact, he detested it. He made his own familiar, in Spain.'

Katie looked again at her email. Her boss had signed himself, as he always did, 'Best, T.' The T was for Terry. Terry rode an upmarket motorbike to work from the house he had bought in north London, with views out into Hertfordshire. There was no wife in the house, only a series of girlfriends, and a staff of three, one of whom polished the two Maserati GranTurismos in the garage. He too had made his own familiar, having grown up in a crowded household in Deptford, one child out of seven.

'I was saying to Mum,' Katie said, 'that I have to be in court for the next two days. But I'll go out to Spain on Friday night.'

Sebastian said carefully, 'I'll talk to Anna.'

'Yes.'

She thought of saying, 'You should make going to Spain a *priority*,' and for some reason, didn't.

'Maybe I could manage to go early next week,' Sebastian said.

'Jake will have got it all sorted by next week.'

Sebastian said with some energy, 'Fuck Jake.'

'You can't have it both ways. You go now and organize everything your way, or you go next week and put up with what Jake has done.'

'And you?'

Katie gave a little yelp of laughter. 'Me?'

'Yes,' Sebastian said. 'What are you proposing to do?'

Katie took the telephone away from her ear for a moment and closed her eyes. Then she replaced it, under her hair.

'Everything,' she said shortly, to her brother. 'Like usual.' She thought of adding, 'Pick up the pieces of the mess you men have made,' and quelled the idea. It was a crude reaction, she knew that, and unjust as well. Jake's presence would make Monica feel much better and safer and more cheerful, and that was what Katie wanted – or should want – so petty resentments and jealousies should be trampled underfoot. Stamped on. Firmly.

She said to her brother, 'Ignore me. I didn't mean it.'

He said sadly, 'Sometimes even Anna says things like that. She can't bear feeling put upon or exploited.'

'No,' Katie said.

'So if you're going at the weekend and so is Bella, and Jake is there now, maybe I'll try and go on Monday. Or next week somehow.'

'Yes,' Katie said, feeling that the conversation had taken a long time to come full circle. 'Yes. I must go. Love to Anna.'

She clicked her phone off and put it face down on her desk. Then she put her hands over her own face, not in despair but more for privacy, to be able to think. She must wait, she told herself, wait for all the whirling thoughts to stop filling her brain with panic at the urgency of all of them and settle themselves into some kind of sequence. Or, if not exactly a sequence, a more manageable series of priorities.

The day had started badly. It had started in the unfortunate way that too many days seemed to start in Katie's family these days. Katie couldn't identify exactly the moment that she and Nic had started to get on each other's nerves rather than being the team they had originally so successfully been, and she supposed that the drift apart had just begun in that imperceptible way of most relationship divides, and then gradually widened as attitudes became habits and habits had hardened. Monica was insistent that Katie and Nic's not being married lay at the root of their troubles, an insistence that Katie now found close to unendurable rather than just an irritation. Just as she found insupportable the insinuation, emanating from some of their friends whose wives didn't work, that Katie's being the main breadwinner must lie at the root of their evident troubles. But the fact was that they were not getting on well as either parents or lovers. They just weren't. And that morning had been a perfect example of the unhappy state of play between them. Nic had left the house early because he said he needed the headspace that could only be found, apparently, in a coffee shop near the college in which he taught creative writing, before his first class of the day. That left Katie with all three girls to get up, dressed and off to school before she could even think of switching from harassed mother mode to her working role as a solicitor specializing in intellectual property. The two younger girls wore – technically at least – school uniform, but Daisy, her eldest, was doing her A levels and was thus liberated from uniform. Liberated, Katie thought most days, meant in fact imprisoned instead by the modern demands of makeup and clothing. Daisy, who was both clever and slender, spent hours every morning straightening her hair and applying precise lines round her eyes before shrouding her body in carefully chosen layers of black. She was, at this moment, declining to eat breakfast. She said she couldn't face eating anything at seven thirty in the morning, which made her next sister down, Marta, feel that she too was incapable of eating even a banana. Only Florence, the youngest, for whom food was one of life's chief necessities, never mind its pleasures, competently and regularly boiled herself a morning egg, and ate it at the table, with relish.

So there had been the breakfast battle, and the school uniform hunt for black tights that were neither too laddered nor unacceptably ripped at the crotch, and Florence's wailing discovery of nit eggs in her plastic hairbrush, on top of Katie's own voicemails from the day's distressed clients and the inexorable ticking of the clock. Seeing all three of them scattering their arguing way down the street towards the bus stop should, Katie told herself, have been the moment of her own liberation. The moment when she could switch from the domestic to the professional, where she could dismiss the image of the disordered kitchen and unmade beds from her mind, and focus instead on the workday ahead and the need to manage her clients' public reputations amid the swirling and perpetually ingenious inventiveness of modern technology.

And in the midst of it all, there was the news about her father. It wasn't, either, just the news itself, it was all the attendant emotions that rose up in her because of it, those feelings of responsibility and guilt and anxiety and inability to decide. Monica had been initially calm and clear on the telephone.

'He's fine. He really is. He's in a wonderful place being wonderfully looked after.'

'When did you say it happened?'

'Tuesday morning.'

'But it's Wednesday! It's more than twenty-four hours later!'

'I told you,' Monica said levelly, 'I told you that Pilar was magnificent. He was in the hospital by mid-morning. I deliberately didn't—'

'*Deliberately?*'

'Yes. I deliberately didn't ring you at once because what could you do, from London?'

Katie said, lamely and fretfully, 'But I needed to know. We all did.'

'Now you do,' Monica said with almost an air of triumph. 'Now you all do. And Jake will be here for supper.'

Katie took a deep breath.

'Ma. Are *you* OK?'

'I'm better,' Monica said. 'Much better than I was.'

'Meaning?'

'I simply meant . . .'

'Yes?'

'That I got a fright. Of course I did. But Pilar was here and that made all the difference. She was wonderful.'

'So you said.'

'And he's in the best place. They think he'd had the stroke only an hour before I found him, so when he got to the hospital – honestly, the ambulance was here before we knew it – he was given a thrombolytic drug.'

'A *what*?'

'It breaks up blood clots, apparently. And he has tubes everywhere.'

'Can he *talk*?'

There was the smallest pause. Then Monica said brightly, 'Not at the moment. Not clearly, at any rate.'

'Oh, Mum.'

'He has high cholesterol, they said. And high blood pressure. He's going to have to change what he eats.'

'If he'll listen.'

'Yes,' Monica said. Her voice sounded abruptly uncertain. 'Yes. If he'll listen.' She gave a half-laugh. 'That'll make a change after forty-five years!'

'I'm so sorry.'

'Yes. Well, there it is. God bless the Spanish care system and the new hospital in Ronda. And Pilar.'

'Of course,' Katie said, 'Pilar.'

'All her nieces and friends are doing the nursing, really. They've made a rota. You know how the Spanish don't really have nurses, they expect the family to muck in. So as we haven't got family out here, Pilar's family are filling in.'

'Yes,' Katie said again.

'It makes me want to cry. How wonderful they're being. One of them is always there—' She broke off and Katie could hear her breath coming unevenly between suppressed sobs. Then she said, more collectedly, 'I'm fine, Katie. I really am.'

'I wish I was with you,' Katie said hopelessly.

'Yes. Yes, I wish it too. But you can't be. And you can hear how well we're being looked after. Both of us. Don't worry.'

Katie waited for the 'darling'. It didn't come. She tried very hard not to think that Jake would get many 'darling's. She said, 'I'll be there late Friday. I'll hire a car at Gibraltar.'

'How nice,' Monica said. 'Lovely. How comforting.'

'Ma. Mum . . .'

'Yes?'

'Try not to worry too much.'

'Oh!' Monica said. 'I'm not worried. He's in the best possible place, after all. I'm just shocked. That's quite different. It rather – takes your breath away, does shock.'

'I know,' Katie said.

'I must go. And I'm sure you should have stopped talking to me long ago. See you Friday.'

When she had rung off, Katie went on holding her phone, staring at it. Then she laid it down, quietly and almost reverently, and turned back to her computer.

'A friend of mine,' her client had emailed, 'thinks we should make a formal complaint to the Independent Press Standards Organisation. Why haven't we?'

———

After the plane had landed, and Jake could switch his phone back on, he saw that there were three missed calls from his older brother. He was about to return Sebastian's call when he suddenly halted, and decided that after all, he wouldn't. He would call Bella to say that he had arrived, collect his hire car from the desk in the huge, empty airport foyer, and then perhaps text Sebastian to announce – cheerfully – that he would be at the vineyard for supper and would take Mum to see Dad in Ronda the following morning.

It was a grey day, if warm, and the top of the Rock was shrouded in grey mist. Mum, if adhering to her time-honoured habit, would have taken her tea out onto the terrace that morning, and observed that the Rock was cloaked in mist and then started fussing about the diamond rot on the canariensis palm, or something. Jake remembered the palm arriving, probably twenty years ago when the house was up but hardly finished, just a slender sapling of a tree, and being planted on the terrace in the centre, in its own bed, and Monica saying to him, reverently, that it would grow to thirty feet high, it really would. And now it had, and it had got this fungus, which meant that the affected leaves hung down in a brown, unhealthy, skeletal way and caused Monica intense distress. She fussed over that palm the way he and Bella fussed if there was anything the matter with Mouse.

He hitched his bag onto his shoulder and rang Bella from the hire-car queue.

'Phew. You're there,' she said.

'I am. I'm just waiting to collect the car. How's Mousie?'

'Asleep, thank goodness. She kept asking where you were.'

'Did you tell her she'd see me at the weekend?'

'Of course I did,' Bella said. 'What do you take me for? I showed her a picture of an aeroplane.'

'Which picture?'

'The photograph one. Don't worry, I didn't confuse her by showing her an over-simplified drawing.'

'Good.'

'Is the sky bright blue? It's dismal here.'

'Bright blue,' Jake said, too heartily. 'Even makes awful old Gib look OK. Bright blue sky and a neon orange windsock I can see.'

'We miss you.'

'Three days. Tell Mousie I rang. Big kiss from Papa.'

He reached the front of the queue and dropped his phone in his pocket. Then in rapid colloquial Spanish, he spoke to the hire-car clerk.

'Hi there, mate. I booked a Jeep or something like it? Name's Beacham.'

'I know you,' the clerk said. 'You're a friend of Francisco's.'

'That's me.'

The clerk beamed at him. 'You were at school with my cousin, Manuel.'

Jake smiled back. He said again, 'That's me. The Englishman who speaks local Spanish.'

'Can you talk posh if you want to?'

Jake adopted a Castilian accent. 'Certainly I can.'

The clerk looked impressed. 'Wow,' he said, 'I can't do that.' He looked at his screen. 'I've got a Jeep Wrangler. Will that do?'

Jake liked being back in Spain. He sometimes thought that he preferred being in Spain to being in England, and when Bella suggested that that was because he liked his Spanish persona better than his English one, he was inclined to agree with her. It was easier, after all, to be sunny in the sunshine, and Jake liked being sunny, he liked things to go well, to be easy and fun and pleasurable. His sister Katie had said to him once – and not smilingly – that he was like one of those Elizabethan sundials that have engraved on them, 'I onlie count the sunnie houres', as if clouded or dark times could be brushed aside as hardly mattering. In Jake's view, they did matter, but they should never be allowed to dominate, let alone spoil the sunshine. Jake was, by temperament, designed for optimism, for the positive, and his determined view of his father's stroke was to regard it as bad but could have been so much worse.

'I mean,' he'd said to his mother on the telephone, 'he could have *died*. Couldn't he? And there's this brilliant brand-new hospital. Pretty miraculous, really. Don't you think?'

Monica plainly did think likewise. She'd answered the phone sounding tremulous and shaken at first and so much older, but by the end, Jake said to Bella, she was practically laughing. And agreeing with him that to have some time off from the old bugger was really pretty wonderful. Jake had no intention of allowing an atmosphere of anxiety and tension to dominate the next few days. His mission was, as he saw it, to open a bottle of their best wine, give his mother a substantial glass, and light the barbecue on the terrace in order to grill the excellent huge prawns he had instructed Pilar to purchase. He'd had several conversations with Pilar, with many jokes – even if they were, in essence, about Gus's stroke. He had, after all, been at school with two of Pilar's brothers in the village and could, in every way, speak their language. When he'd turned thirty, eight years ago, he'd had a whole string of parties to celebrate the birthday, including a Spanish one in the village, to which his English family was forbidden to come. That had been quite a night. Just as well, he sometimes thought, that it had pre-dated Bella. Bella's Spanish was now quite good, but it would always be English Spanish. And his, around people like Pilar, was local; accent, vocabulary and all.

He settled himself into the car and looked approvingly at the premium sound system. Then he texted Sebastian.

'At Gib. Will be at BB for supper. Mum sounds fine. Will report more later. J.'

The car was automatic. He slid the gearstick into 'Forward' and moved towards the amateur confusion of the Spanish border. Good to be back, he thought and then thought, odd but I always have a sense of homecoming here, a sense I almost never have in England. He slid the driver's window down.

'Cheer up,' he said to the nearest border policeman, yawning at his post. 'It's raining in London.'

———

Anna, Sebastian said to anyone who would listen, was much better at technology than he was. It was Anna, after all, who had been on a course to learn how to manage a business, and had come home with a knowledge of spreadsheets which she said was impossible, and therefore pointless, to pass on to him. So it was Anna who dealt with all the administration of Profclean, Anna who spoke comprehensively to the accountant, Anna who filed the tax return and arranged for an annual audit. Sebastian was volubly proud of Anna's skills and abilities, but in his heart of hearts, he was also a little frightened of them. Increasingly, they seemed to represent a vital element of the company that was unreachable to him. As Anna herself seemed sometimes to be.

Their two sons, named for two great-uncles on Anna's side who had both been lost at the battle of Monte Cassino in the Second World War, seemed to be as formidably focused as their mother. They both attended a prestigious school of ancient foundation in north London, and if they were led astray by their contemporaries, they showed little outward signs of it. Sebastian knew that Dermot and Marcus derived a certain cachet from having a first cousin, in Katie's Daisy, who was generally considered hot, and he also knew that Daisy had accepted a spliff at a party all the cousins had attended, but Anna had told him, in that effectively quiet way of hers, that he was not to interfere. Teenagers, she said, must be left to be teenagers as far as possible. It would be far more worrying, she said, if Dermot and Marcus had never been drunk and never experimented with weed. They were clever boys who knew their parents were watching in silence, and that silence, Anna told Sebastian, was not only golden but imperative. Sebastian, whose own adolescence had been an intermittently parented period of confusion and anxiety, could only defer to her. She must be right. Of course she was. And anyway, it was, as it had now been for eighteen years, a relief to be married to anyone so certain.

If he was honest with himself, Sebastian knew that Anna had grave reservations about his parents. She thought, even if she seldom said so outright, that they had not been what she considered good parents; that Gus had always been too consumed with trying to please his father to be any use to his own children, and that Monica had made the wrong choice in putting her husband's welfare and wishes first. She had thought her late grandfather-in-law a monster – 'Quite frankly, Seb, you are as much in need of rescue as anyone I've ever met. It amazes me that you are related to those old horrors in any way' – and her father-in-law weak, having allowed his emotional development to be crippled by old Gus. But the real problem, subtly, was Monica. Anna disliked her mother-in-law as much as Monica feared and resented her daughter-in-law. Monica wasn't resentful of Sebastian's dependence on Anna, but merely baffled that her eldest son had chosen someone so alarmingly self-confident and – frankly, Monica thought – chilly. It was, as a situation, a classic case of incompatibility between mother-in-law and daughter-in-law, and the resulting animosity between Monica and Anna had, if anything, only intensified over the years. In truth, it wasn't Profclean that prevented Sebastian and his sons going out to Spain all these years: it was Anna. Profclean was just a useful excuse, an acceptable hypocrisy. Anna hadn't said outright, 'I can't bear your mother, and she can't bear me, so the less we have to see of each other, the better,' but she didn't need to. Nor did she or Monica seem to feel any obligation to explain how they felt about each other. It was just there, dislike simmering away and only threatening to boil over if a meeting was mooted.

Sebastian had informed his family of Gus's stroke. The boys had glanced at their mother to gauge the appropriate reaction and Anna had said, 'Oh dear. I am so sorry. I really am. What a good thing your mother found him so soon after it happened.'

Dermot muttered something about poor Grandpa and Marcus made an inarticulate sound or two, which appeared to be sympathetic. Then Anna nodded in her sons' direction and they melted out of the kitchen. Five minutes later, the sound of Dermot's drum kit being played thudded through the ceiling, accompanied by Marcus on his keyboard. Marcus, the music master at school assured Sebastian, had the makings of an impressive jazz pianist.

Anna was slicing leeks.

'You'll have to go out to Spain,' she said to Sebastian.

'I know.'

'In fact,' Anna said, turning to tip the leeks into a casserole on the hob, 'you ought to go soon. Before Jake gets there and takes over.'

Sebastian said unhappily, 'He went today. He texted me to say he'd be at the bodega by suppertime.'

Anna didn't turn. She said softly, 'I bet he did.'

'There's a brilliant new hospital in Ronda. Dad's there. Mum was full of praise for it.'

Anna said nothing. Sebastian regarded her back view, the smooth bob of dark hair, the apron tied neatly round her admirably trim waist.

'Look,' he said, 'I know you think I'm feeble, but there wasn't anything else I could do. Katie's going out on Friday night. I suppose I could go on Monday.'

'Why don't you go on Friday night too?' Anna said, stirring leeks. 'With Katie? Then you could drive up there together.'

Sebastian said nothing. Anna turned.

'I don't have to come,' she said. 'You know I don't want

31

to. I am genuinely sorry about your dad and all that, but your mother doesn't want me there. She wants you, she wants her children, especially Jake. Go. Go on Friday.'

'It's a mess.'

'It's been a mess since you were Dermot's age. I mean, honestly. Starting a vineyard in Spain at the age of forty-seven, older than you are now! Did they think about old age then? Did they think about what it would mean for their children in due course? And don't, do *not*, get me started on Brexit.'

Sebastian said mildly, 'There was no inkling of Brexit in 1993. And in any case—'

'What?' Anna said furiously.

'In any case, there'd have to be a wholesale repatriation of all nationals right across Europe to affect them seriously, and that simply isn't going to happen.'

Anna opened the fridge door and took out a supermarket tray of cubed meat.

'All the same.'

'OK,' Sebastian said soothingly, 'OK.'

'Shall we just get back to practical matters?' Anna said, ripping open the cubed-meat tray with her leek-slicing knife. 'You getting to Spain? You have to go.'

'I know. In fact, part of me wants to.'

She regarded him, knife poised.

'Good. Go on Friday, with your sister. I'll watch the boys play rugby on Saturday.'

'If you're sure . . .'

'Of course I'm sure. Ring Katie.'

'After supper.'

Anna pointed at him with her knife.

'Now,' she said, with emphasis.

CHAPTER THREE

The young consultant – almost certainly too young to be a consultant, and in Monica's view, also much too good-looking – explained to Jake in rapid Spanish that Gus had had an ischaemic stroke, and that ischaemic meant an inadequate supply of blood to some part of the body, in this case the brain. It was a very good thing that Monica had found him when she did, and an even better thing that he could be admitted to hospital so soon afterwards as that meant that he could have an injection of alteplase very quickly – a very effective treatment for restoring blood flow to the brain as long as the stroke wasn't haemorrhagic, which a swift brain scan had confirmed that Gus's wasn't.

They had wondered, the young consultant said, baring his very white teeth at Jake, if they would need to perform a thrombectomy and insert a small catheter into Gus's groin, but happily that had not proved necessary. What would be suggested was a lifetime course of both aspirin and apixaban or dabigatran to prevent further blood clots, but the first forty-eight hours – the crucial period for strokes – had been managed with optimum speed and success. He turned his wide white smile on Monica and congratulated her warmly. She was appalled to feel herself blushing.

He was glad, the consultant then said, turning back to Jake, to see that his father seemed to have no trouble in swallowing – a common effect of strokes – because future nutrition was extremely important. Gus would remain in hospital for another week since any further strokes were likely to happen soon, if at all, and in any case, the hospital needed to monitor Gus's blood pressure, speech problems and ability to raise his arms. But it was not, he was glad to say, a severe stroke. More of a warning one. Perhaps some things, like taking more exercise and losing some weight, needed to become priorities?

'You tell him,' Jake said to the consultant. 'You try putting some small fear of God into him. My father is so stubborn, he makes a mule look obliging.'

The consultant smiled. He said, 'Perhaps it's a characteristic of fathers?' and they both laughed. Then the consultant shook Jake's hand, and then Monica's with Continental gallantry and a small half-bow, and left them with a swirl of sharply laundered white medical coat.

Monica gazed after him. 'Goodness.'

Jake put an arm round her shoulders.

'Bit of a bonus, eh, to have Dad looked after by George Clooney?'

'I'm just so relieved,' Monica said, 'that Dad isn't worse.'

Jake began to turn her towards the hospital corridor. 'Let's hope the next stage is amenable.'

'What do you mean?'

'I mean,' Jake said, nimbly steering, 'that it's going to be a merry old game getting Dad to take his health remotely seriously. Can you imagine his reaction to suggesting he might swim now and then? Or walk anywhere?'

'Perhaps he won't be able to drive.'

'Steady on,' Jake said. 'That sounded a bit happy.'

'It wasn't. I can't think of anything worse than your father not driving, not being able to indulge every whim and impulse . . .'

'Now you sound quite fierce.'

'I *feel* it,' Monica said, 'I really do. Now that I'm over the shock of finding him, the shock of him having had a stroke, I just feel full of dread.'

'Steady on,' Jake said. He tightened his grip on her shoulders. 'No more talk like that. No more *thinking* like that.'

'I can't help it. I can't. You have no idea how awful he is to live with. And with his freedoms curtailed, he'll be worse.'

Jake stopped walking. He turned his mother to face him, holding her shoulders firmly.

'Mum. Look at me.'

'I am,' she said, not doing it.

'*Look* at me.'

She glanced up. 'Better?'

'Hold it there,' Jake said. 'Do not look away.'

She gave a half-nod.

'Now,' Jake said, 'take a deep breath. Take several deep breaths. You've had a shock, a severe shock. But Dad is alive, it wasn't a severe stroke, and he is going to be fine. Do you hear me? *Fine*. He'll have to change some things in his life, but they aren't huge and he can do it. He's had a shock too, remember. He isn't Mr Invincible any more.'

Monica could feel tears rising up her throat. She said, in

a strangled whisper, 'You have no idea how difficult he is to live with.'

Jake held her gaze. 'This is exactly what I mean. About shock. You've had an awful fright and you're bound to feel a bit shaken after it. Now, come on, Mum. Dad's alive, and his being a bit tricky to handle is a sign that he's fine, the old bugger. If he was easier to handle, *then* I'd be worried, I really would.'

She sniffed, and looked up at him damply.

'Thank you, darling.'

Jake took his hands away and offered Monica his arm.

'That's more like it, Mum.'

'Yes.'

'I hope George Clooney has read him the riot act. Really told him.'

'Yes.'

'I've had an idea,' Jake said. 'We'll check in on Dad, and then we'll go and eat red prawn balls at the Gota de Vino. Wouldn't you like that? Lunch on the terrace, like the old days?'

Monica clutched his arm. She suddenly felt a shaft of light streaking through her, an unspeakably welcome lifting of her spirits.

'Oh yes,' she said. *'Yes!'*

———

Pilar said that it was no trouble. Her family, she said, were tremendously nosy about other people's business and they all had so many cars now, and there were so many of them, that it was no problem at all to maintain a kind of nursing/ visiting rota to Ronda. In fact, she thought they'd be glad of the excuse and the distraction and of course, Gus would be much easier to handle if attended to by anyone other than Monica.

She and Monica were standing either side of the bed they were making up for Sebastian. Plain white sheets, Monica had decided, rather than the embroidered ones she had chosen for Katie's bed, with white cotton Spanish lace round the pillowcases. Jake had colonized his father's room and organized Pilar to bring a cot in, for Mouse, and a mattress to put on the floor which he intended to occupy so that Bella could have the bed. Sebastian would sleep in the little room at the back which had been intended, on the original plan, as a laundry room with a permanently erected ironing board, and Katie would be in the official guest room, with its view and the embroidered sheets, and a vase of prettily drooping plumbago beside her bed. Jake and Pilar seemed to have arranged it all between them and Monica, pushing a pillow into its white cotton case, felt at once thankful and obscurely resentful.

'I bring you *calabacín* from Dad's *huerta*,' Pilar said. 'On the kitchen table. So many!'

'Thank you,' Monica said absently.

'What's *calabacín* in English?'

'Courgettes.'

'You should griddle them for a salad with pine nuts.'

'Maybe.'

'You know,' Pilar said, snapping a sheet out of its laundered folds, 'it makes so much difference having Jake here. There is *energy* in the house at last.'

Monica laid the pillow on the bed. 'I know.'

'I haven't seen Sebastian for three years. And Katie since

Christmas. Mother of God, that it should take this to bring them here!'

Monica straightened up. 'Stop it, Pilar.'

'Stop what?'

'Stop pointing out my family's inadequacies.'

Pilar tucked the sheets round the mattress with brisk hospital corners.

'Not inadequate,' she said. 'Just strange. Strange to us Spanish for whom family is *everything*.'

'I am really, really grateful to your family. But I don't want implied criticism of mine.'

'Implied?' Pilar said. '*Implícito*? I don't understand you.'

Monica put a second pillow on top of the first.

'Yes, you do, Pilar. The verbs are, I believe, *implicar, insinuar*. Don't do it.'

Pilar said nothing. She spread a white cotton cellular blanket over the sheets in eloquent silence and then she crossed the little room to the window and banged the shutters closed in a manner that she knew Monica disliked.

'Sun,' Pilar said decisively. 'Sun. It is the enemy, here in Spain. And this is the first time your family have been here all together for *five years*.'

—

Sebastian, Katie thought anxiously, looked older. He stooped a bit which, coupled with new rimless spectacles and clothing which could only be described as apologetic – plainly crease-free fabrics in dim colours – was definitely ageing. And not in a cheerful, authoritative, confident way, either. Just – sad. She hadn't managed to connect with him on the London end of the flight as she was late on account of Florence suddenly throwing a huge strop at being left in the care of her thirteen- and seventeen-year-old sisters until their father returned from college, so the sight of him at Gibraltar airport, explaining to the desk clerk in his careful, accurate Spanish what kind of car had been reserved, was her first.

She dropped her bag on the floor beside him and kissed his cheek.

'Seb. So sorry not to see you on the flight. It was all a bit of a dash.'

Sebastian stopped explaining about a small four-door Seat and turned to greet her.

'Katie.'

His skin felt smooth and papery and he smelled, as he always had, of soap and pepper. She smiled at him.

'Are you OK? Dad sounds better. What about the car?'

'All organized,' Sebastian said. He turned to the clerk. 'I *hope*. Nothing fancy, we aren't driving hundreds of miles. Just something cheap and reliable. Got it?'

'Nic hates hire cars,' Katie said. 'He hates the unfamiliarity and not knowing how they work. Modern cars with no ignition key or handbrake are his idea of a car nightmare.'

'I'm rather with him. Yes, Dad sounds fine. So does Mum. I rang her yesterday and she'd had lunch in Ronda the day before with Jake and they'd got through *two* bottles. At lunchtime, would you believe. Then Jake drove her home. Honestly.'

'Sounds rather fun,' Katie said wistfully.

'Mum was still on a high.'

'I bet she was.'

The desk clerk handed Sebastian a key and said the car, a Renault, was parked behind the wire fence.

'But I asked for a Seat.'

'There are no Seats available. Seat cars are made by Volkswagen, anyway. This car is better. It's an upgrade, for the same price. Sir.'

Katie touched her brother's arm.

'It's fine, Seb. Let's go.'

'But I specifically asked—'

'Let's *go*.'

'I hope,' the clerk said to her, 'that you find your father better. That's a good hospital.'

Katie managed to lead Sebastian away. He said, fretfully, 'It's very annoying.'

'I know it is, Seb. But it's better value to have a better car. And don't forget the point of being here. It's to see Dad. And make sure he and Mum are OK.'

'Two bottles of wine,' Sebastian said. 'At lunch! She sounded fine.'

'It's good that she was cheered up by a boozy lunch. Isn't it? I mean, what's better, Mum happy and a bit tipsy or Mum in a state because Dad's had a stroke and she can't cope with anything?' She looped her bag handle onto her shoulder and took his arm. 'Come on, Seb. Look on the bright side. Or the *brighter* side.'

Sebastian stopped walking. He said, 'I'm not happy. About any of it.'

'I know. It's a shock. Think of the shock for poor Mum.'

'It isn't that so much,' Sebastian said, walking on again and out into the balmy dark of the Gibraltar evening. 'It's the way it's been handled.'

'You mean Jake.'

'Yes,' Sebastian said. '*Yes*. He does the usual thing of rushing out here and then taking over. Just taking over. He didn't even call me.'

'Did he text?'

'Yes. The usual kind of cheery brush-off. I'd rung him *three times* to ask him to call me.'

Katie took his arm more firmly.

'Don't dwell on it, Seb. Don't focus only on resenting Jake. I mean, apart from anything else, what does that achieve?'

'Nothing,' Sebastian said angrily.

She waited a moment and then she said, 'Aren't you pleased to see me?'

He stopped walking again and looked down at her. His spectacles caught the lights of the runway arc lamps.

'What on earth is that supposed to mean?'

'It means,' Katie said, 'that I am patiently trying to deflect you from your own negative obsessions. I am your sister, remember? The sister who lives in the same city even though we hardly see each other?'

Sebastian said lamely, 'I've a lot on my mind.'

'So have I.'

'Of course I'm pleased to see you.'

'We're in *Spain*, Seb. Our father isn't going to die of his stroke and we have a weekend ahead in a lovely place and Mum to ourselves. When did we last have Mum to ourselves?'

Sebastian sighed. He began to walk again. Katie didn't take his arm. She said, instead, 'To be frank, Seb, you can't see Mum properly if you're with Anna, so can we just make the most of this opportunity? Silver linings and all that?'

He didn't reply, but began to walk faster.

'You're as bad as Nic!' Katie shouted after him. 'As bad as Dad. If you don't like something that's true, you just pretend it isn't there. Mum and Anna don't get on. Fact. *Fact.* You pretending they do, or ignoring that they don't, doesn't make anything any better and a lot of things much worse!'

Sebastian stopped walking beside a large, sleek black car as high off the road as a horse.

'My God!' he said, and his voice could not disguise his pleasure. 'Do you think this one is really ours?'

———

The house looked wonderful. There were lamps softly lighting their bedrooms, and out on the terrace, Jake had lit a whole host of lanterns, which flickered beguilingly in the darkness. Pilar had laid a table outside, with a rough tablecloth and thick green tumblers and wine glasses with bubbles trapped inside the glass, and pottery plates painted with pomegranates. There were candles on the table, too; fat altar candles in storm lanterns, and napkins which matched the cloth and which had clearly been dried outside in the high, clear, hot air. There was also a smell of herbs and oil from the barbecue.

Monica was wearing a turquoise cotton kaftan she had bought in Chefchaouen in Morocco years before, and she had pinned her hair up with a number of little mirrored combs. She put green glasses of wine into Katie and Sebastian's hands.

'See what you think. It's our new dry muscatel, a bit of an experiment but we can't drink red as Jake is barbecuing a red mullet. It's huge, a whole huge one in a salt crust.'

Sebastian took a deep swallow of his wine. He said, without particular rancour, 'We aren't guests, Mum. We're your children. You don't need to talk to us as if we were tourists.'

Jake put an arm round Monica's shoulders. 'That's you told, Mum!'

'It's so lovely,' Monica said. 'Having you here. Having you all here. And Bella and Mouse tomorrow.' She looked fondly up at Jake. 'Jake's going to collect them.'

'I could do that,' Sebastian said.

Jake smiled easily at him.

'No you couldn't, bro. You're taking Mum and Katie into Ronda to see Dad. I'll nip down to Gibraltar. No problem.'

Sebastian took another gulp of his wine. 'We could go later.'

'The hospital is expecting you at eleven. Spanish eleven. We fixed it with George Clooney.'

'Who's George Clooney?'

'Dad's doctor,' Jake said. He let Monica go and turned back to the barbecue. 'Ten minutes, team. This'll be one wondrous fish.'

Monica said, 'Bread made by Pilar, courgette salad made by me from Pilar's father's garden.'

'Why George Clooney?'

'He's very handsome, darling,' Monica said. 'Very dark and very handsome.'

'But is he a good *doctor*?'

'Yes,' Jake said, from the barbecue.

Monica waved her glass. 'He's wonderful. The hospital is wonderful. Pilar's family are wonderful.'

'Then,' Sebastian said crossly, 'you hardly need us, do you?'

There was a silence. Katie, who hadn't spoken, looked down into her wine glass.

'I think,' Monica said deliberately, 'that we all need, as it were, to go out and come in again. Don't you?'

Sebastian muttered something.

'What, darling?'

'He said, "Sorry,"' Katie said.

'No, I didn't.'

Monica moved across the terrace and put her hand on Sebastian's arm. She said, 'What did you say, darling?'

He didn't look at her. 'Nothing.'

Monica didn't move. She stayed where she was, looking up at her eldest son, her hand on his arm.

'I'm waiting, darling.'

'I didn't want to come in the first place,' he said reluctantly. 'That's what I said.'

'None of us did,' Monica said. 'None of us wanted this to happen. But it has. And we have to cope with it. And none of it stops me from appreciating having all three of you here together. For the first time, Pilar was reminding me, in five years.'

'Ready!' Jake shouted from the barbecue. 'À table! Fish coming up!'

In her pocket, Katie's phone vibrated with an incoming message. It was from Florence.

'I don't want to belong to this family any more,' Florence texted. 'I hate my sisters and I don't like Daddy much either. I am in despair. Come HOME.'

Monica paused in guiding her eldest son towards the table and turned to Katie.

'Everything all right at home?'

Katie dropped her phone back in her pocket and headed for her place at the table.

'Fine,' she said.

———

Later, in the quiet glow of her bedroom, she texted Florence back.

'I am going to see Grandpa in hospital tomorrow. I'll be home on Sunday night. Big kiss.'

Then she rang Nic. He sounded as if he hadn't a care in the world, and if there was a care, it was nothing to do with him.

'Where's Daisy?'

'I have no idea,' Nic said. 'It's Friday night, after all. Isn't that the one night she can be free?'

Katie got onto her bed among the embroidered pillows, and pulled the gauzy folds of the mosquito net, hung from a circle attached to the ceiling, around her. She said, 'Have you been smoking?'

Nic laughed. 'No.'

'I don't believe you,' Katie said. 'Have you been smoking weed? You sound kind of silly.'

'I have had two glasses of Syrah with my Friday night pizza with your daughters.'

'Our daughters.'

'Katie,' Nic said, as if collecting himself. 'How is your dad?'

'Fine,' Katie said. 'He sounds fine. He's in a new hospital being looked after by a very competent doctor who apparently looks like George Clooney. Seb and I are going to see him tomorrow.'

Nic said reflectively, 'I like your father.'

'So do I.'

'I'm glad you're there.'

'There was a text from Florence. Saying she was miserable and you were all being horrible to her.'

'Florence,' Nic said, 'is pretty good at being horrible herself. She's a fight-picker of Olympian standards.'

'Where is she?'

'Currently asleep. After a mega-bath.'

'And Marta?'

'Checking her Facebook page, last time I looked. I thought they were all into Snapchat and Instagram, but Marta updates her Facebook page every single day, it seems.'

'I'd like Daisy to be at home.'

'Don't fret,' Nic said. 'She will be. You just enjoy Spain.'

'I would enjoy it more if I could be sure that Daisy was home and you were being a responsible parent.'

'Ooh,' Nic said. His voice was shaky with sarcastic laughter. 'Responsible, now, is it?'

'Yes.'

'Shall I tell you what I propose doing now? Shall I? I shall pour another glass of Syrah, and then I shall turn up some bossa nova really loud on my Spotify and I might – I might just dance with a cushion. All around the house. Shall I do that?'

Katie took her phone away from her ear and looked at it. Then she clicked it off and put it under her bed. She closed her eyes and lay down. She was in Spain, she told herself, Spain. In her parents' guest bedroom with blue blossoms by her bed and a wonderful landscape outside the windows to wake up to. It was time, wasn't it, to think about her father, not about where Daisy might be or with whom. As long as she isn't frightened, Katie thought. Then the same reflection struck her about her father, lying there in hospital in Ronda. She opened her eyes and sat up. Oh God, she thought. Suppose he is frightened too?

She fought her way clumsily out of the mosquito net and slid her feet to the floor. The house was as quiet as only a house in remote countryside can be; quiet in a positive way, definitely and certainly quiet. Through the wall to her right, her mother would be lying in her own bed, and beyond that – such nonsense, this ridiculous pretence that her parents still shared a bedroom – Jake would be in Dad's bed and probably, being Jake, would be sound asleep and snoring. If he was, he'd be the only one of all of them. Monica would be awake; so, for different reasons, would Sebastian, probably; and as for her – well, now being frightened had occurred to her as a possible state of mind, it seemed a likely scenario for all of them, from Gus in his hospital bed through everyone at the vineyard, to the possibility of Daisy, scared and helpless, in someone's back bedroom or a multi-storey car park or a club where her drink had been spiked.

Katie padded over to the window and pulled the shutters open. The night outside was thick and black and balmy. Peering to the right revealed no light spilling out of her mother's room and certainly none beyond it. She thought about the generator Gus had initially installed, a petrol-driven temperamental machine that had rattled away in its own outhouse until it was replaced by another, more up-to-date version, and finally and expensively, by mains electricity which Gus had to contribute towards, being three kilometres from the village.

Monica's light might be off, but she wouldn't be asleep. She'd be lying in bed with her eyes wide open, worrying about the future. None of them had mentioned the future that evening. It had, as an unspoken topic, hung above the table like a thundercloud and they had all skirted round it with the skill that was second nature to them, swerving the conversation away whenever it veered towards 'What happens next?'

It was to save Monica's feelings, of course. That, and Jake's perpetual insistence that there was nothing that couldn't be turned to general optimistic advantage, that every bad thing that happened was really a catalyst for good – in the end. But what *would* happen? What future was there for a business whose mainspring – Gus – was looking at a very changed way of living his life? What if he couldn't carry on, what if he and Monica couldn't even stay in Spain? Why hadn't they all thought of this, as a possibility, why hadn't they talked about it, why hadn't she and her brothers even discussed what might happen when their parents grew too old, too frail, to manage a vineyard on the slopes of a mountain in southern Spain?

Katie put her head down on her arms on the windowsill, the tiled windowsill that was cool now, but certainly not cold. It was shameful to have been so careless, to have been so wrapped up in the demands of their own lives that they hadn't really considered this, let alone planned for it. Jake was as he always had been, perpetually positive and irritatingly blithe about everything, but she should have talked to Sebastian more, she should have made him focus, harnessed his sense of what was due to their parents. And now, of course, Sebastian had his own worries, his own anxiety about his relationship with Anna and his position in his own family. He was as anxious to hide any difficulties as her parents were, but he was a fool to think that Katie was deceived for a second. She knew Anna, after all. She had seen the gradual, inexorable shift in Anna and Sebastian's relationship, just as she was sure Anna had noticed the development – no, she thought, face it, the *deterioration* – in things between her and Nic. What a mess, she thought now, head on her arms on the tiled windowsill, what a bloody, unholy mess the whole family has got itself into.

Under her bed her phone vibrated briefly, indicating that a text message had arrived. She fled back to her bed and yanked her phone out, almost dropping it in her eagerness. There was a text from Daisy. 'Home', it said. No kisses, nothing but the one word. It was redolent of exasperation, of an impatient indulging of entirely unnecessary fuss. Katie put the phone to her mouth and pointlessly, idiotically, kissed it. Then she looked across at her bedroom wall, the wall that divided it from Monica's room. There was no way, let alone one word, that could grant her mother the swift and instant luxury of peace of mind.

Katie subsided onto the edge of her bed, clutching her phone. Perhaps she should go in to her mother? Should she? Should she go into Monica's room and tell her to spill every worried bean about her father, about the future? Was there even enough money? Was the vineyard mortgaged? Had Gus borrowed to finance improvements and not said, because he never said anything anyway, and was fiercely private about his business affairs to the point of obsession?

It was all huge. The more she thought about it, the more unmanageably huge it became. It was, in truth, a nightmare situation and one o'clock in the morning was not the time to think about it, let alone confront it. She would not disturb – disturb! What a useful delusion – her mother. She would see how the land lay in the morning, when they had seen her father. She looked down at her phone. Its screen shone blackly, empty of further messages. 'Sleep well,' Katie typed to Daisy. 'Sweet dreams. XXX.'

CHAPTER FOUR

The speech therapist in the new hospital in Ronda said that Gus's speech would probably return in a few days. His present difficulties in speaking were compounded, she explained, by a very common consequence of having a stroke, which was a weakness in the muscles around the mouth.

They nodded, staring at her, side by side like the schoolchildren they had once been. The therapist, who was neat and dark, and possessed of impressively accurate English, went on, 'This inability to make himself comprehensible is of course frustrating for your father. As is the aphasia.'

Sebastian thrust his neck forward, like a turtle. 'Aphasia?'

'It is a general term to cover all cognitive difficulties. Like short-term memory problems. Or not being able to plan, or organize himself. Or reason.'

'Good God,' Sebastian said.

Katie put a steadying hand on his shoulder. She said to the therapist, 'But you can help him?'

The therapist indicated the iPad under her arm. 'With the help of this, I hope so.'

They both looked miserably at the iPad.

'Oh?' Katie said.

'It is a system we call Visual Attention, which has proved very effective for stroke patients. We have had remarkable results in cases of aphasia.'

'I thought,' Katie said, slightly desperately, 'that Dad had only had a mild stroke.'

'He has.'

'But if he can't speak, or reason, if—'

'Most of these capacities,' the therapist said, 'will return to him. He can swallow after all. He can raise his arms.'

Katie moved her hand down to grasp Sebastian's. She said unhappily, 'So we wait.'

'But,' Sebastian burst out wildly, 'for how long?'

The therapist regarded him coolly.

'If we ever knew that, in the medical profession, our lives would be very easy.'

'Excuse me,' Katie said. 'We are in shock. The whole family is in shock.'

'So is your father.'

'We know.'

The therapist looked intently at them without much warmth. 'Just as long as you remember that it is your father who has had the stroke.'

———

The hospital cafeteria was off the immense central lobby of the building, and clattering with families. Katie found a table, told her brother to sit, and went off in search of coffee. When she looked back at him across the cafe, he was hunched where she had left him in his plastic chair. He had despair written all over him. She picked up a tray and joined the queue for the coffee machine. It had been a terrible half-hour with Gus. Poor Sebastian. Poor Dad. Poor all of them.

When she put the tray down in front of Sebastian, all he said, with a kind of dull horror, was, 'He can't speak properly.'

Katie unloaded two cups of coffee. She said, as steadily as she could, 'I know. But he probably will be able to. You heard what the therapist said.'

Sebastian leaned forward. He gripped Katie's wrist.

'But I know what he was trying to say!'

Katie seated herself awkwardly opposite her brother. 'Do you?'

Sebastian let go of her wrist. 'Yes. Yes I do. And I can't.'

Katie pushed the tray to the far side of the table. 'Can't what?'

'I can't take over the vineyard.'

Katie paused in picking up her coffee cup. She said firmly, 'Seb. He wasn't. He absolutely wasn't. He wasn't trying to say anything like that.'

'Yes,' Sebastian said vehemently. 'He was. He *was*.'

Katie shook her head. 'No, he wasn't. That's just what you imagined he was trying to say because it's the last thing you want to hear.'

'Katie,' Sebastian said with emphasis, 'he *was* asking me. And I can't.'

She sat back. After a moment or two, she looked at her brother. She said, reluctantly, 'Of course you can't. None of us can.'

Sebastian said nothing but his eyes were misting. To forestall any weeping, she went on quickly, 'We've all got lives in England, Seb. All of us. Children, jobs, other people.' She glanced round her. 'I mean, Spain, living in Spain was always their idea. It wasn't, ever, a family decision.'

Sebastian cleared his throat. Then he said, more robustly, 'But now it's become one. This stroke of Dad's has made it one. For all of us.'

Katie picked up her coffee cup. 'Yes.'

'I can't live here,' Sebastian repeated.

'No,' Katie said, 'you can't. Nor can I.'

'Could – could Jake?'

She shook her head. 'I don't think so. Not even Jake. And actually . . .' She stopped.

'What?'

'I don't think Mum wants to. Not any more. Not really.'

He was astonished.

'Not live here? But she loves it. She's lived here for over twenty-five years.'

'Dad wanted to,' Katie said.

'But . . .'

'She's of her generation, Seb. Wives like her followed the drum, they went where their husbands' lives or professions or personalities took them.'

Sebastian looked down at his cup. 'I've never really liked Spanish coffee.'

Katie held her hands out. 'Give it to me, then.'

He lifted his cup. 'Are you sure? All that caffeine . . .'

'Today,' Katie said, 'I'm taking everything going. Caffeine, alcohol, bring them on. Jesus, Seb.'

'I know.'

'I've got friends,' Katie said, pushing her own empty cup aside, 'who've been dealing with parent crises forever – disabled parents, sick parents, demented parents, alcoholic parents, just generally hopeless parents. And I've sympathized, I've made all the right noises, done all the supportive things like have their children to stay, made casseroles, generally done my bit. But while I was doing it, I suppose I was thinking all the time, that because Mum and Dad had made this very distinct and different decision to move to Spain, that they had made themselves remote from all the usual responsibilities of family and that we were somehow free of the consequences of their choices. But we aren't, are we? This happens, out of the blue, and suddenly we're landed with our parents, and they're kind of infantilized, aren't they, and looking to us like – like *fledglings*. It's awful, Seb, awful. And I feel extra awful that I didn't see it coming, that I pretty much chose not to see it coming. I mean, last night . . .' She paused and then continued, staring at the table top, 'Last night, I wondered if I should go into Mum's room, to see if she was OK. And I didn't. I decided not to, because, if I'm honest, I didn't want to. I didn't *make* myself. But she's seen Dad. She must know the score. She must know it's very unlikely he'll recover enough to be able to run the vineyard again. And that must scare her. I mean, what's the future for her? And for Dad? What's he thinking? It's beyond awful for them, it really is. Here they are in the ruins of what once looked like a bold and adventurous dream. One stroke and crash, the whole house of cards collapses. No wonder they're frightened. As frightened as we are.'

He was watching her intently.

'Yes,' he said.

'And we,' Katie said, still staring at the table, 'are their children. Whatever they've done, whatever choices they've made and however irrespective of us those choices were, we are still their children.'

Sebastian put a hand on Katie's arm to get her attention. 'But why do we have to be responsible for the consequences of those choices that most certainly weren't ours? Or even considerate of us?'

She sighed, then said sadly, 'What I feel isn't logical. I know it isn't. It's instinctive. And probably personal. After all, why should I expect you to feel something that I feel, just because you're my brother?'

He squeezed her arm briefly. 'I *do* feel something just because I'm your brother.'

She gave him a wan smile. 'Thank you. But don't let it become an obligation.'

'It isn't.'

Katie took her hands off the table and put them briefly over her eyes. She said, 'Honestly, I just want to scream. I can't bear all this. I know it'll get better as I get used to it, but at the moment, all I want to do is scream and scream. Like a banshee, whatever that is.'

'Katie . . .'

She took her hands away from her face and looked across the table at him. His tone of voice had altered.

'Yes?'

Sebastian hesitated. Then he leaned forward again and said, hoarsely, 'I don't think Anna wants to live with me any more.'

—

Jake was sitting in his father's swivel chair in the office, below the wine award framed in corks. He had papers strewn all round him, layers and layers of paper on a surface already thickly covered with them. The light, from a single unshaded bulb hanging directly over Gus's desk, shone brightly and harshly down on the scene and illuminated the crown of Jake's head, where the hair was beginning, remorselessly, to thin.

From the doorway, where Monica usually stood, Sebastian cleared his throat. Jake didn't turn round. He said, 'Who told you I was here? Bella?'

'Bella's asleep,' Sebastian said.

'Where's Mouse, then?'

'She's with Mum. They're trying on Mum's jewellery. Katie's asleep too. Very Spanish, I suppose.'

Jake looked over his shoulder. He said jauntily, 'Come to spy on me, then? See what you might be missing?'

Sebastian moved into the tiny cluttered space of the office, flattening himself against a bookshelf of box files.

'No,' he said, 'actually. But Mum said you were here and I thought you could do with some moral support.'

Jake looked back down at the papers.

'It's a mess. It's frankly a terrible mess. Dad's got personal debts and a biggish bank loan and God knows if he's mortgaged the house too. I haven't got to that. But he's making good wine. The wine is selling. It's winning awards still and it's *selling*.'

Sebastian inched closer to his brother. 'I thought a girl came in from Ronda to help.'

Jake made a dismissive gesture. 'Oh, her. She's fine but she's a bookkeeper really. And no one could stand up to Dad if he wanted things done his way, and he was determined that his way prevailed when it came to this place.' He picked up a sheaf of papers. 'You know what these are? They're printouts. Printouts of invoices sent out electronically. There are spreadsheets on this thing' – he gestured towards the computer screen – 'and then he prints them out too, and files them in this general muddle, layers and layers of unfiled mess.'

Sebastian peered at the top invoices. 'Goodness,' he said. 'The Caribbean!'

'And most of the Baltic countries. Never mind Spain itself. Or Italy. Or the UK. He makes good wine and he sells it. From this dump.' He looked about him. 'It's dreadful, Seb. The waste! This place is essentially a gold mine.'

Sebastian looked round him. 'Could I sit somewhere?'

Jake waved an arm. 'There's a stool over there.'

'Where?'

Jake didn't move. 'Under those lever-arch files.'

Sebastian edged round behind his brother and lifted the files. 'What are these?'

'Dunno,' Jake said. 'Haven't got to them yet.'

Sebastian put the stack of files on the floor in the tiny space available, and lifted the stool in the air. 'Could you shove over a bit? So I could put this down?'

Jake moved a few inches to the left. Sebastian said, 'Katie and I saw Dad this morning.'

Jake was staring at the computer screen. He said, 'Of course, I know. I fixed it. While I was fetching Mouse and Bella, you two were in Ronda.'

Sebastian manoeuvred himself onto the stool. He said, his eyes on the screen as well, 'I was horrified.'

'Why?'

'Well, by Dad of course. He was – hopeless, really. He was trying to speak, and he couldn't.'

Jake said reasonably, 'He's had a stroke, you know.'

'I've never seen anyone who's had a stroke before.'

'Nor have I. Probably time we did.'

Sebastian looked down at the chaos of paperwork. He said, with difficulty, 'Katie and I had coffee afterwards, after we'd seen the therapist.'

'I saw her,' Jake said. 'She was pretty upbeat. She said Dad stood a good chance of recovering his speech and a whole lot besides.'

'So you know.'

Jake said heartily, 'Of course I know.'

'Katie said, on the way home, that there's something else you should know. Something that I am absolutely sure Dad was trying to say to me.'

Jake's gaze didn't waver from the screen. 'Which was?'

'Could you look at me?'

Jake turned his head towards his brother. He said in the same easy tone of voice, 'Fire away.'

Sebastian was unprepared to find his brother's face so close to his own. He drew back a little, defensively.

'Come on,' Jake said impatiently. 'Spit it out, whatever it is.'

Sebastian was hampered by the stool's position, and there being no space to adjust it. Leaning back in an attempt to create a distance between their faces, he said, 'Katie said I should tell you that Dad asked me this morning if I would take over running this place. And I can't.'

Jake's expression didn't flicker. 'Did Dad say that?'

'He tried to. I know he did. He's very traditional, after all, and he'd want his eldest son to take over.'

'But you said no.'

'I didn't say no *then*. I didn't say anything. I – I just held his hand. And kind of stroked it. It would have been too cruel to refuse him then and there. Heartless.'

Jake went back to looking at the screen. 'So Dad thinks you'll take over running this place from him?'

'No. Well, yes, perhaps he does. But the thing is, I can't. I can't live here – I can't leave London.'

Jake began typing with rapid competence. He said, 'And Katie?'

'She's the same. Anyway, she's a partner now. And her girls are all at school in London.'

'Like your boys.'

Sebastian said nothing. After a pause, Jake added, still typing, 'Did you say Bella was asleep?'

'Yes.'

Jake glanced at his mobile phone to get the time. He said, 'And Mouse is with Mum?'

Sebastian nodded.

'Anything else?' Jake said. He didn't look at his brother. 'Anything else Katie said you ought to tell me?'

Sebastian opened his mouth to reply, and shut it again. He got to his feet with difficulty and edged towards the door. He said, 'I'll go – I'll go and see José Manuel. I suppose one of us ought to and he'll be here on a Saturday anyway, won't he?'

Jake said, to the computer screen, 'Don't bother, Seb. I've done it. I've already seen him. Everything to do with wine-making is under control.'

———

Mouse was sitting on Monica's knee in front of the dressing-table mirror. It was an old-fashioned dressing table, kidney-shaped, which Monica had had since she was a girl, and under its glass top a series of faded photographs lay trapped, photographs of Sebastian and Katie and Jake as children and a new one of Mouse herself, naked on a bath towel at three months. She was fascinated by it.

'I expect,' Monica said, 'that you'll hate it when you get older. You'll hate it that we took your picture when you hadn't got any clothes on.'

Mouse gazed at her baby self without recognition. If she raised her eyes just a fraction, she could see herself in Monica's dressing-table mirror, with Monica's pearls round her neck, lots and lots of pearls including some particularly fascinating ones that popped apart and together with an extremely satis-factory sound. In fact, if she turned her head, she could see three of herself in Monica's triple mirror, three sets of red-gold curls and three sets of pearls. It was very pleasing, it really was. Back and forth, up and down, curls and pearls. The baby on the bath towel was, however intriguing, nothing to do with her. Not the now her. She bent forward to get closer to the mirror, and felt Monica's hand on her ribcage.

'Careful, darling,' Monica said.

Impatiently, Mouse tried to prise Monica's hands away. She leaned closer to the mirror and opened her mouth to protest. Then the glass of the dressing table rose up and smacked her sharply on the forehead. The deliberate shrieking became something entirely natural and Mouse roared, cradled against her grandmother's shoulder.

'What's happened?' Sebastian said. He was standing in the doorway.

Monica swivelled on her dressing-table stool, holding the sobbing Mouse.

'She fell forward, poor baby. Trying to get closer to the mirror.'

Mouse didn't really know Sebastian, but he was a man and something about him had the familiarity of Daddy. She craned towards him, out of Monica's arms, wailing. He closed the door behind him and came across the room. He said, almost shyly, 'I always wanted a daughter.'

'Take her,' Monica said. 'She wants to go to you. Poor baby. Horrid bump. Horrid dressing table, to bump you.'

Sebastian lifted Mouse into his arms and she immediately curled herself into his shoulder, tucking her wet face into his neck.

'Goodness,' he said, pleased. 'Hello, Mouse. Hello, Mousie. Do you have a real name? I've forgotten what it is.'

'It's Molly,' Monica said.

Sebastian walked to the window, jiggling the baby.

'Was she christened Molly?'

'She wasn't christened,' Monica said briefly.

'Ah. But I thought Jake and Bella got married. In fact, I know they did. I was there.'

'Bella,' Monica said carefully, 'is a humanist. She was married in church to please her parents.'

'And Jake?'

'Jake,' Monica said, 'wants to please everyone all the time. As you know.'

Mouse began to whimper in Sebastian's arms. Monica held out a limp square of greyish cloth.

'This is what she wants. It's her doodoo.'

'What?'

'Bella describes it as an object of transition. It's what she goes to sleep with.'

Sebastian subsided onto the edge of Monica's bed. Mouse seized on the cloth and immediately put her thumb in her mouth and closed her eyes. He smoothed back her hair.

'She's going to have quite a bruise.'

'Something real for Bella to fuss over, then,' Monica said briskly.

Sebastian looked down at his niece. 'This is nice. I like this.'

'I'm glad to hear it. It's time something happened that somebody likes.'

'Oh, Mum.'

Monica put her head back as if she was defying tears to fall. She said, slightly unsteadily, 'Whatever the reason, it is lovely to see you, darling.'

Sebastian said, with awkward politeness, 'It's – lovely to be here, Mum.'

'I think,' Monica said, too brightly, 'that we're the only ones awake. Bella's asleep, Katie's asleep . . .'

'Jake's in the office.'

'Ah, yes. Do you want to talk about the office? Is that why you came to find me?'

Sebastian shifted a little to get Mouse into a more comfortable position.

'Actually, no.'

'Do you want to talk about seeing Dad this morning? Do you—'

'No,' Sebastian said. 'Not that, not either of those things, even though I know how important and urgent they are. This is something else, something I told Katie this morning, and she said I should tell you, whatever else is going on. She said mothers need to know everything.'

Monica said nothing. She went over to the window, to the view, and stood looking out at it for some moments. It was difficult to tell if she was seeing anything, registering what lay before her. Sebastian regarded her back view in silence while Mouse, slipping into slumber, grew heavier and heavier in his arms. Then Monica turned.

'Darling,' she said. 'What is it?'

———

Monica did not feel like putting the mirrored combs in her hair that night. In any case, Mouse had found them when she needed a dressing-table rummage to distract her from the unpleasantness of waking from her nap in Sebastian's arms, and had thrust them all anyhow into her own hair and would not be parted from them.

'I think you've lost your combs, Granny!' Bella said brightly, coaxing Mouse to eat mashed avocado for her supper. 'Bye-bye combs, Granny!'

Jake had made Monica a gin and tonic in a tall glass with a wedge of lime in it and big square ice cubes from the tray she had bought for Gus and he refused to use. The gin – Jake had been generous with it – was very welcome. Monica gestured with her tumbler.

'All I need back, sometime, are the real pearls. Mouse is welcome to everything else.'

'Mm,' Bella said, her head on one side. 'Don't know about that. Do we, Mousie? Not sure we'll want to part with anything, will we?'

Jake, passing through the kitchen on his way to the terrace, paused in front of his daughter's high chair, deftly extracted the string of real pearls from the collection around her neck, and handed it, smilingly, to his mother. Mouse appeared not to notice. Monica slipped the pearls over her head and did not catch Bella's eye. Katie said loudly, 'Is supper one of Pilar's paellas?'

Monica said firmly, 'It was very sweet of her to make it.'

'So oily.'

'Not by Spanish standards.'

'Bicker, bicker,' Jake said, coming back from the terrace. 'Do you wonder why we don't get together as a family more often?'

'I'll lay the table,' Katie said.

Jake grinned at her. 'Done it. And lit the candles.'

Katie made a face at him. 'Mr Perfect.'

'Not at all,' Jake said breezily. 'Merely doing what needs to be done.'

Katie looked at Bella. 'Is he always like this?'

Bella scraped avocado off Mouse's chin. She didn't look up. 'Pretty much.'

'Insufferable,' Katie said. 'It must be awful to live with someone so wonderful.'

Bella said nothing. Katie looked across at Sebastian, who was in turn watching Mouse distracting herself from eating her supper by fingering the combs in her hair. Katie raised her glass.

'To us. To all of us. For getting through today.'

'Hear, hear,' Sebastian said softly.

Jake, crossing the kitchen yet again, paused and lifted the bottle he was carrying. 'Perhaps we should drink to Dad. After all, he should be here and none of us would be here, in any sense, if it wasn't for him.'

Monica said, choking a little, 'Oh, darling.'

There was a silence, then Sebastian roused himself and raised his own glass. 'To Dad.'

Mouse picked up her sippy cup and brandished it above her head.

'Look!' Bella said. 'Isn't that just adorable?'

Jake put the bottle he was carrying down on the kitchen table. Then he turned to look at them all.

'Perhaps,' he said, 'now is the moment. I wasn't planning to say anything, for some time, but maybe I should speak up now.'

He looked round the room again. Everybody was silent, watching him, even Mouse, who had lowered her sippy cup to the tray of her high chair and successfully fended off another swooping spoon of avocado.

'What?' Katie said.

Jake turned so that his back was to the kitchen table and spread his fingertips out along its edge, either side. Then he said, as if he was addressing a meeting, 'You know that the work I do – the promoting, the networking and so on – can be done online, don't you? I have an office in London, but I don't need to have one; I don't need anything except good Wi-Fi, actually, in order to work anywhere in the world. So I am free, freer than either Katie or Sebastian, who really have to be in London because their lives are in London, that's where their work is, that's where their children are. Whereas my child – Mousie, I'm talking about you, poppet – is small enough to take anywhere. So, what I propose . . .' He paused and took a deep breath. 'What I propose is that Bella and Mouse and I move here, out here, and I run the vineyard. Seb doesn't want to, Katie can't, but I can. And that is what I am proposing to do.'

He stopped and looked round him once more, slowly. Monica began to cry, blotting her eyes with the backs of her hands and gasping, 'Thank God, thank God.' Jake's glance travelled to his brother and sister.

'OK?'

They gazed at him mutely, stunned into silence by his apparently effortless audacity. Then Bella said to him, 'Jake. You've forgotten one thing.'

'Have I?'

She didn't move from where she sat beside Mouse's high chair, but she raised her voice.

'Yes,' Bella said, the avocado spoon still in her hand. 'You are forgetting that I don't want to live in Spain. And I don't. Ever.'

CHAPTER FIVE

Monica was sitting up in bed, with her spectacles on, reading a magazine. When Katie came in, she lowered the magazine to her lap. She sounded astonished.

'Katie!'

Katie closed the door behind her. 'Mum.'

Monica patted the bedclothes beside her knees.

'Come and sit down.'

'There?'

'Why not? It's a big bed, after all.'

Katie sat down awkwardly, somewhere near her mother's feet.

'Well,' Monica said, sliding the magazine behind her radio, 'this is very nice and a great surprise.'

'I should have come last night.'

'Should you? I was probably asleep, you know.'

'Were you?'

Monica sighed. She took her reading glasses off and put them beside the radio. Then she said tiredly, 'I haven't slept at all really, since Dad had his stroke. It's the shock, you know.'

'And the worry? About the future?'

Monica raised her eyes to the ceiling. Then she lifted her hands as well and let them fall, as if in praise and thanksgiving.

'I don't mind telling you that I *was* fussing rather about the future. Then darling Jake . . .'

'That's what I came in about,' Katie said. 'Jake and Bella.'

Monica made a gesture of dismissal.

'Oh, Bella will come round.'

'Mum,' Katie said, 'she might not. And what's more, why should she?'

'She's Jake's wife, Katie.'

'She may have married Jake, but she has all the independence he has. She isn't lesser in terms of human value just because she isn't a man. Nor is Anna.'

Monica rolled her eyes. 'Anna!'

'I know Sebastian told you.'

'*Poor* Sebastian. He's had so much to bear, to endure. She's been what my father would have described as tricky, all along.'

'Mum.'

'What?'

'Suppose these daughters-in-law have a point? Suppose that Bella really doesn't want to live here, and Sebastian really does drive Anna round the bend?'

Monica folded her hands in front of her. Katie could hear the faint chink of her rings, loose now, on her fingers.

'Marriage isn't a bed of roses, Katie. It just isn't. You wouldn't know, because you haven't done it.'

'What Nic and I have amounts to a marriage.'

Monica closed her eyes for a moment as if what Katie had just said had to be endured, however ludicrous.

'Be that as it may, Katie. The point is that marriage means

that inevitably, now and then, you get irritated, almost to screaming point sometimes, and you don't always want to do exactly what the other person—'

'The husband. The *man*.'

'—is determined to do, but you remember the promises you made, the words you said. And you make the best of it. You *must*.'

'Bella didn't promise to obey Jake,' Katie said. 'Nor Anna Sebastian.' She stopped, just before she said, 'It would have been so old-fashioned.'

Monica looked down at her knees. She said, scornfully, 'I expect you want to tell me that promising to obey your husband is very old-fashioned. Well, I promised it when I married, of course I did. Everyone did then. Everyone.'

Katie leaned forward and tried to put her hand on her mother's.

'Mum, I wasn't being critical. Or at least, I had no intention of it.'

Monica didn't take her hand away, but she didn't respond to Katie's gesture either. She said firmly, 'But you came in to tell me that my sons' wives have every right to throw them out at the very moment that both boys are stepping into the breach and, in their separate ways, saving the family?'

'No,' Katie said. 'No. I just wanted to remind you that Anna and Bella have quite as much right to decide their own lives as Sebastian and Jake do.'

Monica looked directly at Katie in a way that made Katie withdraw her hand.

'No,' she said, 'they don't.'

'Mum . . .'

Monica raised her voice a little. 'Poor Sebastian. Poor, poor Sebastian,' she said loudly. 'He stands to lose his boys and his home and his whole *existence*, as a family man. And Jake has offered to rescue us, to rescue the business that has been your father's whole *life*, that he built up from nothing to be something very successful. What is more, Jake is free to step in. You heard him. He can run his business from anywhere and Mouse is of an age to go to the village school here. It's a perfect plan. *Perfect*. Which silly Bella will come round to, in the end. Of course she will.'

Katie stood up, slowly. She looked down at her mother.

'OK, Mum. But what about you?'

Monica looked deliberately amazed. 'Me?'

'Yes, you. What does your ideal future hold?'

Monica gave a bark of mirthless laughter. 'Ideal!'

'Well, OK, not ideal, but possible, bearable.'

'I haven't the foggiest.'

'You must have. You must have thought—'

'Katie,' Monica said, 'I haven't got that far. I haven't thought; I haven't dared to think. Could you kindly just allow me to revel in the sheer relief of knowing that Jake will take over the vineyard? Isn't there enough to worry about with Dad's situation alone, never mind Sebastian's and mine?'

Katie took a step towards the door. 'I didn't mean—'

'Oh,' Monica said crossly, 'you always say that. You come in and lecture me about my failings and then you try and say that you never meant to tick me off.'

'I didn't. I'm not.'

Monica pointed at the door. 'Just go, Katie. And take all your women's liberation nonsense with you.'

'Please, Mum.'

'What?'

'I didn't come in to say any of how the conversation has turned out,' said Katie, her hand on the doorknob. 'I came in to ask you if you were OK.'

Monica glared at her. 'I was,' she said, 'and now I'm not. Good night.'

———

Jake was making coffee in the kitchen the next morning. Pilar had come in – because, Katie thought, Jake was there – and had cleared away the debris of last night, and washed the wine glasses. Monica, in dark glasses, was sitting out on the terrace with a pot of tea on a tray beside her, and Mouse, still wearing the mirrored combs, was busily sorting a pile of pebbles at her feet.

Jake was humming. He had put on a canvas apron that a houseguest had given Gus, with a crude drawing of the central section of a naked woman's body printed on it, and was managing to create some kind of breakfast while the coffee heated up, marshalling pots of jam and slicing bread in a purposeful manner.

Katie looked out at the terrace.

'She OK?'

'Of course she is,' Jake said. 'Why shouldn't she be?'

'Where's Bella?'

'In the shower. Mouse has had milk and a banana. You look rough.'

Katie yawned. 'I didn't really sleep.'

'Excuse me,' Jake said cheerfully. 'Nobody sleeps well, after that much wine.'

Katie subsided into a chair. 'Where's Seb?'

'I haven't seen him yet. He's probably gone for a walk. His bed's empty.'

'Jake . . .'

'Yes?'

'Is Bella OK? I mean, after last night.'

Jake arranged slices of bread in a wicker basket. He said, pleasantly, 'Why don't you leave Bella to me?'

'I'm on her side.'

'*I'm* on her side,' Jake said.

'That's what clients say when they're trying to control other people, and those people aren't falling conveniently into line.'

'Says the lawyer.'

Katie got up. Jake went over to the open glass door to the terrace and called to his mother, 'More tea?'

Monica smiled and shook her head. Then she bent down and offered Mouse her sunglasses.

'Look at that,' Jake said fondly. 'They adore each other.'

Katie went out of the kitchen, carrying her coffee mug. Sebastian was in the hallway, taking off his trainers.

'Did you go for a walk?'

'Bloody hot,' he said. 'Even this early. I don't think I'm much good in this climate.'

'Seb,' Katie said. 'What are you going back to?'

Sebastian sighed. He stood up, his bony bare feet on the tiled floor.

'More of the same, I guess.'

'If it's any consolation to you, me too. Do you want to come and stay at mine?'

He said worriedly, 'I don't really want to rock the boat.'

'But if Anna wants you gone?'

'She hasn't *said* so. She just – behaves as if she can hardly bear having me around.'

Katie leaned on the nearest wall. 'Mightn't it be a good thing to take some action yourself? Not just wait for Anna to do something?'

'I don't think so.'

'Seb. Where's your pride?'

He stared at her. 'Pride?'

'Yes. Pride. Standing up for yourself, for one thing.'

He bent to pick up his trainers.

'I know you mean well,' he said, 'but sometimes you sound just like Anna.'

———

On the drive down to Gibraltar airport, Katie texted her daughters. She hadn't even offered to drive as it was plain that Jake had told Sebastian that she was in no fit state to drive anything anywhere, and Sebastian had the car keys in his pocket anyhow, from Friday night.

'On my way,' she typed. 'Should be landing about six, your time. Can't wait to see you!' She added three kisses, and then wrote more laconically to Nic, saying she should be home about eight and didn't want supper.

Pilar had been at the vineyard when they left. She came out of the house to embrace them and tell them not to worry. Katie felt real gratitude to Pilar coupled with an inexplicable and unmanageable resentment, and she stood in Pilar's embrace with all the reciprocal warmth of a coat hanger.

'We look after them,' Pilar said to her earnestly. 'We look after them like they are our own.'

Bella looked pale and tired, standing on the edge of the group with Mouse on her hip.

Katie said, kissing Bella, 'I'm always there, if you need me. If you want to talk.'

Bella said severely, 'I can talk to Jake. Any time.'

'I thought . . .'

Bella raised her chin a little and adjusted her hold on Mouse.

'Last night was hard for all of us. Wasn't it, Mousie? And we'll see Grandpa tomorrow, in the hospital. Won't we? Then I think we'll all know more where we are.'

Katie regarded her for a moment. 'OK.'

Bella lifted one of Mouse's hands. 'Wave to Auntie Katie. Wave bye-bye.'

Katie flapped a hand at her niece. 'Bye-bye, Mouse.'

'I think,' Monica said, her sunglasses firmly back on, 'that we'll all feel better tomorrow. Yesterday was an ordeal for everybody. Don't you think?'

Katie leaned to kiss her. 'Mum.'

Monica patted Katie's back. 'Give my love to the girls.'

'Of course I will.'

'Tell the girls I found my old Donny Osmond poster the other day, in a drawer. They'll never have heard of him, but they should know I was young once and had crushes just as they do! I adored the Osmonds, even if I was much too old to go on adoring anyone after I met Grandpa.'

'Will you ring me?' Katie said. 'Will you ring me about anything? Any time?'

Monica didn't take her dark glasses off. 'Of course I will. Now go. Go. You don't want to miss the plane.'

'We've got hours, haven't we?' Katie said now, to Sebastian.

'I mean, we didn't really need to leave when we did, did we?'

He was grasping the wheel tightly, leaning slightly forward, and she could see his jaw was tense.

'I did,' Sebastian said. 'I needed to leave yesterday.'

Katie put her phone on her lap and looked sideways at him. 'Seb . . .'

'Do you mind,' Sebastian said, 'if we don't talk? If we just don't talk at all? About anything?'

She looked at him for a few seconds longer and then she turned her head to study the landscape, the looping lines of the hillsides, dropping dramatically down to the coast.

'OK,' Katie said. Her voice sounded to her like that of a sulking child.

———

Florence said, 'You aren't at all *brown*, you know. In fact, you look really, really tired.'

She was sitting heavily on Katie's lap, and playing with her hair.

Katie yawned. 'I am. I didn't get much sleep.'

'Nor did I,' Florence said, starting on a plait which would hang directly down in front of Katie's face. 'I couldn't get comfortable and Marta wouldn't turn the landing light off.'

'You should shut your door.'

'I *hate* having my door shut. And I hate the light being on. I could make little plaits all over your head, like cornrows.'

'Please don't.'

'It's not up to you,' Florence said. 'It's up to me. I'm in charge.'

'And I must do some work.'

'Do not move.'

'There are at least fifteen work emails,' Katie said, trying to dislodge her daughter, 'that I have to read tonight.' She staggered to her feet. 'Did you have supper?'

Florence nodded. 'Mac and cheese. Your hair looks really weird.'

Katie put a hand up and felt the plait. Disentangling it, she said, 'Did you all have mac and cheese?'

'No. Just me and Daddy. Daisy's out and Marta said she wasn't hungry. Marta's *never* hungry.'

'Daisy shouldn't be out. There's school tomorrow. It's Sunday night.'

Florence spread her hands. 'You know Daisy. She doesn't say anything, she just goes.'

Katie ran her fingers through her hair. 'Not if I'm here.'

'Mummy,' Florence said, 'was it sad in Spain?'

'Yes. Yes, actually it was. Sad and complicated.'

'The ageing body,' Florence said. 'You just can't rely on it.'

'Who said that?'

'Someone on telly.'

Katie dropped a kiss on her head. 'I'm glad you had supper at least. And that you are your familiar self, like this kitchen is. It's all a huge relief.'

'From what?'

'From my parents and my brothers.'

'Don't you,' said Florence, rolling a tangerine across the table, 'like them much? I don't like Marta and Daisy and I only sometimes like you and Daddy. In fact,' she said, fielding the tangerine, 'I liked you much more when you weren't here. I really missed you.'

'Thank you, darling.'

'Oh look,' Florence said, 'this is all warm. Feel it.' She held out the tangerine.

'No, thank you. I must go and look at my emails.'

'Polly's mother is at home all the time. She makes pizza and jam tarts and stuff.'

Katie paused in the doorway. 'What are you saying, Florence?'

Florence threw the tangerine at the table top. She said, carelessly, 'That I'm going to be a lawyer when I grow up.'

'Sure?'

The tangerine rolled off the table onto the floor.

'Yeah,' Florence said, diving to retrieve it. 'Very sure.'

———

Nic was using Katie's laptop. She said, 'I think you'll find that this is *my* computer?'

He stretched his arms above his head and smiled up at her.

'I prefer it to mine.'

'Nic,' Katie said, 'I am close to the end of my tether and I need to get to my laptop.'

He rose from the study chair with elaborate indolence. He said, grimacing at her, 'Was it grim?'

'In a word, yes,' Katie said, sitting down immediately in the chair Nic had just vacated. 'Yes with knobs on. And then . . .' She shook her head. 'Oh, it doesn't matter.'

Nic stayed where he was, just behind her. 'What? Tell me.'

Katie said, 'It's nothing, really. It's so - so stupid, like the last straw really. Seb wouldn't sit with me on the plane coming back. We weren't together because we booked our seats at different times, but the plane wasn't full and I said to him, let's try and sit together and he said he didn't want to.'

Nic didn't move. 'Didn't *want* to?'

'He said to me – I think I'm quoting him exactly – "Do you mind if we don't because I have had it up to here with family, one way and another." It was fine, it really was, but I was so hurt and so furious and so – so . . .'

Nic moved to the door. 'Do your emails. I'll be back. I'm going to sort the girls and then I'll be back.'

Katie didn't look up. 'Florence says Daisy is out. She knows about the Sunday night curfew, she *knows* it.'

'She's seeing a friend. She'll be back soon. She promised.'

'And Marta didn't eat any supper.'

'Sort your emails,' Nic said. 'I'll be back.'

———

It was Sunday night, so Anna was out at choir practice. She had a good – but only good-ish, she insisted – mezzo soprano voice and was a keen member of the local choir. Anna was, Sebastian often told people, admirably committed to community effort. She was as competent outside the house as she was within its walls.

The boys were in their bedrooms, apparently working. Dermot was in the lower sixth of his academically ambitious school, and Marcus was two years behind him.

Sebastian opened Dermot's door six inches and put his head in.

'I'm back. Supper?'

Dermot raised his head but didn't get up. 'Oh. Hi, Dad. No thanks. Not hungry.'

'I'll see if Marcus is.'

'He won't be,' Dermot said laconically. 'We had late lunch. Huge. Roast potatoes and stuff.'

Sebastian knew he was doing himself no favours by asking. 'Here?'

'Yup,' Dermot said. 'Mum cooked it.'

'Just the three of you?'

Dermot let a beat fall.

'Some mates came.' He paused and then he said, 'We had crumble for pudding.'

Sebastian had a sudden memory of Katie saying to him that he should stand up for himself. He said loudly, aware that there was a note of querulousness in his voice, 'Don't you want to know how things are in Spain?'

Dermot waited a deliberate moment or two, then he turned to face his father with a bright, false smile.

'How was Spain, Dad? How is Grandpa?'

Sebastian looked at him. He was tall and thin, and had shaved the sides of his head in a way that would never have been permitted below the sixth form.

'When you are ready to talk to me,' Sebastian said, 'you will find me downstairs making an omelette.'

And then he shut the door and went resolutely down to the kitchen.

———

Among the emails were three from Katie's current client, demanding to know why a formal application hadn't been made to the press regulator, complaining about inaccurate reporting and demanding reparation. They were the kind of emails which required a soothing and measured response from Katie, pointing out that as neither racism nor paedophilia was involved, the press regulator would not see the matter as urgent, and that response should be drafted now, toned down in the morning and not finally sent for twenty-four hours. It was also necessary to imply, without spelling it out, that distortions of fact were in a different category altogether from deliberate invention, and the client had to realize that inconvenience and misinterpretation were a very different matter from an outright lie.

'If it happened,' Katie had got very accustomed to saying, 'it did, however much you may now wish it hadn't. The best that I can do for you is to diminish your being publicly defined only by that one thing.'

Nic came quietly into the room and put a mug of tea on the desk beside her laptop.

'Daisy's home.'

Katie was focused on her screen. 'Good.'

'She was actually home by ten to eight. She's now in the shower. Florence is in bed and Marta nearly is.'

'Where's Marta?'

Nic sat down in the padded chair close to Katie's laptop. 'Brushing her teeth in our bathroom. Daisy's using the shower in theirs.'

Katie said tiredly, 'This bloody woman.'

'Look at it again in the morning.'

'If only she hadn't got all this money to spend on legal fees.'

Nic took a swallow from his own mug. He didn't look at Katie. He said, 'Tell me about your dad.'

Katie typed in silence for a while. Then she pushed her chair back and said in a rush, 'Well, it isn't Dad, really. I mean, of course it is, but he's in the best place for him right now. It's more the bodega, and Jake. And Bella. And Sebastian and Anna. And – and, oh God, it's Mum, really. It's Mum.'

Nic said, not looking at Katie, 'I've always felt rather a bond with your mother. She and I irritate you like anything.'

Katie gave a little snort. 'You irritate me all right. But she's in another league. She doesn't even like me much.'

Nic grinned into his tea mug. 'The trouble is that she knows you know. She can't fool you like she can your brothers and she knows you have a point about all the traditions and conventions she clings to. It's very annoying indeed to be seen through, and it's very hard for you to be punished for being perceptive.'

Katie turned to look at him. 'Wow,' she said. 'What made you change your tune?'

'I don't know what—'

'Oh yes you do. You know perfectly well. What is it? What do you want me to agree to?'

He looked up at her. He said, soberly, 'Nothing.'

'Come on.'

'No,' he said earnestly, 'nothing. I'm not trying to soften you up. I want to help, I really do.'

'Why?'

His glance flicked away. 'You know why.'

Katie turned her whole body to face him. 'Go on. Tell me why.'

He said, reluctantly, 'Because I want to help in a bad family situation. I want to help because – well, you are the mother of my girls and I admire you and . . . and I love you.'

'Do you?'

'Yes. Yes I do.'

'Just not enough, most days, to use your considerable intelligence to imagine what it's like to be me? To put yourself in my shoes?'

He said, leaning forward but not trying to touch her, 'That's exactly what I'm trying to do now. Your whole family has been devastated by this, and all kinds of things have crawled out of the woodwork at the same time, like Anna and Sebastian, and Bella announcing she has no intention of living in Spain. And you've plainly had a dreadful weekend. Look at you, poor Katie. You're shattered. And you've got work tomorrow. So when I say I would like to help you, I mean it. I mean it as much as the reason behind meaning it. We've been together nearly twenty years, after all.'

Katie looked at him for a long time in silence. Then she said, 'OK. You mean it. You want to help.'

'I do.'

'How?' Katie said flatly. 'How do you propose to help?'

Nic stood up. He bent to take Katie's nearest hand and pulled her to her feet. Then he said, still holding her hand, 'I think we should ask your mother to come here. As a start, anyway.'

CHAPTER SIX

Monica dreamt of her childhood in Scotland, of being out on the loch and sitting in the stern of the boat gutting the mackerel her father and brother were catching. She had wondered, as she did on every one of these mackerel-fishing expeditions, why she and her mother always did all the gutting while the men of the family had the fun of the catching. But she hadn't asked, in her dream, any more than she ever did in life, and in any case, the dream was so vivid, so powerful, that when she woke and stared up at the gauzy folds of her mosquito net, she couldn't, for a moment, remember where she was. Then the recollections swam into her mind one by one, like little bright fish, followed by the realization that her room was light because sunlight was falling strongly through the shutters and lying in dusty bars on the tiled floor.

She fought her way out of the folds of the mosquito net and fumbled for her watch on her bedside table. The watch said ten to nine. Ten to nine! It was outrageous. It had been years since she had slept beyond six or six thirty, years since she had been greeted by a fully fledged day rather than watching it dawn. And I slept, she thought. I actually slept!

I haven't had a sleep like that, a long, deep, uninterrupted sleep, for as long as I can remember.

She went across the room in her bare feet, and pulled back the shutters, releasing the sunlight they held back to fall warmly and brightly into the room. On the terrace outside, Mouse, in a pink and white striped sunhat, was pushing a moth-eaten toy dog on wheels that had belonged to Jake over thirty-five years before.

Monica folded her arms on the sill. 'Good morning, darling.'

Mouse went on determinedly pushing. She was, apart from the sunhat, wearing only a pull-up printed with international flags. Monica disapproved of training nappies, and nappies in general not being hidden from view, under clothing. Katie, at that stage, had had knickers, Monica remembered, made of the same fabric as her dresses. Mouse would look so charming – so much *more* charming – if she were wearing a sundress, say, of the same fabric as her hat, plus matching knickers.

Bella materialized out of the shade at the far side of the terrace. She was wearing sunglasses and shorts, with an elasticated bandeau top which exposed her pale flesh above the waistband of the shorts.

She called, 'Don't worry, Granny! We're covered in factor 50!'

Monica waved vaguely. When she was Bella's age, she had worn a bikini, the kind of minimal bikini that Bella would now deeply disapprove of, and she had been tanned much more darkly than was now regarded as healthy. She remembered sitting on a beach, comparing the palm of one hand to the back of the other, with the greatest satisfaction. Dark tan, white smile, long hair. Wonderful.

She said, in a conciliatory manner to Bella, 'You know what you're doing, Bella. I know you do.'

Bella watched Mouse for a moment. She said, 'Jake has rearranged your visit to see Gus a bit later. Because you were sleeping.'

'It was a magnificent sleep. Best for years and years. We're all going to Ronda, aren't we?'

Bella bent to turn the dog so that Mouse could push him back across the terrace. 'I'll stay here with Mousie.'

'Oh, but I thought . . .'

'Well,' Bella said, 'I don't think poor Grandpa is what Mouse needs to see.'

'Don't *you* want to see him? I'm sure Pilar and Carmen would look after Mouse for a couple of hours.'

Bella straightened up again. She didn't look at Monica. 'I shall stay here and give Mouse her nap.'

Monica felt at a sudden disadvantage in her nightgown at the window. 'Very well, Bella.'

Bella looked out across the view. She really was very pale, Monica thought crossly. Pale and very slightly bulging.

———

It was one of those workdays, Katie realized, when she was both vulnerable to being caught out and just waiting for it to happen. She might have been fully trained for one thing, and a partner in the firm for over a decade for another, but some days it seemed to her that neither counted for anything and she was just bound to be found out, to be exposed as an incompetent fraud, and sent packing amid jeers and catcalls. Those were the days when the inevitable – as it seemed – humiliation would have been welcome; when she would have felt a rush of relief at being no good, inadequate at even pretending to be a professional person fit to charge hundreds of pounds an hour for legal advice.

The day crawled by at a pace that made her wonder if the digital clock on the wall in front of her desk needed its battery changed. She gulped too many cups of coffee and ate a slice of someone's birthday cake – a mistake, she knew, even as she bit into it – and then punished herself for the cake by skipping lunch. What she should have done was drink water and eat salad, she told herself, but she didn't, and the result was that she reached home in a state that could only be sorted by – one of Monica's favourite phrases from Katie's childhood, the one she'd used after Sebastian's outburst on Friday evening – 'going out and coming in again'.

Daisy was standing by the fridge eating yoghurt out of a plastic pot with a teaspoon. Katie crashed her bag and a canvas carrier of lever-arch files onto the kitchen table.

'Hello, darling.'

'Hi,' Daisy said, spooning yoghurt and not looking at her mother.

Katie looked at her. 'Nice yoghurt?'

'Uh-huh.'

'What flavour?'

'Strawberry,' Daisy said. 'My favourite.'

'Could you look at me?' Katie said. 'Could you be civil? Could you, for example, offer to put the kettle on?'

Daisy put the yoghurt pot and the teaspoon on the table. She said, as if Katie's tone had been warm and friendly, 'Of course.'

'I've had a grim day. After an awful weekend. I really, really need a cup of tea.'

Daisy went, without hurry, over to the kettle and carried it to the sink. With her back to her mother and the tap running, she said, 'Actually . . .' and then stopped.

'Actually what?'

Daisy carried the full kettle back to its base and switched it on. 'Maybe now's not such a good time.'

'For what?'

'To talk to you,' Daisy said.

'To talk to me about what? About your going out on a Sunday night?'

Daisy waited. She got a mug out of one cupboard and a teabag out of a Kilner jar in another and dropped one into the other. Then, with her back still turned to her mother, she said, 'Marta.'

Katie was taken aback.

'Marta! You mean the not eating, the constant saying she isn't hungry when her school bag and waste-paper basket are full of chocolate wrappers?'

'No,' Daisy said. 'Not that. Her not eating is to stop you seeing what's really the matter.'

Katie stared at her. 'What?'

'I feel awful telling you. Marta doesn't know I'm saying anything. In fact, I don't think she knows I know, she just thinks she and her friends, who are doing it, have got some little exciting secret or something.'

Katie felt for a chair and sat down in it. 'Doing what?'

Daisy busied herself with making her mother's tea.

'Doing what, Daisy? Drugs? Is it drugs?'

Daisy carried Katie's mug over to the table and set it down. The teabag, grossly swollen, bobbed on the surface.

'Not drugs,' Daisy said.

She went over to the fridge and extracted a litre carton of milk from the door. Then she turned back and set the milk down by Katie's elbow.

'Not drugs,' she said again. 'Cutting.'

Katie gasped. 'Cutting!'

'Haven't you noticed?' Daisy said. 'She's always got long sleeves on.'

'But . . .'

'Mum,' Daisy said, 'don't say why. Parents always say why.'

'They say it because it's important. Of course it is. Why? Why is Marta cutting herself? If, of course, she is.'

Daisy was nodding. 'Oh she is. She's been doing it for weeks.'

'*Weeks?*'

'Mum, she's careful. Of course she is. It's part of it, not being caught.'

'*Part* of it? Part of what?'

Daisy sighed. 'Part of the relief.'

'*Relief?*'

'They do it because they can't stand stuff. So there's relief for a little bit after they've done it. Then it all builds up again and they need more relief.'

Katie put a hand out and gripped Daisy's arm. 'Daisy. Does Dad know?'

Daisy moved her arm out of Katie's grip and massaged it. ''Course not,' she said. 'Only you. Honestly. You ask the weirdest things.'

———

The doctor who looked like George Clooney had been replaced by a geriatrician who was also, she explained, a neurologist, having specialized in problems affecting the brain and nervous systems before becoming a consultant for the elderly. She was called Ana Ramirez and she came from a family of doctors. Monica was simultaneously certain of her competence and regretful she wasn't an attractive man.

Dr Ramirez said in her careful English that Gus was doing well. He could swallow, and sit up without support, and his speech was gradually coming back to him although some of the words he used were correct but not in the right context, as the family would see. She was afraid that there was some permanent brain damage which meant that there would be a missing space in Gus's brain that he wouldn't be conscious of, but which would mean that he lost some abilities, some of which would never return. The one change that they must brace themselves for was that Gus would no longer be able to drive.

Monica seemed unable to take it in. Jake leaned forward. He said to Dr Ramirez in Spanish, 'Are you saying that my father won't ever be able to drive again?'

She nodded. 'I'm afraid so.'

'Crikey,' Jake said in English. 'He'll go mad.'

Dr Ramirez said politely, 'It is hard. Very hard.'

Jake turned to Monica. 'Did you get that?'

She looked dazedly at him. 'Not sure, darling.'

'Dr Ramirez says that Dad won't be able to drive again. Ever.'

Monica gaped at him. 'What?'

Jake took her nearest hand. He said to Dr Ramirez, 'This really is dreadful. This news.'

'I know. It is a terrible thing for everyone who hears it. But with hemianopia, it is the only decision to take.'

'Hem what?'

'Hemianopia. It means that the vision is severely reduced, and occurs with the swelling of the brain.'

Jake shook Monica's hand gently. 'Poor old Mum. A lot to adjust to.'

Monica whispered, 'If he can't ever drive . . .'

'I know.' He looked back at Dr Ramirez. 'And how much longer here?'

She gave a little shrug. 'A few days. Till we are sure he can manage everyday tasks.'

Monica snorted. She said loudly, 'Well, what about *me* and everyday tasks?'

Dr Ramirez looked at her sympathetically. 'I know. That is why we want to make sure he can use the toilet, maybe even dress and shave himself, feed himself, tasks like that.'

Monica closed her eyes. She extracted her hand from Jake's and clasped it within the other, tightly, in her lap. She said, 'And this is a *mild* stroke.'

'It is,' Dr Ramirez said. 'Some patients are unable to walk at all and are so confused that they have to go into residential care.'

Monica muttered something. Jake bent closer.

'What, Mum?' Then he put his hand on hers again. 'No, Mum,' he said. 'No. That wouldn't be better all round. This is the lowest moment, the worst. It'll be better from now on. It'll get easier as we get used to it.'

Monica said clearly, 'Dad won't get used to it. He never will. And he'll punish me for his misfortune.'

Jake turned, smiling, to Dr Ramirez.

'I'm afraid my poor mother—'

She waved his protestation aside. 'Please don't apologize,

it is a great shock. It is a shock for everyone, especially the husband or wife.'

Jake put an arm around Monica's shoulders.

'Come on, Mum. Come on. Time to see Dad now. Time to see what Dad can say.'

Monica struggled to her feet. 'I know what he'll say.'

'You do?' Dr Ramirez said politely.

Monica looked at her.

'He only has one word at the best of times,' she said, 'and I gather it's easy to say, when you've had a stroke.'

Dr Ramirez smiled courteously. 'Which is?'

Monica licked her lips. She didn't look at either the doctor or Jake. She said, in a tone that indicated the word had nothing to do with her, 'Fuck.'

———

Gus looked uncharacteristically neat and organized. He had been carefully shaved, his hair had been combed, and he was wearing not a hospital gown, but a well-ironed blue cotton shirt. He was evidently pleased to see them, and when Monica bent to kiss him, he pulled her towards him with surprising strength in order to press his mouth to hers. He smelt, she could not help noticing, of soap and toothpaste rather than alcohol and tobacco, but she did not like feeling his tongue pushing against her clenched teeth all the same. When he released her, she retreated hastily to a plastic chair at some distance.

'Wow, Dad,' Jake said heartily. 'You look so much better.'

'Yes,' Gus said, his mouth working elaborately. 'My cup is broken. Very broken.'

'What?'

'Broken,' Gus said loudly. He touched his throat. 'Very broken. Very.'

'I think,' Monica said from the far side of the bed, 'he means his throat is sore.'

'Broken!' Gus shouted, touching his throat.

Jake glanced at his mother.

'It'll get better, this speech thing. Dr Ramirez said it would.'

Monica said distantly, 'It's called dysphasia.'

Jake took his father's hand. He shook it encouragingly. 'It's what speech therapists are for, isn't it? Speech therapists and physiotherapists and God knows what else.'

'Broken,' Gus repeated, more quietly. He looked at Monica and said, clearly and accurately, 'Home.'

She nodded. 'Perhaps by the weekend. Next week anyway.'

'Home.'

'Yes, Dad.'

'Home.'

'I know, darling,' Monica said. 'Of course you want to be home. But we have just got to arrange a few things first.'

'Broken,' Gus said. 'My cup is broken.'

Monica began to cry, tidily and discreetly. 'Oh my God.'

Jake got up and went across to her.

'Come on, Mum. What's all this? Aren't I riding to your rescue?'

Monica nodded and blew her nose. 'Sorry, darling. It's just seeing him, like this . . .'

'I know. Poor old Dad. Poor you, too.'

Monica took his hand and pressed it to her cheek. 'I couldn't face or do any of it without you, darling.'

'Don't overdo the gratitude, Ma. I wouldn't be doing this if I didn't want to, now, would I? But actually, I'm pretty excited about the future. And to be honest, it's easier if Dad can't do it all his way, any more.' He raised his voice and said cheerfully to his father, 'You old bugger, you.'

Gus looked up, not back at Jake, but straight ahead of him, as if he couldn't see. And something, some kind of spasm crossed his face and briefly illuminated it.

'Look at that,' Jake said, still holding Monica's hand. 'Look at that, will you? The old bugger's even smiling!'

———

At supper, Bella said she only wanted a single glass of white wine, otherwise she'd just have water, thank you. She got up several times to ostentatiously refill the pottery water jug. She looked very pretty, Jake told her, in an embroidered white blouse with a cardigan knotted loosely round her shoulders. When he complimented her, she merely lowered her lashes and smiled as if at a private joke.

Jake had lit the candle lanterns again all round the terrace. He had given Monica a generous glass of red wine and told her to go and have a bath while he barbecued supper. When she emerged, in another kaftan from twenty years before, there was a smell of rosemary from the twigs laid on the barbecue coals and the terrace was glimmering with candle-light. The table had been laid – by Pilar, Jake said – and Jake himself, in a fresh shirt, was sitting beside Bella, with his arm stretched protectively behind her.

'Ma,' he said warmly, when Monica appeared. Neither he nor Bella moved.

Monica settled herself in one of the cushioned terrace chairs. 'Did you tell Bella?' she said.

'Tell her what?'

'That Dad won't be able to drive again.'

He glanced at Bella. 'Oh no,' he said, 'I forgot. Poor old Dad can't drive any more.'

Bella sipped her single glass of wine. 'Sad for Gus but a bit of a relief for everyone else, I should think.'

Monica didn't look at her. 'Not for me, Bella.'

Jake said easily, 'There's so many people to drive him here though, Ma. They all drive. They can drive Dad. Bella's right. He was beginning to be a menace.'

'It's the *psychology* of it, though.' Monica looked ahead. 'If he can't please himself at every turn. He's so used to obeying his impulses.'

'Well,' Jake said cheerfully, 'he'll have to learn, won't he? Like we all will. New life, new conditions.'

'He'll just take it out on me,' Monica said, to no one in particular.

'No he won't,' Jake said. 'I won't let him. I'll be here, after all, and so will Bella and Mouse. Dad can't bully you if we're all here to stop him.'

Monica, emboldened by the wine, looked directly at Bella.

'But will you be here? I thought you said you didn't want to live in Spain.'

Bella took a small sip of wine. 'I don't,' she said.

Jake put his arm round her. 'But because of me, she's going to give it a try. Aren't you, angel? Just a try. Six months, we said.'

Bella nodded. 'Six months.'

Monica regarded her. 'And if after six months, you decide you can't stand it?'

Bella leaned against Jake and gazed up at him. 'Then we'll think again. Won't we, Jakey?'

He bent to give her upturned face a quick kiss. 'We absolutely will. Promise.' Then he heaved himself to his feet. 'Now for those lamb steaks. Pinkish, don't you think?'

———

Nic said he'd had no idea. No idea whatsoever. He'd been worried about the possibility of anorexia, although he was aware of all the crisp packets and sweet wrappers, and all parents nowadays were alert for drug use, but self-harming had not occurred to him. He'd noticed the long sleeves, but he'd assumed that they were Marta's reaction to Daisy always pushing her sleeves up above the elbow. But cutting . . . Cutting! He'd looked it up, at once of course, on the internet, and there were photographs of young forearms criss-crossed with razor slashes as well as endless diagnoses and analyses of why it happened.

Daisy had looked at the photographs, too.

'That's what Marta's arms look like. Exactly that. In exactly the same place.'

Nic and Katie were sitting either side of the kitchen table with her laptop between them. She had closed the laptop, as if closing it would somehow obliterate the photographs. 'I feel so guilty,' she said.

He had his elbows on the table and his hands over his eyes. From behind them he said, 'Why?'

'I don't know. I just do. Something to do with failing her, letting her down, not noticing.'

'Balls,' Nic said briefly.

'Suppose I didn't work, though. Suppose I was like Polly's mother and stayed at home making jam tarts.'

Nic took his hands away. His eyes were red. 'Double balls,'

he said. 'You are a wonderful mother. We are wonderful parents. This isn't about us. It's about Marta, about that gang at school.'

'Um . . .' Katie said doubtfully.

'You know how intense teenagers are. How melodramatic. They can dice with death because they are too far away from it to think it'll ever happen to them.'

Katie blinked. 'Self-harming is different from death, though, isn't it? It's a cry for help.'

'Or a cry for significance. In this *X Factor* culture. The need to be famous.'

Katie whispered, 'Poor little Marta, though.'

'I know.' He reached across the table and said, commandingly, 'Hold my hand.'

She sighed. She put out a hand reluctantly and held his. 'I don't think we should try and feel better. I don't think we are allowed that luxury.'

'It's not about feeling better. It's about togetherness, about being Marta's parents together. About having a united front.'

'Front?'

'Strategy, then. Plan. To tackle this.'

Katie withdrew her hand. 'First, we have to tell her that we know,' she said slowly.

'Without telling her *how* we know.'

'Yes. And then, depending on what she says, what she gives as a reason, we take her to see a specialist. Oh God, Nic! Oh God.'

He said robustly, 'You can take it. You can deal with it. You *can*.'

She drew a long, shuddering breath. 'Can I?'

'Yes,' he said.

'Nic . . .'

'This is an awful time. Let's face it. It's an awful, awful time. Gus's stroke and all that fallout and complications, poor old Sebastian and now Marta. But Marta is the priority. Your priority. *Our* priority. Marta is what concerns us; Marta fills our foreground and our middle ground and our background. You are Marta's mother before you are anyone's daughter or sister. OK?'

Katie nodded. 'Yes,' she whispered.

'And I am Marta's father. As her parents we go forward together. As a family we go forward together and as a priority. Our family *first*.'

Katie nodded again. 'OK.'

'So first we have to tell Marta that we know.'

Katie looked at him across the table. He looked as gaunt, as haggard as she felt herself. She nodded a third time. 'Yes,' she said. And then, 'But what about Spain?'

'What about it?'

'Jake says Dad can't drive any more. And Mum is in despair at how Dad'll be, not driving.'

Nic stood up. 'Forget it,' he said.

'I can't.'

He came round the table and pulled her to her feet.

'You have to,' he said. 'It's Marta that matters and only Marta.'

She said, obediently, 'Yes. Marta.'

'Who we're going to confront.'

'Gently.'

He paused. He said, 'I shouldn't have used the word confront.'

'No. Except it's what we have to do, isn't it? To be face to face with things we can't avoid however much we wish we could. And oh Nic, how I wish that right now!'

She stopped and brushed her hand across her eyes. Then she said, half crying, 'God, life is hard. Isn't it?'

CHAPTER SEVEN

Sebastian asked gravely, 'Did you say your name was Luminata?'

The girl nodded. She was slender and pale.

'Bulgarian?'

'Romanian,' the girl said. 'My friends here call me Lumi.'

Sebastian consulted his computer screen. 'You are very overqualified to work for Profclean, Luminata. It says here that you are a teacher.'

'I was a teacher in Cluj-Napoca,' the girl said. 'But here I need other work.'

Sebastian looked at her. 'Where are your parents, Luminata?'

'In Cluj. With my sisters who are still at school. My father worked at the Bosch factory there where my brother works now.'

'And why did you leave?'

Luminata gave a little sigh. 'My boyfriend.'

'Ah.'

'He is a musician. He lives for music. He is the DJ in an international club in Paddington.'

Sebastian sat back and interlaced his fingers. 'And what do *you* live for? Your boyfriend?'

She shrugged slightly. 'Pretty much.'

Sebastian remembered earlier that morning, and his sons sniggering over a photograph on Marcus's phone, which turned out to be of Daisy, at a party, in a clinch with a boy. Sebastian was sure that Katie wouldn't have liked either the clinch or the boy, never mind that the photograph had been taken at all and then sent to everyone in Daisy's ever-expanding circle. He had remonstrated with Marcus.

'It's a cool picture,' Marcus said, grinning. 'Daisy won't mind.'

'I wasn't thinking of Daisy,' Sebastian said. 'I was thinking of her mother.'

Marcus and Dermot had rolled their eyes at one another, and then Anna had come in and held her hand out wordlessly for Marcus's phone. She'd said, looking at the picture of Daisy, 'I'm afraid my reaction is what a little slut,' and then she'd handed the phone back and told the boys to get a move on and what about their athletics kit? They hadn't rolled their eyes at Anna, Sebastian noticed, but just meekly melted from the room. He hadn't just noticed it this time, either. He had seen it and felt a sudden burst of anger, which had brought with it an unexpected energy. He had very nearly followed his sons out of the kitchen and demanded to know what they thought they were playing at, ignoring him as if only their mother's opinion mattered. The energy, or indignation, or whatever it was, hadn't subsided either. In fact, if anything, it had settled into something rather resolute and encouraging in his brain. He found himself two hours later, in the office of the industrial unit where Profclean was based, looking at a pale young Romanian girl whose hormones were dictating behaviour not a million miles from his niece, Daisy's

– even if their public manifestation was, outwardly at least, more seemly – with a pleasing and new kind of confidence.

'But you've been in London for eight months. What have you been doing all that time?'

'I was a waitress.'

'And?'

'My boyfriend didn't like me to be a waitress. It was the way some customers . . .' She stopped.

'I see. So cleaning offices and serviced flats is seen as more acceptable to your boyfriend?'

Luminata nodded. Sebastian thought with a far from unwelcome new impatience that this was not the first time he had come across such a situation. He would probably send this poor girl out on trial with a cleaning team and she would, equally probably, prove herself more than capable, so he would offer her a job and she would accept it and peace would be restored – for a while – with the boyfriend. The boyfriend and his music, his wretched, damnable music. Sebastian looked at Luminata with a mixture of pity and exasperation. It was on the tip of his tongue to confront her, to demand that she just look at her situation in the light of her boyfriend's evident bullying, when he was halted by the abrupt realization that Luminata's situation uncomfortably mirrored his own. He gaped at her, briefly rendered speechless by the power of his own realization. What could he say? What *should* he say? And then, as if to rescue him from an awkward predicament, his mobile phone began to ring in his pocket. Sebastian pulled it out, in confusion and relief, and stared gratefully at the screen. It was Jake calling, from Spain.

———

Jake was pleased with his day's work. He had had something of a breakthrough with Monica whom he considered was failing in her wifely duty towards Gus, in that she had managed never to see him since the stroke without someone to accompany her. He had thought about pointing this out to her but had decided that a simple course of action was best, and so he had driven her into Ronda, pulled up in front of the hospital's new and impressive entrance and said cheerfully to her, 'Well, here we are. Out you get.'

Monica had been waiting for him to drive on to the visitors' car park. She turned a bewildered face to him.

'What do you mean, darling – out you get?'

'Absolutely, Ma. Out you get. Chop-chop.'

'Are you going to park the car, then? I don't at all mind coming with you.'

'No, Ma. I'm not parking the car. I'm going to see a friend for coffee. While you see Dad. On your own.'

'On my . . .'

'Own, Ma. Go on. Out.'

Monica was clutching her bag with both hands. 'But I thought . . .'

'You thought wrong, Ma. You need to see Dad alone. Dad needs to see you alone. I'll pick you up in an hour.'

'An hour!'

Jake leaned across his mother and opened the car door. He was smiling still but silent. Very slowly, Monica crept out of the car and stood up, still holding her bag as if it were some kind of talisman. Then she straightened her spine.

'See you in an hour,' she said brightly. 'Enjoy your coffee.'

Jake turned the car with unnecessary speed and as he drove away, he looked back in his mirror at the hospital entrance.

Monica was still standing there. It struck him that if he had been near enough to see more clearly, his mother's knuckles were probably white with tension.

He turned the radio on. Radio Ronda was playing Ed Sheeran's 'Perfect', which Jake could sing along to. He rolled down the driver's window and rested his elbow on the sill, beating time to the song on the steering wheel. This was not only the life, he thought, but the future. Beacham's Bodega was looking at a very bright new prospect, modernized and energetic, reinvented by one Jake Beacham. And the meeting that lay ahead did not, in fact, involve coffee with a friend, but rather an encounter with someone Jake had met online, who had revived an ancient grape variety called Garnacha and was producing wine which was reported by some to be as good as the old French Burgundies. Spanish wines – and by implication, his father – were stuck in a Tempranillo rut, but Jake wasn't going to join them. No sir. And this meeting, arranged by email and with an ingeniously edited version conveyed to Sebastian in order to tick the principled behaviour box, was just the beginning.

———

If Gus hadn't been in a cream linen shirt instead of a blue cotton one, he might not have been moved from the chair where she had last seen him, Monica thought. Again, he looked extremely tidy, with combed hair and, she noticed, clean and trimmed fingernails. She had decided, standing at the hospital entrance, that she would not kiss Gus this time, so instead she picked up one of his uncharacteristically manicured hands and kissed that instead.

'Hello, Gus darling.'

He leaned forward, puckering up his mouth. He said, quite clearly, 'Kiss me.'

She regarded him.

'No thank you. I've kissed your hand and that's quite enough.'

He stayed where he was, leaning forward, staring at her. 'I'm better.'

'So I see. Good.'

'Kiss me.'

'No, Gus. No.'

'Why not?'

'Because,' Monica said clearly, 'I don't want to. I don't want to kiss anyone except Mouse.'

'Mouse?'

'Your granddaughter. Jake and Bella's little girl.'

Gus leaned back in his chair and put his hand to his forehead. He said again, 'Mouse?'

Monica extracted her mobile from her bag and scrolled to find a photograph. She held it out.

'There.'

Gus looked at Mouse's picture without interest. 'Oh.'

'You'll remember,' Monica said, 'when you see her. You'll remember who she is.'

Gus leaned forward again. He fixed his gaze on Monica's face. 'Home,' he said urgently.

'When they say you can. When you're ready.'

'I'm ready now.'

Monica drew back a little. There seemed to be an endless series of shocks to get used to: the stroke itself, the aftermath, the weekend with the children, the worries about the future, Gus's driving ban. And now there was the prospect of Gus coming back to the vineyard; Gus realizing he was forbidden to drive; Gus submitting (or not) to sessions with physiotherapists, occupational therapists, speech and language therapists, to visits from expat health insurance companies that he had always grumbled were a waste of money; Gus being told that José Manuel had taken the dogs home to live with him for the moment. No sooner, it seemed to her, did one alarm or problem get mitigated or solved, than several others rose up urgently in its place. If it wasn't for Jake . . . Monica closed her eyes. She must be sensible about Jake, she must, she really must. She must acknowledge that Jake wasn't perfect, wasn't some kind of god, and that her thankfulness at his apparent ability to solve his parents' problems was in part due to the depth of the traumas she had suffered in the last week or so. She swallowed. Calm down, she told herself; breathe, breathe slowly and deeply, think of Mouse pushing her father's old stuffed dog on wheels across the terrace.

'Home,' Gus said again, as a command.

Monica opened her eyes. Gus was staring at her accusingly, his eyes fixed defiantly on her face.

'In time,' Monica said. 'When the hospital says you may. When you are ready.'

'Fuck,' Gus said.

Monica felt an unmistakable glow of familiarity.

'You can swear at me till you're blue in the face, if you want to. It won't make any difference. You have had a stroke, Gus, and nothing is going to be the same. *Nothing*. Do you hear me, you stupid, stubborn old man?'

———

Jake had left a voicemail message for Katie. In it, he said that he had spoken to Sebastian about future plans for the vineyard and that they had agreed on a way forward, and that if it was OK by Katie, he, Jake, being on the ground, would just implement what he and Sebastian had agreed? He then said something about there being no problem about his perpetual availability, but Katie couldn't really focus on the second part of what he was saying, partly because it didn't seem important, but mostly because of Marta.

She and Nic had had a session with Marta, in which Marta had wept throughout and refused to show her parents her arms, saying, over and over between sobs, that she didn't know why she had started it, but she knew that she felt better, briefly, after she had. She stood in the kitchen at the end of the table, declining to sit down, and gripping the cuffs of her sweatshirt with her fingers so that her hands and arms were almost completely covered.

'We're not cross,' Katie said pleadingly, 'I promise we aren't. We're just horrified that you're so unhappy and that it's come to this.'

Nic had rung a number given online which claimed that an anxious parent was calling about self-harm every few seconds. He had also contacted their local doctor, the local hospital and a clinic in Harley Street that specialized in adolescent psychiatry. He had said to Katie that everyone professional was ready to spring into action the moment Marta agreed that she needed help, but until she did, she, Katie, was absolutely *not* – did she hear him? – to even mention that any research had been done or that the merest offer of help had been put in place. There had been an element in Nic's planning and forcefulness that had made

Katie feel, obscurely but distinctly, that she was almost being treated as the enemy, as if she was somehow to blame for Marta's troubles.

Nic had also been adamant that Daisy's volunteered information about Marta should not even be mentioned.

'I wasn't going to,' Katie said.

'No, I know. I know. But it's crucial to keep Daisy right out of it.'

'I know, I—'

'It is vital,' Nic said, 'that we do nothing that could even begin to harm their relationship.'

'I *know*, Nic, I know!'

He'd focused on her sternly. 'You say you know. And I absolutely believe in your commitment to justice and to your daughters. But you mustn't even hint—'

'Jesus, Nic, I *know*!'

When it came to it, Marta didn't ask how they knew. She stood, shivering and sobbing, at the end of the kitchen table, her dark head bent, her eyes swollen and pink. Every so often, she reached forward to snatch a tissue from the box on the table, and blew her nose ferociously while never letting her grip on her sleeves relax for a second.

Katie stretched a beseeching arm out towards her daughter along the table top.

'Darling . . .'

Marta hiccupped but said nothing.

'Darling,' Katie said again, 'can I ask you something about friends at school?'

Marta nodded.

'Are there – lots of you, at school? Doing this, I mean. Are there—'

'Katie,' Nic said warningly.

She glared at him. Then she looked back at Marta. 'I just wondered,' she said, 'I just wondered if – if it was kind of catching?'

Marta shook her head. She mumbled, 'Just me.'

'Are you sure, darling? Are you sure it – it isn't something you don't want to be left out of?'

Marta gave a yelp of anguish. Nic leaped up and put his arm round her shoulders.

'There there, sweetie, there there.'

'It's just me!' Marta shouted. 'Just *me!*'

'Tell us,' Nic said. 'Tell us how we can help you.'

Marta wailed, 'I don't know! I don't know!'

'We want to help you,' Katie said. 'We just want—'

Marta put her forefingers in her ears, her palms and other fingers still gripping her sleeves. 'Stop it!'

Nic kissed the side of her head.

'The thing is, sweetie, that we do know now. We know that you are very unhappy about something and we want to help you to deal with it. We won't do anything you don't want us to, but now that we know, we can't just stand by and not help you. Don't you see?'

Marta took her fingers out of her ears. She whispered, 'OK.'

'OK, what?' Nic said gently. 'OK, we can help you?'

Marta shook her head violently. 'No!'

Katie stayed where she was, her arm along the table. 'Are you saying that we might know now but we can't help you? That you don't want us to help?' she said, trying to keep the urgency of fright out of her voice.

Marta said nothing. Nic bent his head over hers so that his mouth was almost touching her.

'Marta?'

Silence.

'Marta,' he said again, very softly, 'Marta. Answer us.'

'Are you saying,' Katie said again, 'that you don't give us your permission to help you? Is that what you're saying?'

Marta gave an enormous sigh. Then she straightened up in the circle of her father's arm, and nodded her head decisively.

'Yes,' she said. 'That's it. I want to be left alone.'

———

When Katie was just a junior in her firm, she had been taken by Terry to meet a wealthy and important client. Terry had explained on the journey there that it was rare to meet Petro Kravchuk in person and that mostly Terry only met with one of his people, usually the man who acted as Kravchuk's chief of staff. Kravchuk had been born in the Ukraine, but had been sent to England when he was seven, to be educated. He had ended up going to an English university and had taken British citizenship, but because of his name and his birthplace, Western media referred to him constantly as an oligarch.

'He can't stand it,' Terry had explained to Katie. 'He absolutely can't. He's made his money in commercial property, and being lumped in with all the wide boys Yeltsin gave the country's oil and gas rights to drives him crackers. He employs us to keep an eye out for any mention, and stamp on it. That's all we're required to do.'

Katie had liked Petro Kravchuk. He sounded and looked to her completely English. He had married an Englishwoman and had had three sons, who were all at English schools.

Kravchuk had plainly approved of Katie in return because his requests – or demands – became specifically directed at her, even though, as Terry had said, she hardly ever saw him.

The latest newspaper outrage involved his eldest son, who was described not only as 'falling out of a nightclub' but also as the son of Kravchuk 'the Russian oligarch'. There was, Katie knew from past experience, absolutely no use in pointing out the transitory nature of media attention, nor the clichéd idleness of almost all tabloid journalism. Kravchuk would demand that the news item be taken down immediately and destroyed forever. Which wasn't, Katie knew, either practical or possible. The most she could do was to ensure that when the son's name was entered into a search engine, the first news item that came up about him was not the offending piece about the nightclub and the parentage. She looked long and hard at the boy's open and unformed face in the media photograph. He looked, she thought, not much older than Marta. But then, everything was relevant to Marta just now, everything and everybody. Marta's face, Marta's straight dark hair, Marta's covered arms dominated everything at the moment.

Quite apart from work and Marta, she told herself that she must also ring Sebastian. Bella had brought Mouse back to London, but Jake was still in Spain and said he would be staying out there to help Mum settle Dad into being home. Once more Jake had said, in his irritatingly breezy way as if nothing was a problem to him, that a friend of Pilar's called Lucia was a trained nurse and had just sent her youngest off to full-time school, so was perfectly prepared to come in each day and help Gus to wash and dress and eat breakfast. He had, he said, vacated his father's bedroom and moved what he referred to as his clobber into the bedroom Katie had occupied.

'Perfect, really. Sandwiched between the parents, God help me. And there's plenty of room for Bella in due course.'

Katie had asked him about the vineyard.

'The what?' he said genially, as if the vineyard was of no consequence.

Katie waited, her phone to her ear, her eyes on the photograph of Kravchuk junior.

'Oh, the *vineyard*,' Jake said, finally and blithely. '*That*. It's all absolutely fine. Don't worry. José Manuel is doing his thing, as are all the workmen, and I am slowly wading through the chaos here in Dad's office.'

Katie waited a moment. Then she said, 'Anything else?'

'No-o-o,' Jake said. 'At least, nothing that can't wait till Dad gets home.'

Somebody had ironed the shirt young Kravchuk was wearing and he had taken care with rolling up the sleeves. They had a precision about them, as did his haircut and the box-fresh newness of his trainers. Poor boy. Poor little rich boy, doomed to be misunderstood forever because of his father's name, just the way his father himself had been doomed.

She pulled herself back to the phone call. 'Have you spoken to Sebastian?'

'Yes, actually,' Jake said. 'I wouldn't take any decision without consulting you two. You know that.'

'What I know,' Katie said, 'is that you are in Spain and Seb and I are here. You are in Spain, Jake, with two very shell-shocked parents.'

Sudden tears sprang to her eyes. What were she and Nic

if not shell-shocked parents? What on earth was she saying? She might feel an immense reluctance to tell Jake about Marta, even if Marta had given her permission to tell anyone, but that didn't prevent her mind falling flat every time that Marta occurred to her. Which was, it currently seemed, almost continually.

'It's because they're in such a state that I'm staying,' Jake said. 'I mean, that's precisely why.' His tone grew injured. 'In fact, I'd rather hoped that you and Sebastian would be pleased.'

'I am,' Katie said. 'I'm thankful to you. I just seem to have conflicting emotions about the whole thing at the same time. When I ring Mum she either sounds unnaturally jaunty or in despair.'

'Despair isn't allowed round here,' Jake said. 'Definitely not. It'll be better than she thinks, once Dad's back. God, I miss Mouse!'

'I'm sure you do.'

'Katie, I promise I'll tell you the moment there's anything to tell. We're just jogging along, keeping things going day to day. You know.'

'No plans?'

'God no,' Jake said heartily. 'Have I got time or energy to think of anything as enterprising as a plan?'

'I'm not a fool,' Katie said. 'I don't miss much. You can't pull any wool over my eyes.'

Jake's voice changed as he stepped out of Gus's office and into the sunlight. 'I wouldn't even try,' he assured his sister warmly. 'Hah! The very idea!' He broke off and then said hurriedly, 'Gotta go, Katie. They've decided to run the bloody sheep through. Sheep and geese! Thank you, Dad.'

Slowly, Katie dialled Sebastian's private phone. He answered cautiously: 'Hello?'

'Seb, it's Katie. Doesn't my name come up on your screen?'

He said defensively, 'I didn't look at my screen.'

Katie sighed. 'I've just been talking to Jake.'

'Oh yes?'

'You don't sound very interested.'

'I'm not,' Sebastian said shortly.

Katie closed her eyes. 'Seb, these are *our* parents in Spain. Who happen to have a vineyard which employs seven people and a farm shop which employs goodness knows how many more part-time. And our father has had a stroke.'

'I know all that.'

'But Seb, we have a problem resulting from *all that*, as you call it. And we have the problems in our own lives. You can't just withdraw interest.'

'I haven't withdrawn it,' Sebastian said. 'I just can't feel it.'

'You can't mean that.'

'I do,' Sebastian said gloomily. 'I promise you that I do.'

'For God's sake,' Katie almost shouted. 'What is the *matter* with you?'

Sebastian said nothing.

'Is it the Anna thing?' Katie said. 'Are you so miserable about the Anna thing that you can't worry about anything else?'

'Actually,' Sebastian said annoyingly, 'she's been quite nice to me since I got back. She even told Dermot to speak respectfully to me this morning. After the Daisy photograph episode.'

Katie felt a clutch of fear.

'What Daisy photograph?'

There was another silence. Then Sebastian said, 'Sorry, Katie. I probably shouldn't have mentioned it.'

'*What?* What photograph?'

Sebastian cleared his throat. 'It was of Daisy at a party while we were in Spain.'

'What was she doing?'

'Oh,' Sebastian said vaguely, 'just, you know, partying.'

'Send it to me.'

'I can't. I don't have it. It was on Marcus's phone this morning.'

'Get him to send it to me,' Katie commanded. 'What was Daisy doing?'

'In my day,' Sebastian said unhappily, 'it would be called snogging.'

'*Snogging? Daisy?*'

'Yes. She looks extremely pretty, however.'

Katie had an impulse to hurl her phone across her office. She said, between clenched teeth, 'And your sons were sniggering over this picture, were they?'

'Not sniggering, Katie. Marcus said Daisy would be completely cool about it.'

'Well,' Katie said, '*I'm* not.'

'No.'

'I'm sorry I shouted at you just now.'

'Think nothing of it. It's all such a strain. One has to crack sometime.'

'Can I ask you something?'

'Of course.'

'Do you really not care what happens to Mum and Dad in Spain?'

There was a pause, as if Sebastian was thinking. Then he

said, 'Oh I care. I care all right. It's more that dealing with the situation and all these different personalities and what is and isn't acceptable is often just too much for me. If Mum listened to me ever, it would be a different matter. But she doesn't. She only listens to Jake and there's nothing I can do about that, so I've stopped even trying. I try to stop minding, too, although I'm not very successful. So despite the fact that I know you think I'm wet and useless and defeatist, I'm actually just trying to elude being stamped on by everyone else, flattened, obliterated. It may sound pathetic to you, but I just want people to be kind. Kind to me, and to each other. That's all.'

CHAPTER EIGHT

Marta's door was closed. She often shut it against Florence but this time it had the look of being closed against all comers. Nic, holding a mug of coffee and a notebook and pen, considered on the landing for a moment and then knocked sharply.

There was no reply. He waited and then knocked again. Still silence. He called through the door, 'Marta!'

Florence appeared in the adjacent doorway of her own bedroom. She was wearing a yellow T-shirt and multicoloured pyjama bottoms and on her feet were huge nylon fur slippers, bright green and fashioned to look like frogs, with popping plastic eyes. She said conversationally to her father, 'She's in there.'

'I know,' Nic said.

'I'd just go in.'

'It's her room.'

'It's your *house*,' Florence said reasonably. 'She only lives here because of you and Mum.'

Nic took a swallow of his coffee. 'What do you know about the concept of privacy?'

Florence flapped a hand airily. 'Outdated.'

'Is it? Or is it only outdated for everyone else and really important for you?'

Florence glared at him. 'I hate you.'

Nic shrugged. 'Then I'll have to try and live with that.'

'You are probably,' Florence said crossly, '*the* most annoying father in the whole world. What are you doing now?'

'Writing a note to Marta.'

'Why?'

Nic went on writing, balancing his coffee mug deftly as he wrote. 'None of your business. Nor is the content of the note.'

'You are so mean.'

Nic stooped to slip the paper under Marta's door. He said to Florence, 'And you are so nosy.'

'Marta is my *sister*, I'll have you know.'

He straightened up again and took another sip from his mug. He grinned at Florence.

'Ask Mr Google about the principle of Need to Know.'

'What?'

He bent to kiss her. 'If you ever have a problem – which I devoutly hope you never do – I would never discuss it with Daisy or Marta.'

Florence said eagerly, 'Do you want to talk to Marta about eating all that junk so she's too full for meals?'

He regarded her. 'Something like that.'

Florence retreated into her room, wagging her hands either side of her head. 'OK, OK, I get it.'

'Good,' Nic said. He looked back at Marta's door. Then he said to Florence, 'If you see Marta, if she opens her door, tell her I'll be in my study.'

'We're not supposed to interrupt you in your study,' Florence said sanctimoniously.

He winked at her. 'I'm just marking. Eminently inter-
ruptible.'

———

Gus was shouting. He'd shouted a good deal since coming
home, with, Monica noticed, liberal use of the F-word. When
he shouted at Pilar, or Lucia – who had some English, having
done a nursing exchange in a hospital in Norwich – they
appeared to take little notice and merely went on shaving or
dressing him, nattering away to each other in Spanish as if
Gus hardly existed. It was the same with Jake, who had
instructed everyone to put their car keys in their pockets.
When Gus ranted at Jake, Jake said hearty things like, 'I know,
Pa. Very rough on you. But there it is and it ain't gonna
change,' and went whistling on to the next thing.

But Monica couldn't brush Gus's bewildered rage aside
like that. She had tried to explain to him why having a stroke
was connected to his no longer being allowed to drive, and
he had bellowed back at her in a tirade laced with obscenities.
She had been amazed at the language he used and amazed
he should use such words to her. She said to him once, almost
wonderingly, 'Do you actually remember who I am?'

And he had muttered an incoherent reply and slammed
unevenly out of the room, banging into the doorframe as he
went, which made him howl with pain. She rushed after him
to see if he was really hurt, and there were Pilar and Lucia
already soothing and patting and talking to him in Spanish.

Lucia called out to Monica, 'Don't worry, madam! All is
well!'

'I wish,' Monica said to Pilar, 'that she wouldn't call me
madam. Can you tell her?'

'Of course,' Pilar said.

But Lucia took no notice and when Monica complained to Jake, he said, not raising his eyes from the computer screen in Gus's office, 'Forget it, Ma. In the great scheme of things what does a tiny irritation like that matter?'

Monica leaned against the door-jamb.

'But it makes me feel ridiculous. It's kind of false and grand. It makes a distance between Lucia and me.'

Jake didn't turn, but he lifted his gaze from the screen and rested it on the wall ahead.

'Ma . . .'

'Yes?'

'Do you want to look after Dad all by yourself? Do you want to be his sole carer?'

Monica was flustered. 'No, of course not, I couldn't.'

'Exactly. And Lucia can. And will. She is paid to do what a trained nurse can do. She is *prepared* to because she isn't related to Dad so it's easier for her psychologically.'

Monica said in a small voice, 'Could you turn round? I've spent twenty-five years, after all, talking to the back of your father's head.'

Very slowly, and in a manner alarmingly reminiscent of Gus, Jake swivelled round until he was facing his mother. He did not stand up.

'I know you think I'm making a fuss about the wrong things, but you should realize that I have to get used to these huge changes too.'

Jake smiled up at her. 'I know.'

'It's been just me and Dad for so very long now, up here on this hillside. And now it seems to be lots of people, all the time, and poor old Dad.'

'There was always Pilar every morning,' Jake replied, smiling. 'And José Manuel and all the vineyard workers. And Carmen and her crew.'

Monica said desperately, 'Oh I know. I know all that. But really, basically, it was just us. And now it's not that, it's no longer just us, but also Dad is different. Of course he is. He's changed.'

She stopped abruptly. Jake waited, still smiling up at her but somehow managing to be entirely unhelpful at the same time.

'The thing is,' Monica went on, 'that Dad is being so difficult. He always has been in a way, at least for the past ten years or so, and now of course it's worse. But at the same time, I feel for him. I really do. I feel his frustration and his fury and his – his *impotence*. I feel it at the same time that I can hardly bear being in the same room as him.'

Jake made to turn his chair back again.

'Look, Ma,' he said. 'You're just going to have to get used to life now, like we all are. It's no good coming whining to me.'

'I'm not whining! I just need to tell someone.'

'. . . whining to me that life is different and difficult now. I *know* that. I've changed my whole life to accommodate this new situation after Dad's stroke and –' he closed his eyes and held his hand up to silence his mother – 'I don't want any thanks for that; I'm glad, really glad, to do it, but I can't take on your little troubles and problems as well.'

Monica said stubbornly, 'They're not little.'

Jake swung his chair back to face the computer screen. 'Sorry, Ma. I've got to get on.'

Monica swallowed. She said, tentatively, 'I gather some new vines are arriving soon.'

'Yup.'

'I don't think Dad is very keen on any vine that isn't Tempranillo.'

Jake said evenly, 'It might not always be exclusively his decision.'

'Oh.'

'Seb and Katie are onside.'

Monica said, 'You – you rang them?'

Jake's voice was suddenly its easy, sunny self again. ''Course, Ma.'

'Oh,' Monica said again. 'Good.'

Jake bent towards the computer and away from her. 'Sorry,' he said, 'but I really must get on. See you at supper.'

———

Marta stood silently in the doorway to Nic's study. She was wearing leggings and a huge sweatshirt that came down to mid-thigh, and her feet were bare. Nic was aware of her standing there for several seconds before, without raising his eyes from his marking, he said quietly, 'Nice to see you.'

Marta said, 'I got your note.'

'Yes.'

'I – I don't want any supper.'

Nic went on with his marking. 'I didn't think you would. Florence ate enough for two people anyway. I am so depressed about these chapters. Creative writing isn't *therapy*, for God's sake. Why do so many people treat it as a confessional?'

Marta subsided onto the floor in the doorway. She said, 'I thought you were supposed to write about what you know.'

Nic still didn't look at her. He said, 'The trouble is that modern society sanctions what you know as being defined by the worst fears of your immature personality. Or so it would seem from this lot.'

Marta said, 'You sound a bit tetchy.'

He laughed, and turned to face her. 'Bingo. That's me told. Grumpy old man.'

'Where's Mum?'

'At a work dinner. Do you want to talk to her?'

Marta bent her head and began, without letting go of her cuffs, to pick at her toenails.

'No.'

Nic said, good-naturedly, 'I don't suppose you want to talk to me, either.'

Marta's voice was muffled. 'I don't know why.'

Nic managed still not to look at her. 'Why . . . ?'

'Why I do it. I can't tell Mum why. I don't know.'

Nic said gently, 'You said that the other day. That you didn't know why.'

'It's no good asking me, I don't know. I don't *know*.'

'Well,' Nic said, keeping his voice as calm and matter-of-fact as possible, 'you can probably imagine why Mum's first instinct is to ask you why. Because her second instinct would be to try and help you.'

'I don't want help,' Marta said.

'Don't you?'

'No.'

'So,' Nic said kindly, 'you like what you're doing to your arms? You enjoy it?'

She said defensively, 'You haven't seen my arms.'

'No, I haven't. But the internet is awash with photos, so I'm imagining that yours look fairly similar.'

Marta put both arms protectively round her knees and

then lowered her forehead to rest on them. She was, Nic noticed, still gripping the sleeves of her sweatshirt. Her hair, long and dark, divided to swing one section over her face. She muttered something.

Nic bent forward. 'What, Marta?'

Marta lifted her face but didn't look at her father.

'There's this gang.'

'What gang, sweetie?'

'At school,' Marta said.

Nic didn't move. He said, in as nonchalant a tone as he could manage, 'A gang you're part of?'

Marta looked as if she might cry. Nic said softly, 'Perhaps a gang you would *like* to be part of.'

Marta said unsteadily, looking straight ahead, 'They go everywhere together. All the cool places. And they post, every-where they go, from all the clubs, all the parties . . .'

Nic said, 'Can I get this straight? These people at school make sure you see all the pictures of whatever they're doing but you're never asked to join in?'

Marta said nothing. Nic moved from his desk to sit beside her on the floor. He didn't touch her. He said softly, 'Have I understood you? Are you saying that these kids are posting pictures of all the fun they're having but they're deliberately excluding you? That they're kind of – kind of taunting you?'

Marta said hurriedly, 'It isn't why I do this.'

'Of course not.'

'It's got nothing to do with that.'

'No.'

Marta glanced at him and mumbled something. He leaned towards her slightly.

'What, sweetie?'

She tossed her hair back but she didn't look directly at him. She repeated herself. 'I said, don't tell Mum.'

—

When Katie came out of her legal dinner, she switched her phone back on. There was a message from Daisy which sounded as untruthful as most messages from Daisy did, nothing from the rest of her family, two work-related voice-mails and a missed call from Spain. She stood on the wet pavement in Chancery Lane and peered at the lit screen of her phone. Monica had rung at nine thirty, Spanish time. Two hours later would mean that dinner in Spain would have been eaten and, with luck, Monica might be alone in her bedroom with the mobile phone she had been so reluctant to buy.

'I don't need it,' she'd said to Katie. 'Why do I need such a thing? What's the matter with the telephone line in the house?'

'It isn't for you or about you, Mum. It's for us. So we can reach you, so we know where you are.'

'But suppose I don't want you to be able to spy on me.'

'Ma,' Jake had said. 'Stop right there. You're having a phone. Period. Speaking personally and purely selfishly, I need to know I can get hold of you whenever I want. OK?'

She'd given in, at once. Of course she had. Jake had arranged with José Manuel to buy his mother a mobile phone in Ronda and shown her how to use it. It turned out, inevitably, that Gus had had a phone for years, but claimed it had never crossed his mind that Monica should have one too. 'Parents,' Katie had said at work, recounting the story. 'Honestly!' That had been ten years ago, when Gus was active and fit and Monica was beginning to dream up the shop. It felt not just another age, but also another world.

She stood there on the wet pavement in the flat shoes she had swapped her heels for after the dinner, her handbag and her capacious work bag on her shoulder, and rang her mother.

'Hello?' Monica said cautiously.

'Mum. It's me.'

'Oh!' Monica said. 'Katie! How sweet of you to ring!'

Katie said tiredly, 'You rang me.'

'Did I?'

'Yes, Mum. There was a missed call from you on my phone. I've just come out of a dinner.'

'How lovely. What kind of dinner?'

Katie tried not to sound exasperated. 'The Association of Women's Solicitors. Mum, are you OK?'

'Of course,' Monica said. 'Why shouldn't I be?'

Katie said patiently, 'You rang me, Mum. And I know Dad got home this week.'

'Yes,' Monica said. 'Yes. I did. He did.'

'And?'

'And what?'

'And,' Katie said, 'I imagine it's all pretty difficult. I imagine that's why you rang.'

Monica was silent. Katie couldn't tell if she was crying or trying not to cry. She began to walk towards Fleet Street.

'Mum . . .'

'I'm fine,' Monica said. 'Fine. It's just – a shock. Another shock. To get used to. Lucia . . .'

'Lucia?'

'She's a friend of Pilar's. A trained nurse. She's coming in every morning to get Dad up and shaved.'

'*Shaved?*'

'He can't shave himself. Or won't. I don't know. He's in such a rage about not driving that I don't know what's temper and what's the after-effect of his stroke.'

'Oh, Mum . . .'

Monica was crying now, openly.

'He's in such a fury about everything, all the time. And I do see, I do. I understand why he's in such despair, poor old Gus. But he is so awful too, swearing all the time, especially at me. And now Jake—' She halted abruptly mid-sentence.

Katie stopped walking.

'What about Jake? Mum? What has Jake done?'

Monica said, more steadily, 'Of course he was right. He was completely right.'

'About what?'

'I've just got to accept these changes,' Monica said briskly, as if she hadn't been in floods of tears only seconds ago. 'Of course I have. It's no good my whingeing on wishing things were easier or even like they used to be. Dad's had a stroke and as a consequence, can't drive any more, and he has got to accept that just as I have to accept the changes in everything that was known to me.'

Katie said, 'What did Jake say to you?'

'He was sweet,' Monica said. 'And he was quite right. It's no good my wishing to have the past back and it's no good my not being thankful for Lucia.'

'Hm,' Katie said. She waited a moment while she digested the implications of Monica's disclosures and then she said, 'Would you like me to come out again?'

'Lovely of you to offer,' Monica said, recovering her social voice. 'But no thank you. There's nothing to be done, nothing to be achieved except getting used to this new way of doing things.'

'But if Jake—'

'He's exhausted, Katie. I'm telling you that he has his hands fuller than full trying to sort out the mess your father left. You can imagine. Or perhaps you can't – it's dreadful, the chaos. It's wonderful of him to just give up his own life for this. And that's what he's done, just given it all up.'

Katie began, slowly, to walk again.

'Mum . . .'

'Yes?'

'Mum, why did you ring me earlier?'

'D'you know,' Monica said brightly, 'I can't remember. I really can't. Senior moment, as Jake would say.'

'OK.'

'How are the girls?'

Katie blinked. 'They're fine, Mum. Teenage fine. You know.'

'Give them my love,' Monica said. 'And don't worry about anything here. We are under control, promise, and what can't be cured must be endured, as my prissy old granny used to say.'

'OK,' Katie said reluctantly. 'If you're sure.'

'Of course I am. I'm far more sure tucked up here in my own bed than you are getting a late taxi.'

'Tube, Mum. I travel by public transport.'

'Please,' Monica said. 'Don't give me something else to worry about, picturing you on some awful late-night bus full of drunks and drug addicts.'

Katie felt despair and exasperation rising up in her like a scorching tide.

'Night night, Mum.'

'Text me when you're home?'

'Of course.'

'I shall be lying here, worrying about you.'

'Please don't,' Katie said. 'Don't burden me with that too.'

'Burden?' Monica said sarcastically. '*Burden?* You don't know the meaning of the word.'

———

Daisy was in the kitchen, at the table, eating cereal absent-mindedly while her eyes were fixed on the screen of her phone, propped up against the fruit bowl. When Katie came in, she didn't look up or move but said, 'Hi,' round her mouthful. She was wearing skinny jeans and a voluminous checked shirt, and her hair was artlessly scooped up on top of her head and skewered with what looked like a chopstick.

Katie dumped her bags on the table.

'Hello, darling. Are you the only one still up?'

Daisy didn't take her eyes off the screen of her phone. 'Looks like it.'

Katie glanced at the phone. 'What are you watching?'

'A movie.'

'What sort of movie?'

Daisy sighed theatrically.

'A horror movie, Mum. A really horrible horror movie.'

'Well,' Katie said pleasantly, 'would you like to pause it and talk to me instead?'

Daisy stretched out an arm and pressed a button on her phone. Then she looked at her mother.

'Better?' she said, in a surprisingly conciliatory tone.

'Much. I really need a cup of tea.'

'And a biscuit?'

'Goodness,' Katie said. 'Are there any?'

Daisy got up. 'I hid them from Marta.'

'Oh,' Katie said faintly.

'D'you know,' Daisy said, reaching to the back of a cupboard, 'I can actually do the decent thing sometimes? I can tell you about Marta. I can stop looking at my phone and talk to you. Look. Chocolate digestives. A whole packet.'

Katie carried the kettle across to the sink. Daisy said, 'Dad always uses filtered water from the jug.'

Katie ran tap water into the kettle.

'Yes, I expect he does. Daisy, we really value that you told us about Marta. We really do.'

Daisy laid the packet of biscuits on the table and sawed through it with a bread knife.

'But,' she said. 'I'm waiting for the but.'

Katie plugged the kettle in and switched it on. Then she came back to the table and stood close to Daisy. She said quietly, 'What are those photos?'

Daisy had bitten into a biscuit. She stopped, mid-chew.

'What photos?'

Katie cleared her throat. 'Sebastian told me that his boys were laughing over some photographs of you kissing a boy at a party at the weekend.'

Daisy resumed chewing. She didn't look at her mother.

'We weren't *kissing*,' she said with emphasis.

'Oh? Well, who was he, anyway?'

Daisy waved vaguely. 'Some boy.'

'You mean, a boy you don't even *know*? You don't know his *name*?'

'Will something, perhaps. Or Adam.'

Katie put her hand on Daisy's arm.

'Daisy. Look at me. Do you mean to tell me you were photographed kissing a strange boy at a party and you don't even *care?*'

Daisy shrugged. 'Nope.'

Katie stepped back and took off her mac. She slung it over the back of a chair. She said calmly, 'I don't believe you.'

Daisy took another biscuit. 'Well don't then.'

'I think,' Katie said, taking a mug out of a cupboard and crossing the kitchen towards the kettle, 'that you are pretending not to care, but actually, you care very much indeed that you were photographed making a fool of yourself with a stranger and then your cousins were laughing over the pictures. Were you very drunk?'

Daisy shrugged again. 'Don't remember.'

'I'll take that as a yes.'

'Whatever,' Daisy said rudely.

Katie dropped a teabag into the mug and poured boiling water over it. She said, her back to her daughter, 'Tell you what.'

Daisy collapsed into a chair. 'What?'

Katie turned round, her back to the kettle.

'I think I won't tell Dad. I can't promise that he won't find those photos for himself somewhere, but I'm not going to say anything about them to him.'

'OK,' Daisy said indifferently.

'But even though I can't stop you making an idiot of yourself in public again, I could perhaps ask you to look out for someone photographing you while you do it.'

Daisy broke her second biscuit in half and swept the crumbs into a small ridge.

'Daisy?'

She muttered an almost inaudible 'OK' as Katie opened the fridge for milk.

'I spoke to Granny this evening,' Katie said.

Daisy licked a forefinger and pressed it into the biscuit crumbs.

'Is she OK?'

Katie paused. This was no time for inappropriate unburdening. She took a gulp of her tea.

'Not very, to be honest. Grandpa's back from hospital and is very fed up not to be allowed to drive.'

Daisy grinned. 'Is he swearing?'

Katie smiled back. 'A lot, Granny says.'

Daisy licked the crumbs off her forefinger. She rose to her feet.

'Think I'll go up. Poor old them.'

'I know.'

'At least Jake's out there.'

'Shouldn't you refer to him as Uncle Jake?'

Daisy made for the door. She was still grinning.

'Nah.'

Katie pointed to her cheek. 'Kiss good night?'

Daisy came back and planted a kiss on her mother's cheek with emphasis.

'Love you, Dais.'

Daisy made a gesture of something inexplicable in the air.

'Nighty night, Mum.'

—

Nic and Katie's bedroom was dark and quiet. In the dimness, Katie could make out Nic's long outline under the duvet, sleeping on his side turned away from her, as was his wont.

When she slid into bed, he stirred and rolled towards her, without opening his eyes. He said, his voice slurred with sleep, 'How was it?'

'Fine,' Katie said in a whisper. 'Interesting people either side of me, luckily. Everything OK here?'

He nodded without opening his eyes.

'Fine, too.'

'What about supper? Did anyone eat supper?'

Nic yawned. 'Just Florence and me, as usual.'

'Not Marta?'

'No,' Nic said. 'Not Marta.'

He reached out and put an arm across her. It lay there as heavy and unyielding as if it had been a tree trunk.

Katie put her face close to his. 'Anything else? Anything else to tell me?'

'Not a thing,' he said. 'Not a thing.'

CHAPTER NINE

Jake's new wine friend had suggested that he might like to try planting some Godello vines as well. Godello, he learned, had originated in north-west Spain, probably in the sixteenth century, and produced intense white wine which was long-lived and interestingly mineral-rich. The vines, Jake's new friend said, ripened early and thrived in dry places. The fact that Godello vines were also susceptible to fungal disease was not, to Jake's mind, any kind of obstacle, nor was the other inconvenience of the grape's preferred location being hundreds of kilometres further north. Jake had instructed two of the men in José Manuel's team to plough up several more hectares ready for planting, and when José Manuel pointed out that this ground was not only exposed openly to the sun but also even further from the river, Jake merely clumped him on the shoulder and said, 'Ideal, old buddy. As you will see.'

He did not trouble to inform either his brother or his sister that he was planting Godello as well as Grenache vines on land he had reclaimed from the hillside. It was land his father owned, after all, and it was no trouble to reassure himself that not only was a little leeway a natural and inevitable consequence of being in charge – or, to put it another way, having sacrificed a complete other life to rescue the situation that suddenly had befallen the aged parents – but the end product, some glorious and profitable white wines, would occasion both Katie and Sebastian to be deeply grateful and appreciative. It was, Jake found, quite easy to anchor his confused and muttering father in the office, with a deluge of inexplicable paperwork, and leave himself the liberty of the vineyard. Monica had never been out in it, as far as he knew, and showed less than no inclination to start now.

In fact, dealing with his parents was proving to be much easier than anyone had predicted. Jake himself had always inclined to the it'll-be-all-right-on-the-night point of view, but both Gus and Monica seemed so stunned by their new circumstances that they were, if not exactly docile or biddable, reasonably easy to handle. Bella, however, was proving another matter altogether. She had gone back to London, taking Mouse, after the first ten days, in order to put their London affairs in order and let their flat. Jake had assumed – or, as he told himself more aggrievedly, Bella had encouraged him to assume – that she and Mouse would be back in Spain within a month, and Bella would then set about starting the holiday trekking company that Jake was certain would be absolutely the answer to all her doubts about committing herself to a life in Spain.

But Bella was not acting with the purpose and energy that Jake expected. In fact, she seemed to be making very little effort at all, either to find a tenant for their flat, or to see their accountant or their solicitor. She was also exasperatingly elusive, and only answered her phone for a FaceTime call if Mouse was awake and could, as Bella put it, 'talk to Daddy'. It was very irritating. Irritating and puzzling. And Bella's behaviour compounded Jake's indignant realization that neither of his siblings had actually picked up the phone to him since the weekend after their father's stroke. When he came to think of it, it was he, Jake, who had bothered to ring them about the purchase of the new vines. Neither of them had troubled to ring him about anything, certainly not to ask how he was doing, at the coal face of the situation with both parents to cope with. And the situation was, after all, a *family* one. They were, all three of them, equally responsible and liable for what had happened and for which he, Jake, had shouldered almost all the consequent burden.

When he thought about it like this, Jake grew warm with affront. It was outrageous actually, he told himself, and he wasn't one whose back was easily put up. He glared at the email from his new wine friend, the email that suggested adding a number of Godello vines to the order, and thought angrily to himself that it was superfluous to even bother telling Sebastian and Katie what he was planning. In fact, their conduct, their supreme indifference now that he was conveniently holding the fort, more than justified any inclination he had to mildly exploit his autonomy. He leaned forward and deliberately and carefully doubled his order. It crossed his mind, briefly but alluringly, that when the new planting bore its spectacular fruit, and the wine was selling like hot cakes, he might not even trouble to pass on either the news of his success or the profit. He felt, briefly, fired up with righteous indignation. Then his gaze fell upon a photograph of Mouse that he had stuck to the wall just behind Gus's computer. She wasn't smiling, merely regarding him with her open, trusting, serious gaze.

Jake groaned.

'God,' he said to the photograph, 'I miss you. I miss you so much.'

—

Anna had left supper for Sebastian in a low oven covered with a saucepan lid to prevent its drying out too much. Anna herself had gone to a special choir practice – singing in a charity concert performance of the Holy Sonnets of John Donne, music by Benjamin Britten, a part originally intended, she said, for the tenor voice of Britten's partner, Peter Pears. The boys had eaten earlier with their mother, and had gone out to one of their mysterious destinations that Sebastian never seemed privy to. When he lifted the saucepan lid, he somehow did not feel like what lay beneath, even though he was normally quite partial to Anna's Thai-style fishcakes, but thought, with a spurt of defiance, that he might order himself a forbidden takeaway instead – even, perhaps, an illicit pizza with extra pepperoni and a side of chilli sauce. He would drink beer with it too, he decided, cold beer that he would bring up from the cellar and chill in the freezer section of the fridge. What's more, he told himself, he wouldn't order any vegetables or salad with the pizza. Nothing green. Nothing red, either, except what came with the pizza. He opened the tall kitchen pedal bin with one foot and tipped the fishcakes in quickly, before he lost his nerve. Then he dialled the local pizza place, who were constantly and optimistically posting garish leaflets through the door, and gave his order. The girl at the other end said it'd be with him in half an hour.

In the cellar, Sebastian could find no cans of beer. There were certainly cans there, a dozen cans in shrink-wrapped plastic, but the beer in them was triumphantly labelled as being alcohol-free. Sebastian didn't want no-alcohol beer, he wanted a proper supercharged beer, possibly Belgian – in a bottle, now he came to think of it, beaded with condensation from being so cold. He rang the local off-licence and asked them to send half a dozen beers as soon as possible.

'Which one?' the young man at the other end said.

Sebastian thought.

'I don't know. Belgian maybe?'

The young man sounded as if he was asked this kind of thing all the time.

'Duvel,' he said boredly. 'If you want Belgian.'

'I do,' Sebastian said firmly. 'Half a dozen bottles. Cold. Very cold.'

He felt energized when he'd rung off, energized to the point of being very slightly exhilarated. The effect of discarding his supper and ordering a replacement was emboldening enough to encourage him to ring Spain and to say to Monica, when she answered, 'I know you won't have even started supper yet, Mum, so I just thought I'd ring.'

'Heavens,' Monica said. 'Sebastian!' Then she covered the mouthpiece of the old-fashioned telephone handset, and said audibly to whoever was with her, 'It's Sebastian.'

'Is that Dad?' Sebastian said. 'Is Dad in the room?'

'Indeed he is,' Monica said brightly. 'Gus, it's Sebastian.'

Gus said loudly, 'I heard you the first time.'

'How is he?' Sebastian asked. 'How are you?'

Monica said, 'Oh, we're fine. Really fine. Aren't we, Gus?'

'No,' Gus said audibly and crossly.

Monica said to Sebastian, 'He's longing to talk to you. I know he is. Aren't you, darling?'

'He'll say no,' Sebastian said.

'No,' Gus said clearly.

'Jake's still working,' Monica went on as if neither her husband nor her son had spoken. 'He's in that office morning, noon and night, if he isn't out in the vineyard. I know he misses Mouse terribly. How are the boys?'

'Out,' Sebastian said. 'But good.'

'Out?'

'At some jamming session. Jazz. Band practice or something, you know.'

'And are you and Anna about to have supper?'

'Yes,' Sebastian said untruthfully. 'Anna's fishcakes. Asian style. Delicious.'

Monica sounded as if anything Asian was fine for some but definitely not for her. 'Lovely.'

'In fact,' Sebastian said, 'she's just dishing up. I should go. I just wanted to see how you are.'

'Sweet of you,' Monica said. 'We're fine. Aren't we, Gus?'

There was a silence. Sebastian said, 'Mum?'

'What, darling?'

'Are you OK? I mean, you specifically?'

'Oh yes,' Monica said. 'No complaints.'

'It can't be easy.'

'It isn't. But having Jake makes all the difference.'

There was a roar from Gus.

'Mum?' Sebastian said again. 'What was that?'

'Nothing.'

'But I heard—'

'Do you know,' Monica said, interrupting, 'that we are having squid for supper? Pilar brought it this morning. I love squid. You must go.'

'But I want to know how you really are.'

'Darling,' Monica said, 'so sweet of you to ring. Love from us both.'

Sebastian stood looking at his phone when she had rung off. Then, before he lost his nerve, he rang Jake's mobile. It was switched off. He listened to Jake's jaunty message inviting him to leave his own message after the tone and felt a small bolt of the same emotion that he had experienced tipping the fishcakes in the bin.

'I've just tried to speak to Mum,' Sebastian said to Jake's voicemail, 'and got nowhere. Could you let me know how things really are?'

He put his phone down on the table. Anna had left a place laid for him, knife and fork and water tumbler, beside his blue linen napkin in a ring Dermot had made when he was eight. Metalwork Job Two, it had been, and involved learning to use pliers and a length of wire. Sebastian considered tidying it all away. He would, instead, eat the pizza out of the box it came in and drink the beer out of the bottles. The napkin, now he came to think of it, might be useful for the chilli sauce.

—

Florence said, 'Will you test me on my French vocab? Will you? Will you? It's a test on Friday and she goes *nuts* if you make even the smallest mistake.'

Katie was peering at her mobile. She said, absently, ''Course.'

Florence put her French notebook firmly over her mother's phone. She said commandingly, 'You've got to *concentrate*.'

Katie glanced up.

'Or *you* have. It's you who has to do the test.'

Florence sighed theatrically. 'I'm just asking you to think about *me* for three minutes.'

'I think about you a lot, you know.'

Florence clutched her head. 'If *only* that were true.'

'Darling,' Katie said, 'you and Marta and Daisy are my chief preoccupations.'

'After work.'

'No.'

'Oh yes,' Florence said, nodding. 'Everything comes after work. At least Daddy . . .' She stopped.

Katie put a hand on Florence's exercise book to hold it steady.

'What about Daddy?'

Florence said airily, flapping her hands, 'Nothing!'

Katie put the phone and the exercise book down on the table.

'Why did you say "At least Daddy" like that? What did you mean?'

Florence squirmed.

'Nothing. Really nothing.'

Katie took hold of her shoulders. 'It *was* something. What? Tell me.'

Florence rolled her eyes. 'Jeez, parents! It wasn't anything much.'

Katie pressed down on Florence's shoulders. 'I'm waiting.'

Florence looked sideways. 'It was just the other night. With Marta.'

'Marta?'

'Daddy put a note under her door.'

'And?'

Florence paused. Then she said, in a rush, 'Marta went

down and talked a bit to Daddy. After he'd put the note in her room.'

'Were you eavesdropping?'

Florence looked indignant. 'No!'

'Then how do you know?'

'She went downstairs. I saw her. My door was a little bit open. But I didn't listen, I didn't, I didn't!'

Katie released Florence's shoulders. She picked up the exercise book and held it up so that she could see it properly.

'Spell *essuyer*,' she said.

———

Anna paused by the kitchen table and looked at Sebastian's untouched place setting. The two boys lurked behind her in the doorway, like goofy sentinels. She gestured.

'It doesn't look,' she said to Sebastian, 'as if you've had supper.'

He smiled at her. Two bottles of beer had been very mellowing, particularly with the knowledge that there were another couple chilling in the fridge.

'Oh, I did.'

Anna put her music case on the table. She said, with an emphasis Sebastian could only suppose was for the benefit of the boys, 'You must have eaten the fishcakes with your *fingers*.'

Sebastian kept smiling.

'I didn't eat the fishcakes.' He motioned towards the bin. 'They're in there.'

Marcus gave a gasp. Anna turned briefly in their direction, as if certain of their support. She said calmly, 'You can't mean it.'

'I can,' Sebastian said. 'It's true. I had a pizza. Out of its box. In front of the television.'

Anna fixed him with one of her focused stares. He could not believe his sudden and miraculous imperviousness to it.

Anna said with cold fury, 'Are you *mad*?'

Sebastian leaned back against the rail of the solid-fuel cooker. He shrugged.

'Don't think so.'

Anna turned towards the boys.

'Go to bed,' she said. 'There's nothing for you here.'

Neither moved.

'Go to bed!' Anna shouted.

Sebastian looked benevolently at his sons.

'You don't have to.'

'You do!' Anna said loudly. 'You do!'

Marcus made as if to obey her. Dermot, his ears enlarged by his haircut, was staring at his father as if he had never seen him before.

Sebastian said conversationally, 'I rang Spain. Mum sounded in a bit of a state. I might go out there again soon. I mean, in the next ten days.'

'Do what you like,' Anna said furiously. 'You're drunk. You must be drunk.'

Sebastian looked at Dermot.

'Want to come? To Spain, I mean. Marcus? Want to come to Spain with me?'

'Of course they don't,' Anna said.

Dermot said in a strangled voice, 'I might.'

'I don't think,' Sebastian said to Anna, 'that even I could get drunk on two bottles of beer. As far as I remember, Belgian beer averages about six per cent alcohol at most.'

'You're telling me,' Anna said, 'that you dumped the supper I left you in the bin, and ordered a takeaway pizza instead?'

'And chilli sauce,' Sebastian said. 'I like your fishcakes. I really do. But I just didn't feel like them. And I did feel like a beer. The only beer in the cellar was non-alcoholic so I ordered some proper beer.' He looked at his sons. 'There's more in the fridge if you'd like it.'

Anna sat down unsteadily in a chair by the table. She said, 'I don't believe this.'

Sebastian said reasonably, 'It isn't *such* a big deal. I'm really sorry about the fishcakes. I shouldn't have thrown them in the bin. That was unnecessarily aggressive.'

Marcus said suddenly, 'I'd like a beer.'

Anna's head whipped round. She said, 'It's a school night, Marcus. Anyway, you are far too young.'

Sebastian smiled at his son.

'Friday night, then, lad.'

'Lad?' Anna said. '*Lad?* When have you ever called them that?'

'It probably *is* a bit affected,' Sebastian said. 'But it's diffi-cult to know how to address sons affectionately. Always easier with daughters.'

Anna looked round at the boys again. 'Go to bed.'

They glanced at one another uncertainly but didn't move. Sebastian said, 'Do as your mother says, boys. Go to bed.'

Dermot said hesitantly, 'About Spain . . .'

'We'll talk about it in the morning,' Sebastian said. 'I might walk you to school.'

Marcus said, 'We go on the bus.'

Sebastian let go of the cooker rail and waved an arm. 'Then I might come on the bus with you.'

Dermot blinked. 'Cool.'

Anna was staring at the untouched place setting. The skin of her knuckles, Sebastian could see, was white with tension.

'Go to bed, boys,' she said, between clenched teeth.

They shuffled out of the room. Anna didn't move. She addressed the table, not looking at Sebastian. 'What is going on?'

Sebastian shrugged.

'Don't know,' he said. 'Nothing.'

She gave a snort.

'Nothing? Nothing? You belittle me in front of the children and offer them air tickets to Spain and that's *nothing*?'

He waited to feel the usual tide of humiliated compulsion to apologize. It didn't seem to be coming. He said, instead, 'I was talking to a girl.'

Anna's head shot up.

'What girl?'

'A girl at work. A Romanian.'

'Are you telling me,' Anna demanded, 'that you are involved with a Romanian girl at work?'

Sebastian laughed. 'No.'

'No, what? No, I am not having an affair? No, I am not involved with a girl at work?'

'No, I am not involved with anyone. No, I am not having an affair.'

Anna looked at him with contempt.

'Who'd have you, anyway?'

'Interesting,' Sebastian said, 'to see that you're jealous.'

'Hah!' Anna said with energy. 'Jealous! You *wish*.'

'I don't, actually,' Sebastian said. 'But I wanted to tell you about this girl.'

Anna flung herself back in her chair.

'This girl! This girl who's made you throw your supper in the bin.'

Sebastian left the cooker and took a chair close to Anna's. 'Listen to me, Anna.'

She regarded him warily. 'Why should I? You seem round the bend to me.'

'I think I might have been round some kind of bend before. But not now. And oddly it was this girl who woke me up a bit. By default, I mean. She's done a test clean and passed with flying colours, as I knew she would because she is clever and conscientious and thoroughly overqualified. But she's here because of a boyfriend and what he wants goes, in her life as well as his. It just – struck me.'

Anna was looking at him in a way he had always found intimidating before. She said, 'If you are implying what I think you are implying about *our* relationship, I am far from impressed. In fact, I think you are utterly pathetic.'

'I expect you do,' Sebastian said. 'And you might be right. In fact, as far as the past goes, I'm sure you are right. I *have* been utterly pathetic. I expect I could be again. But I am aware in a way I wasn't before. I'm aware of my capacity – no, let's be honest, my *propensity* – for being hopeless and dismal and pathetic, and it not only makes living with me no fun for either you or the boys, but it isn't much fun to *be* me, either.'

'So this – this display of childish defiance . . .'

'Oh, I agree,' Sebastian said warmly. 'It isn't in the least edifying, or even *normal*, to throw your supper in the bin. But it's a symptom, I suppose. A symptom of waking up to being such a doormat, such a loser, such a—'

'Gus,' Anna said suddenly.

Sebastian looked keenly at her.

'What?'

Anna sat up straight.

'Gus,' she said again. 'It's your father. You're released by his having had a stroke and being incapacitated because of it.'

'Am I?'

She began to get up.

'Well,' she said more confidently. 'Something like that.'

He waited a moment, watching her as she began to clear away his place setting.

'OK,' he said, 'OK. That's your reading. Which I might or might not share. But I am clear about one thing.'

He paused. She was standing the other side of the table, his blue linen napkin and water glass in her hands.

'Well?' she said.

He leaned forward and put his elbows on the table.

'I meant it about going back to Spain,' he said. 'And I meant it about taking the boys along with me. If they'd like to come. Which, I rather think, they would.'

———

There were no crisp packets in Marta's bin. No sweet or biscuit wrappers either, only cotton buds and screwed-up tissues. Her room was, as it had been all her life, quite orderly and impersonal, especially compared with the frenzied sociability of Daisy's bedroom, one wall entirely given over to photographs of friends, and the sheer chaos of Florence's where the cuddly toys of her childhood and every present she had ever been given, let alone every book she had ever read, made it difficult to discern that both a bed and a desk lurked somewhere in the confusion. When all three girls had been younger, Saturday mornings had been allotted as the weekly occasion for tidying. But the resistance to the requirement, and the immense ingenuity of evasion, had triumphed in the end and a tacit truce was called. Even clean and ironed laundry was now left on the landing floor outside all three bedrooms, where it might remain for a week, at whatever cost to Katie.

'Leave it,' Nic would say warningly to her. 'Leave it. Even for a month. They're bloody lucky not to have to do their own laundry, ungrateful little sods.'

Katie had not done her own laundry in Spain, she remembered. There had been a woven basket in the bathroom she shared with her brothers, and the contents had vanished on a daily basis and reappeared, folded and approximately ironed, on her bed the next day. Looking now at Marta's roughly made bed – at least she had made an attempt at pulling the duvet straight – filled her with retrospective shame at the assumptions of her own adolescence and a present shame at being in Marta's bedroom at all, let alone snooping in her waste-paper basket. And snooping it was. No good pretending otherwise. She had even told work that she had a conference call that morning and would not be in the office until midday. She had told the same lie to Nic, and to the girls. And then she had waved them all off that morning, gone back to her laptop with more coffee to check her emails and then, in the strangely silent weekday morning house, climbed the stairs and gone boldly, if self-consciously, into Marta's bedroom.

There was no evidence of her cutting. Nothing. Not a sign.

No bloodied clothing, no razor blades, no marks on towels or tissues. It was, to all appearances, the average bedroom of an average teenage girl, with a few babyish mementos of childhood mixed up with signs of progress towards maturity, academic and adolescent; trainers with glitter laces on the floor, mauve plastic ponies with fantastic manes and tails on the bookshelves, then and now, past and present. I want to cry, Katie thought; I really, desperately want to break down and cast myself on Marta's bed and clutch her pillow and inhale the smell of her hair on it. I want to do something visceral, savage, primitive. I want to kill whoever is making her so unhappy, just *kill* them.

There was a photograph wedged in a mirror frame on the wall. It was a photograph of all five of them taken on a boat off the Croatian coast the summer before. They were all in life jackets because the skipper of the boat, a commanding squat man with blazing blue eyes, had said to the girls that if they didn't put life jackets on, he simply would not allow them on his boat. Katie had watched them meekly do exactly as they were told, even Florence who had all but disappeared into a jacket far too big for her. And here they all were, laughing and carefree in their huge orange padding, and there was Nic too, and her, photographed by the blue-eyed skipper on the blue Croatian sea. Katie had an impulse to kiss the photograph, and only when her mouth was six inches from it did she pull herself sharply backwards. Honestly, she told herself. Honestly. What was she thinking of?

———

She was late back from work that evening. A client wanted to speak to her but was in America on business, so the call had to happen convenient to his meetings in New York. She had rung Nic to say that she would be late and he had reminded her that Florence had a piano lesson and Marta was doing after-school club and Daisy was at a history lecture, so he proposed that he would make pasta for anyone who wanted it later in the evening. He sounded, Katie thought, almost conciliatory, like someone who was really trying to make a difference, to *be* different and more imaginative. She must notice that, she told herself, and not just notice it but acknowledge it, and if the opportunity arose, directly to him. When she walked into the kitchen that evening, Nic was loading pasta bowls into the dishwasher and Brahms was playing on the music system he had insisted on installing when they moved in, and he had switched off the overhead lights, leaving only the two lamps on.

She dropped her work bags on the floor and went across the kitchen to kiss him.

'Hi there.'

He straightened up. 'All present and correct, ma'am.'

She began unbuckling the belt of her mac. 'Are they?'

'Yup,' Nic said. He closed the dishwasher. 'All upstairs. Florence is in bed. The others are doing I know not what. Supper?'

Katie shook her head. 'Not hungry.'

She took off her mac and went back to the entrance to hang it on a hook.

'Good day?' Nic said.

She made an equivocal motion with her hand. 'So-so. You?'

He shrugged, then he picked up his glass of wine and indicated it. 'Wine?'

She shook her head. 'No thanks. Any messages?'

'You mean from your mother? No. None.'
Katie went past him towards the kettle.
'Nic . . .'
'Yes?'
She hesitated. Then she turned to face him. 'Nic,' she said, 'could we talk about Marta?'

CHAPTER TEN

Jake was in a good mood. Bella had told him in the FaceTime call – Mouse was in the pyjamas he had bought her – that she and Mouse would be joining him in Spain in ten days' time. A letting agency had found two women – 'Not girls,' Bella said to Jake. 'Definitely women. Both civil servants over forty. Probably a couple' – as tenants for their flat and it only remained for Bella to stow everything personal in a locked cupboard and pack for a Spanish winter. Jake had said he would come back and help her sort the flat for letting, that he'd like to, he'd be glad to, that his leaving on impulse meant that there were several things he hadn't got with him, never mind people he needed to see.

Bella had said Mouse would be thrilled to fly to Spain with Daddy. She sounded much more like the old Bella, the obliging, sweet-tempered, right-thinking Bella whom he'd married not because she was pregnant, but because she had told him, wide-eyed with determination, that she was going to have this baby whether he married her or not and whatever her parents said. He had loved that. At that very moment, he knew he loved her, and when Mouse was born, he had adored her. He had sat beside her hospital bed, Mouse swaddled beside them in her transparent crib, and felt something for Bella that he had never felt in his life before, a feeling of worship and gratitude and wonder.

'I adore you,' he'd said to Bella. 'I really do.'

He felt something similar now, a rush of exalted and indebted thankfulness to Bella for tidying up their old lives in London and agreeing to embark on a new venture which was, he had to face it, as unfamiliar to her as it was to him. It was not in his nature to regret his past irritation with her – he had never been able to hold a grudge, after all – but very much more in his nature to want to celebrate things going his way once more. He cornered Pilar in the kitchen where she was rinsing out her dusters and asked her to buy the ingredients for a jubilation paella.

Pilar didn't look up from the dusters.

'I can make the paella.'

Jake put an arm round her shoulders.

'No, you can't. I make a much better paella than you do. I just don't want to go shopping, so please do it for me, there's a dear girl.'

Pilar sighed heavily. 'You are impossible.'

He kissed her nearest cheek noisily. 'Bless you. Thank you. I am surrounded by wonderful women.'

'And awful men.'

Jake laughed. He gave her shoulders a squeeze.

'It's the awful men,' he said, 'who make the women look so wonderful.'

—

That evening, he lit all the candle lanterns on the terrace and made Monica one of his speciality gin and tonics. His father, despite being advised not to touch alcohol, had poured himself his usual generous glass of red wine, which he was drinking while watching the British news on his iPad. The British news had always made Gus furious, long before his stroke.

'Why do you watch it,' Jake said, 'if you can't bear it?'

Gus had only grunted, and didn't raise his eyes from the screen. Jake had gone to find his mother.

'Dad's swearing at the screen again,' Jake said. 'Why does he watch the news if he can't stand to know anything about it?'

Monica had laughed.

'That's exactly why,' she said. 'Before the televised news, Dad read yesterday's paper faithfully every day and ranted at that.' She looked round the terrace. 'This is lovely. It all looks so pretty.' She raised her glass. 'And this is lovely, too.'

'Good,' Jake said heartily. '*Good.*'

Monica looked at him. She had put on the turquoise kaftan again and looped her string of pearls round her neck.

'To Bella and Mouse coming next week,' Monica said. 'It will be so lovely to have Mousie back.'

Jake said, 'I ought to go and start the paella.'

'Oh,' Monica said airily, 'it can wait, can't it?'

'Well, it can for a moment,' Jake said. 'Actually, there's something I wanted to ask you.'

Monica was gazing up at her canariensis palm.

'Ask away, darling. Do you know, I think that poor tree doesn't exactly look better but it definitely doesn't look worse. I wonder if I dare hope that I've stopped the rot?'

'Mum . . .'

Monica took a swallow of her gin.

'Yes, darling?'

'Mum,' Jake repeated, leaning forward in his chair, 'could you lend me some money?'

Monica laughed.

'You know, don't you, that I haven't any to lend.'

'But the proceeds of Gramps and Gran's house . . .'

Monica looked dreamily back at the palm.

'I gave that to you three children ages ago, darling. Don't you remember?'

Jake looked at the floor of the terrace.

'I'd forgotten.'

'Anyway,' Monica said, 'what on earth do you want money for? I mean, living here isn't costing you anything.'

'It's *for* here,' Jake said.

Monica seemed to focus for the first time.

'Here?'

'Yes,' Jake said, 'for new planting.' He added, patiently, 'The new vines I told you about. That I told Seb and Katie about.'

Monica said sharply, 'Does Dad know?'

'I told him,' Jake said. 'But I don't know if he took it in.'

Monica regarded him. 'I wonder if you did tell him.'

'Of course I did!'

'He won't like having anything planted here that isn't Tempranillo. I can promise you that.'

'Mum,' Jake said, 'help me. Please.'

She took another sip of her drink.

'Darling, I can't. I can't give you money to defy your father because I haven't *got* any money. Any money I had, I gave to you children. And anything I have now is tied up here and probably useless. Or inaccessible.'

'Mum . . .'

Monica put her drink down and covered her ears with her hands.

'Stop it,' she said. 'Just stop it. Darling Jake, please. I can't bear it. I can't. You sound . . .' She continued, in a lower voice, 'You sound just like Katie.'

———

The first time anyone called Beacham was recorded, Sebastian told his boys, was actually in the Domesday Book. Their ancestor was called Hugo de Belchamp and there he was, written down as having actually existed, in 1086. Both boys looked, despite themselves, interested and impressed. Dermot, who was studying history for A level, said that there weren't really any surnames before 1799, when Pitt the Younger introduced them as being a temporary measure necessary for personal taxation to pay for the expense of the Napoleonic Wars. There hadn't been any income tax before then, either. Sebastian smiled at him.

'Well, there was us, before that. Beachams existed seven hundred years before the Napoleonic Wars.'

'Wow,' Marcus said respectfully.

'We are a very old and continuously recorded family. Getting on for a thousand years of us.'

Dermot nodded solemnly.

'And you are Beachams, both of you,' Sebastian said. 'Descendants of Hugo de Belchamp in the Domesday Book. It is quite something, to be descendants of a family that goes back so far.'

Marcus cleared his throat.

'Why isn't one of us named Gus, like Grandpa? Why aren't you?'

Sebastian said carefully, 'It's the surname that signifies.'

Marcus stared at his father.

'Is it? But why isn't Dermot Gus?'

Sebastian steepled his fingers.

'Dermot was named for a great-uncle of Mum's. As were you. They both died at Monte Cassino.'

'But,' Marcus said stubbornly, 'they weren't *Beachams*, were they? And Dermot and I are.'

Sebastian said lamely, 'You had better ask Mum.'

'I mean,' Marcus said, as if his father hadn't spoken, 'why didn't you insist? You were there, after all. You were there when we were born.'

'I think,' Sebastian said, letting his fingers relax and forcing himself not to put his hands joyfully over his face, 'that this is the very first conversation we have ever had about family history. Don't you?'

Dermot glanced at his brother. Then he said loudly, 'We didn't think you cared!'

Sebastian bent his head. 'Of course I care.'

Marcus was fiddling with a paperclip he had found, opening it up and then trying to bend it back into a clip-shaped oval. He had always fiddled with something, Sebastian remembered, been unable to keep his hands still. There'd been a craze a couple of years ago for little plastic gadgets called fidget spinners, and Marcus had had several small bright discs whose popularity had dwindled as abruptly as it had suddenly flowered. Sebastian reached out and put his hand over Marcus's restless one. Marcus froze.

Sebastian said again, more quietly and steadily, 'Of course I care.'

Marcus slid his hand from under his father's, and jammed both hands into his trouser pockets. He muttered, 'OK.'

'In fact,' Sebastian said, 'I meant it when I said that I'd be going out to Spain again shortly and I would love it if you came. Just for a weekend. If, of course, you want to.' He glanced at them. 'No pressure.'

There was a silence. Then Dermot stood up slowly and looked down at his brother.

'I think – we'd like to. Wouldn't we, Marc? If it's OK with Mum.'

———

The specialist was called Dr Mak. The internet informed Katie that Dr Mak had been born in Hong Kong and had then done all her medical and therapeutic training in America – New Haven, to be precise – and London. Her first name, or names, were Ying and Ley, which the internet helpfully explained meant flower and meadow, and that any woman called meadow was deemed, in most oriental cultures, to be nurturing and sensible. Katie, making the appointment for Marta, couldn't help thinking that a warm and mothering doctor was exactly what she was in need of herself.

The receptionist seemed not only to sense this, but also to have heard it all before.

'You and your husband are welcome to come too, Mrs Ledward, but you must understand that Dr Mak will be talking to Marta and Marta alone.'

'Of course,' Katie said quickly. It occurred to her, as it always did, to inform the receptionist that although she was indeed Marta's mother, she wasn't technically Mrs Ledward. At work she was Katie Beacham and it was as Katie Beacham that she had qualified. It was also how she thought of herself, how she referred to herself. There had been a brief tussle when Daisy was born about whose name the baby should take, and as it was Nic who registered the birth, while the complications and absorptions of the immediate aftermath were so all-pervading, it was only some time later that Katie had realized that Daisy was officially Daisy Ledward.

Nic, taking the baby away one night to give Katie a chance to sleep, had said in a puzzled tone, 'Does it matter? Honestly. Does it? She's our daughter and as long as the three of us know it, who cares what her surname is?'

'But I'm her mother.'

Nic had paused, the baby in his arms. His competence with babies and small children always seemed to Katie to make it extra hard to argue with him.

'I know you are, Katie. And Daisy knows it too, even at three weeks.'

'But when she's at school, when she doesn't have the same name as me . . .'

He nudged the door open with his foot.

'Then call yourself Ledward at these future mythical school gates. What does a name matter?'

'It matters to me!' Katie had cried, and Nic had left the room without replying, carrying Daisy folded into the cobwebby shawl that Nic's mother had knitted for her. It had been almost the last thing she did, knitting that shawl, before she died, suddenly, of a heart attack, just as she was lifting her supermarket basket onto the conveyor belt. The basket had contained teabags and frozen peas and a packet of old-fashioned ginger nuts. Even now, Katie, who had been fond of Nic's mother, could not think of ginger nuts with equanimity.

'I can't *believe*,' Katie had said to Nic, that night in their kitchen, 'that you wouldn't even *tell* me about your conversation with Marta.'

He looked straight at her.

'I promised,' he said. 'She asked me to promise and I did.'

'But Nic, I'm her *mother*.'

He shrugged. 'And I am her father and she must be able to trust us.'

Katie said furiously, 'You are so *pompous*.'

Nic shrugged again. 'People always accuse the principled of pomposity.'

Katie took a deep breath.

'So,' she said with effort. 'Marta is ready, or ready-ish anyway, for some help, you say. What happens next?'

Nic came towards her. He set his wine glass down and although he didn't touch her, he came close.

'If you would like to make the first appointment,' Nic said, looking directly at her, 'you should. And I will tell Marta that you know.'

'Thank you,' she said now to Dr Mak's receptionist. 'Thank you for all your help.'

An email popped up on her screen. It was from the legal department of a national and widely read tabloid.

'We are in receipt of your letter of the 16th,' it said, 'but beg to inform you that we have photographic evidence of the disputed occurrence on the night of the 2nd. Publication of this evidence is entirely within our legal rights and in the public interest. Any legal objection you may have needs to reach our offices by Thursday morning. We await your reply.'

———

'Of course, take them to Spain,' Anna said. She was at her computer and there was a spreadsheet open on her screen.

Sebastian was sitting on an upright chair to the side of Anna's desk. He said pleasantly, 'I intend to. Just for a weekend. They don't want to be away for too long, and nor do I.' He paused and then he said, 'I am only telling you—'

'They told me themselves,' Anna said, tapping her keyboard rapidly.

'I'm only telling you,' Sebastian repeated patiently, 'because I rather hoped you might like to come, too.'

Anna tapped on for some seconds. Then she said, quite gently, 'I don't think so.'

Sebastian looked down at his knees.

'Suppose that *I* would rather like you to come?'

Anna stopped typing. She put her hands in her lap and looked straight ahead. She said again and more firmly, 'I don't think so, Sebastian. Apart from anything else, your mother wouldn't like it.'

'But *I* might.'

'And I might not.'

'Ah.'

She looked away from him.

'I quite see why the boys should go. And you should, of course.'

'May I say,' Sebastian said boldly, 'that this is a change of tune? You would never have countenanced the boys coming to Spain before. Or, indeed, having much to do with their grandparents.'

Anna turned back to her computer. She said, in a different tone, 'Did you say that girl was called Luminata?'

Sebastian repressed a small smile. 'Yes.'

'And she's from Romania?'

'Yes.'

Anna scrolled down her screen. She said, 'And she's good?'

'Very,' Sebastian said with emphasis.

'I can't come to Spain, Sebastian. I really can't. You know why. But I don't want to stop the boys going.'

Sebastian looked at her attractive, decided profile. It was a profile that had always slightly daunted him – in fact, he'd been astonished when she had agreed to marry him. There had always been an aspect of Anna that had seemed to him very finished, very collected and grown-up. Perhaps, he thought now, wonderingly, even Anna had vulnerabilities and doubts. Even Anna was afraid of something.

'Anna?'

She typed on, rapidly and competently. 'Yes?'

'That vineyard in Spain belongs to all three of us Beacham children. Not just Jake. I want the boys to see it, understand what it means to them.'

Anna didn't look his way. 'I know.'

'And Luminata is just a very good and useful and reliable worker.'

Anna said, with slightly less conviction, 'I know that too.'

Sebastian stood up. He looked down at Anna's head, at the smooth, thick hair that always lay against her head and face with such precision.

'I'll just book our flights then,' he said.

She didn't turn her face. 'I could do that.'

'Could you? You're so much better at computers.'

'I'd be glad to,' Anna said. 'Actually.'

Sebastian's gaze didn't shift. He pulled himself rather more upright from his usual slouch. It crossed his mind to comment on her apparent need and desire to be involved somehow in their weekend in Spain, and decided against it. He also resolved not to touch her.

'Thank you,' Sebastian said, unable to keep his voice as neutral as he wished. 'Thank you, Anna.'

———

Dr Mak looked oriental and sounded English. She was small and trim in a dark trouser suit, and she took Marta's hand at once, even as she was speaking to Katie and Nic. She told them that she and Marta would go into her office to talk for a while, and then Katie and Nic could join them.

Marta looked to Katie both young and very troubled. She said, on impulse, 'She's only thirteen.'

Dr Mak didn't let go of Marta's hand. They were about the same height, standing there, but looked generations apart. She nodded.

'I know,' she said.

'Do you mind?' Katie asked Marta desperately. 'Do you mind if we don't come with you?'

Marta looked at the carpet. She shook her head but she didn't speak.

'We will be twenty minutes at most.' Dr Mak smiled and turned to Marta. 'This way, Marta,' and they were gone.

Nic collapsed in a chair and put his hands over his face. Katie stood looking at Dr Mak's closed office door. 'Are we doing the right thing?' she asked uncertainly.

Nic was weeping quietly. After a moment he said hoarsely, 'It's the only thing we *can* do.'

'I'm so afraid.'

'Me too.'

Katie perched on a chair next to Nic.

'You know what I'm thinking?'

Nic took his hands away from his face and pulled a navy blue bandana handkerchief from his pocket. He wiped it across his eyes then blew his nose ferociously. He said, tensely, 'I can guess.'

Katie looked down at her rigidly clasped hands.

'I've got to say it. I've just *got* to say that in my mind, the continuum of self-harming is – is suicide.'

Nic didn't look at her. He said, 'It might be the continuum but that doesn't mean it's accurate.'

'No. But it's a possibility. A possibility that keeps haunting me.'

'Me too.'

'Nic . . .'

'Look, Katie,' Nic said suddenly. 'It isn't because of anything we've done or not done. It just *is*. It's part of now, how life is for kids now.' He glanced towards the closed door. 'Thank God for therapists like Dr Mak.'

'As long as Marta likes her.'

'Yes.'

'She has to like and trust her. She has to feel safe with her.'

Nic looked at Katie. 'That's the main reason I didn't tell you. About Marta talking to me. I wanted her to be certain I was trustworthy.'

Katie looked away. 'Yes.'

'You don't sound very convinced.'

'Oh,' Katie said angrily, 'I don't know what I feel. I don't know what I'm supposed to feel, either. I sometimes – quite often, actually – don't know if I can bear what's happening, whether I can cope with it all.'

'What's the alternative? Abandon us all? Run away and join the circus?'

Katie regarded him.

'Of course not.'

'Well, then.'

'D'you know,' she said abruptly, 'that I can say the unsayable to you. I really can.'

'But you don't like yourself for doing it.'

'That too.'

'And I act it out rather than saying it,' he said, staring at her.

'Yes.'

She looked towards the door again. She said, 'They've been ages . . .'

'I think,' Nic said, 'that it'll take as long as it takes for Marta to feel safe. This is just a beginning.'

'What if Daisy hadn't told us?'

'Don't.'

Katie looked up at the ceiling, blinking away tears. Trying to sound light-hearted, she said, 'At least it has stopped me from fretting about Spain.'

———

Anna booked three return tickets to Gibraltar. She told Sebastian that she had done it, and that if they only took hand luggage then their passage through airports either end of the journey would be both quicker and easier.

Sebastian decided not to say, 'I know.' She didn't pack for the boys but Sebastian noticed that she handed them both international adaptors, which she must have taken the trouble to purchase.

Sebastian rang Monica to tell her the three of them would be arriving on Friday.

'Lovely,' Monica said brightly. 'In fact, both lovely and perfect timing. Jake won't be here.'

'Jake won't . . .'

'No,' Monica said. 'He won't. He's going back to England to collect Bella and Mouse. On Thursday. He's going on Thursday. Aren't you, darling?' She came back to the phone. 'Yes, Thursday. So if you and the boys are here, that's ideal. The boys! I haven't seen the boys for*ever*. Are they as tall as you are?'

'Dermot is.'

'So exciting,' Monica said. 'Dad will be thrilled. Won't you, Gus? Thrilled. To see the boys.'

'Are you OK, Mum?'

'Me?' Monica said. 'Absolutely fine, darling. Jake has been a hero. He really has.'

'How is Dad? Can you say?'

Monica said, more carefully, 'Not really, darling. Not now. More news on Friday.'

There was a subdued roar at the Spanish end.

Sebastian said, 'What was that?'

'Nothing,' Monica said airily. 'Absolutely nothing.'

'Mum . . .'

'What sort of time shall we expect you? Shall I get Pilar to make us some supper on Friday?'

Sebastian could hear Jake's voice raised in protest in the background. 'That would be great.'

'I can't believe it,' Monica said. 'I shall see the boys on Friday!'

'Mum, what's going on?'

'The speech therapist came today,' Monica whispered. 'That's all. It always wears Dad out.'

'Oh Mum . . .'

'But,' Monica said, with a swift change of tone to something altogether brighter, 'there we are. Aren't we?'

Sebastian glanced at his family. Anna and the boys were standing three feet away, regarding him with concern.

He said to his mother, 'Will you be OK? Till Friday?'

'Oh, of course!' Monica said. 'Especially with the thought of you all coming for the weekend. We'll be fine. Won't we, Gus? Bye, darling. Fly carefully.'

'Bye,' Sebastian said. He lowered his phone and dropped it into his pocket.

Anna said, 'How are things?'

Sebastian looked at her. Then he smiled.

'Pretty bad, I think. Brace yourselves, boys.'

CHAPTER ELEVEN

Dr Mak had explained, with emphasis, that the most important element in treating Marta was that she should feel both physically and emotionally safe. She had not only stood close to Marta, in a way Katie found disturbingly intimate, but also said that everything that Marta might use to injure herself must be removed from the house: that meant even not evident things like stray staples, or sharp-edged paper, because even if it was practically impossible to remove every accessible sharp object in Marta's life, it was vital for her to understand the compassion and concern of those around her.

Marta didn't speak at all during the journey home. She sat in the back seat of the car, confined by her seat belt, her sleeves pulled down and her earbuds in, isolating herself from her parents. Her head was bent, too, so that her expression was hard to read.

'It is also very important,' Dr Mak had said, 'that nothing you parents do or say makes Marta feel shame. If she feels any kind of shame she will resort to her usual method of relief.'

Nic was driving. Katie sat beside him and watched Marta covertly in the mirror behind the sunshield. There was, thankfully, music playing – Nic's revered Miles Davis – though clearly Marta was listening to something of her own, separate and unreachable. Katie twisted round in her seat at one point and tried to take Marta's hand, but Marta, although she looked up and gave her mother a half-smile, kept her hands firmly to herself, clamped in her sleeves.

When they got home, Katie said, more robustly than she felt, to Marta, 'I'm not frightened about you, darling, but I am very, very concerned for you.'

Marta didn't look at her. 'I know.'

'There is a difference, you know, between being anxious or scared about someone and minding very much what happens to them.'

Marta nodded in silence.

'I think,' Katie went on, 'that either Dad or I have to tell the school.'

Marta's head whipped up. 'No!'

'But—'

'You can't,' Marta said furiously. 'You mustn't. I'll – I'll *kill* you.'

Nic said, from the other side of the kitchen, 'It's wrong to bully, though. Don't you think?'

'Of course,' Marta said angrily.

'So are you saying that what happened to you wasn't bullying?'

'It wasn't.'

'Wasn't it?'

Marta looked away once more. Nic came across the room and stood beside her. He said again, quietly, 'Wasn't it? Wasn't making sure you knew what you were missing out on a form of bullying?'

Marta still said nothing. Nic peered at her face, even though her head was bent. He said gently, 'Fear shouldn't be any part of real friendship.'

Marta muttered something.

Nic bent closer. 'What?'

Marta said, more clearly, 'They're not real friends.'

Nic glanced at Katie.

'If they weren't real friends, darling . . .' she said softly to Marta.

Marta's head jerked up again. She said suddenly, 'They're cool, though. They – they have *power*.'

'The thing about power or having power,' Nic said, 'is that you mustn't abuse it. Or misuse it.'

'And if,' Katie added, 'we don't tell the school, someone else is going to suffer, like you have done. Perhaps someone who hasn't got a family behind them, like you have. Someone much weaker, more vulnerable than you.'

Nic hitched himself onto the edge of the kitchen table. He said, almost casually, 'Is there anyone else?'

Marta glanced at him.

'What d'you mean, anyone else?'

Nic made a vague gesture. He didn't look at Katie.

'Oh, I don't know. Someone else self-harming.'

Marta said sharply, 'Why d'you ask? Who said there might be anyone else?'

Nic gestured again. He said, almost as if it hardly mattered, 'It's just occurred to me. Thinking about the bullies. Whether there's anyone else in their sights.'

Marta shouted, 'They don't want you to know!'

Katie gave a small involuntary yelp. Nic said levelly, 'In your own time, sweetie.'

'What d'you mean?'

He swivelled to face Marta.

'I mean, take your time in telling us about anyone else at school who is reacting as you are to being bullied.'

'There isn't anyone.'

'Ah.'

'It's just me,' Marta said.

Nic turned to look at Katie. He was looking at her, she thought, as if they were together in something, partners, allies.

'It's just me,' Marta repeated. 'And you mustn't tell the school. You mustn't.' Her voice rose. 'I forbid it!'

———

Later, Nic brought Katie a mug of tea. He set it down beside her laptop and then he paused, looking at her screen. 'What's that?'

Katie went on typing.

'Questions from a senior journalist. For a piece she's writing on working women. I should have answered her last week.'

Nic took up his usual position on the padded arm of the nearest chair.

'Working women.'

'Yes,' Katie said, typing on. 'There were apparently 3.1 million working women with dependent children in 1996 and now there are 4.9 million of us. Where's Marta?'

'In her room. With the door shut. Florence is on the landing outside her door pretending to read a book and fizzing with curiosity, and Daisy is on her iPad behaving as if the whole Marta situation is nothing to do with her.'

Katie stopped typing.

'Well, in a way, I suppose it isn't. Thank God she told us.'

'And, whatever Marta says, we have to tell the school.'

Katie glanced at him. 'I know.'

'Whether or not Marta permits it or knows we're telling them, we have to do it.'

Katie picked up her mug of tea and took a gulp. She said almost tearfully, 'It's such a dilemma. I don't want to break Marta's trust, which is fragile enough, but we have to go against her wishes.'

Nic looked out of the window. 'Yup.'

Katie hesitated. She could feel that she was about to offer to do something her whole being cried out to be spared.

Then Nic said, 'I don't mind doing the telling.'

She had hardly had time to grasp at his offer when her phone rang. She peered at the screen. Her voice was unsteady. 'It's Sebastian.'

'Answer him,' Nic said.

Shakily she put the phone to her ear. 'Seb. Heavens. Where are you?'

Sebastian sounded almost jubilant. 'I'm at the airport.'

Katie stood up from her chair in sheer amazement.

'The *airport?*'

'I'm on my way out to Spain. With the boys.'

Katie looked at Nic, mouthing her surprise. 'With the *boys?*'

'Yes,' Sebastian said cheerfully. 'I have Dermot and Marcus with me and we are flying out to Gibraltar later and we'll be there till Monday.' His voice dropped almost conspiratorially as he said, 'There's a lot to tell you.'

'Can't you tell me now? Is there a crisis?'

'I don't think so. Mum sounded a bit distracted when I rang but that might have been because Jake is coming back.'

Katie suddenly couldn't speak. Sebastian appeared not to notice, because he went on quite cheerfully, 'Just to collect Bella and Mouse. So he won't be at the vineyard when we're there, which I rather think is all to the good.'

Katie sat back in her chair.

'I'd rather forgotten about Spain just recently,' she said, distractedly.

Sebastian's voice was warm and encouraging. 'We can't think about it all the time, we really can't.'

'Why are you going?'

'Oh,' he said airily, 'just to have a look.'

'I thought you never wanted to set foot in the vineyard ever again.'

'I did feel like that,' he went on genially. 'And I probably will again, but at the moment, I'm prepared to go out and see how the land lies.'

'But the boys,' Katie said. 'The boys haven't been for years.'

'We were talking about that. Dermot thinks five years and Marcus thinks three. A long, long time anyway. I just wanted you to know we were going. And of course I'll let you know how we get on.'

Katie said, 'So Jake's back in London? Without telling us?'

'Briefly, yes he is.'

'But he didn't tell *you*?'

'I rang Mum so that's how I know he'll be here.'

Katie closed her eyes briefly. She said politely, 'I hope you have a good weekend.'

'I'm sure we will.' Sebastian's voice sounded uncharacteristically hearty. 'Of course we will,' he said and then, as if he needed to rush for the gate in a purposeful manner, ended the call.

Katie put her phone down. She looked at Nic.

'Crikey,' she said.

'How did he sound?'

'Fine,' Katie said. 'Jolly.'

'*Sebastian? Jolly?*'

'Yes,' she said. 'He did. He had the boys with him and he sounded as if – as if they were going off for a merry boys' weekend.'

Nic stood up. He gestured at Katie's mug.

'You want that tea?'

She looked at the mug.

'Yes, please. Even cold.' She looked up at him. 'Nic, what's going on? Sebastian going out to Spain and Jake coming back without telling us?'

'I'm afraid,' Nic said, 'that I don't trust that younger brother of yours as far as I could throw him.'

She gave him a wan smile.

'Maybe that's why Mum feels so much better when he's around. Because he's just a little bit dangerous?'

'While we're on the topic . . .'

'Yes?'

'Of your mother,' Nic said. 'I meant what I said.'

Katie turned to swing herself back to her laptop.

'What did you say?'

Nic started to move away towards the door. 'I said, why didn't she come here for a bit, just to get away from it all, and perhaps even decide what she wants to do next?' He paused in the doorway. 'And I meant what I said earlier too. I'm perfectly prepared to tell the school about Marta. If you'd like me to.'

———

Sebastian discovered that he was to sleep in the main guest room and the boys were to be in the room he'd occupied the weekend after Gus had had his stroke. The main guest room was now, Sebastian realized, Jake's room, and would be Jake and Bella's room, with a canvas travelling cot set up in the corner for Mouse, already made up with a sheet and pillow-case embroidered with yellow stars. The sheet and pillowcase were new, Sebastian observed, and still bore the creases of their packaging. Someone – Monica, probably – had put a large stuffed koala and a small plush mouse in the cot, too. It was a happy memory, that time in Monica's bedroom with Mouse heavily asleep in his arms.

Monica – or more likely Pilar as instructed by Monica – had cleared a lot of Jake's stuff from the visible surfaces. Sebastian decided not to open any drawers or cupboards, but merely to live out of the small suitcase that he had brought with him and which Pilar had already put on the carved rustic chest at the foot of the bed. He wondered if Jake's presence really did hang palpably and interferingly in the air of the house, or whether he just imagined that it did. He decided, in a way that was both novel and exciting to him these days, that he wouldn't bring his brother's name up voluntarily at all that weekend. If someone else mentioned Jake, so be it. But it wouldn't be him.

He went to find his sons. They hadn't unpacked at all but were sitting on their narrow beds gazing at their phones, and fretting about the possibility of not having Wi-Fi.

'Of course there's internet,' Sebastian said. 'We'll go to the office to check. Have you seen Grandpa?'

They didn't look up from their phones.

'No.'

'He's in the office, I gather. Let's go and find him. Grandpa and Wi-Fi, how about that.'

Dermot said, 'It smells funny.'

'What does?'

Dermot gestured. 'Here. Spain.'

Sebastian smiled deliberately at him.

'Of course it does. It's abroad, it's foreign. It's different to London.'

Marcus said, 'Granny's very small.'

'Is she? Smaller than she was or smaller than you remember?'

'Just small.'

Sebastian said, 'She's had a shock. They both have. Who knows what we'll find with Grandpa.'

Marcus looked round him, shivering slightly. 'Will he be very weird?' he asked.

Sebastian felt something of his old and familiar dread of the unknown, of not being able to cope. He said sadly, 'I don't know.'

Dermot stood up. He spoke in a brisk manner reminiscent of his mother.

'Well, we won't know till we find out, will we? Where's the office?'

Sebastian indicated the window. 'Out there.'

The boys looked in the same direction. Then Dermot said, 'He's our grandfather, whatever he's like.'

'He certainly is.'

Dermot looked at his brother.

'Get up, Marc.'

Marcus shambled to his feet.

'Phone in your pocket,' Dermot said. 'Remember what Mum said.'

Sebastian glanced at him. 'What did Mum say?'

Dermot put his own phone in his jeans pocket. He stood a little straighter.

'She said we were to remember that we were Beachams, too.'

'Did she? Did she actually *say* that?'

''Course she did,' Dermot said. 'Why shouldn't she? It's what we are, after all.'

———

Gus was in his usual seat in the office, his back to the door, facing the computer screen which rose with sleek modernity out of a chaos of papers.

'Hello, Dad,' Sebastian said. His voice sounded false to him. Too jocular.

Gus kept his gaze on the screen. He didn't say anything either. Monica had told them all that Gus was so much better, he really was, the therapists had done wonders and the speech therapist in particular was really pleased with him, which was remarkable of her really, when you considered how awful Gus was with her.

'Awful? What kind of awful?'

Monica had rolled her eyes at her grandsons.

'You know Dad. Bad language. Shocking language, really. But this sweet girl doesn't seem to mind at all.'

'Dad?' Sebastian repeated.

Gus's hands moved restlessly among the papers.

'What are you doing here?' he said finally, disagreeably.

To Sebastian's astonishment, Dermot moved forward into the office until he was in his grandfather's line of vision.

'We're here too, Grandpa. Marcus and me.'

Very slowly, Gus turned and stared up at him.

'Good God,' Gus said.

Dermot gestured to his brother to come and stand beside him.

'Here's Marcus.'

Gus surveyed them both. His mouth worked for several seconds and then he said, 'What the devil – are you doing here?'

'We've come to see you.'

'Why?' Gus said.

From behind his father, Sebastian said, 'I've come too. We've all come.'

'Why?' Gus said again. 'Bloody why?'

Dermot grinned at him. He said, in a much lower tone, 'To see how you are.'

'Huh,' Gus said. His hands, Sebastian noticed, were shaking, and covered with dark age spots like large and unnatural freckles.

Dermot seemed strangely at ease. He lowered himself until he was sitting on the nearest cluttered surface and folded his arms. He said to his grandfather, 'We're your family, you know. And we've come all the way from London to see you. Even if you didn't want us to.'

Gus looked slowly from one grandson to the other. He ignored Sebastian.

'Want to make yourselves useful?' he said. 'You and him?'

'Sure,' Dermot said. 'He's called Marcus.'

Gus snorted.

'I bloody knew that. Marcus. Bloody Marcus.'

'Not so bloody,' Marcus said boldly, joining in. 'Just Marcus.'

Gus eyed him.

'I'll call you what I bloody like.'

'OK,' Marcus said. 'But I mightn't answer.'

'Hah!' Gus said. He was plainly delighted.

'Dad . . .'

Gus turned, with difficulty. He said to Sebastian, 'You bloody keep out of it.'

'I'll handle this,' Dermot whispered to his father.

'But . . .'

'I'll do it,' Dermot said quietly. 'Whatever.' He turned back to his grandfather. 'What would you like us to do, Grandpa?'

Gus gestured at a map of the vineyard pinned to the wall. 'See that?'

The boys stood up and peered at the map.

'Yes,' Dermot said. 'It looks pretty old.'

'It's fine!' Gus shouted. 'Bloody fine! It shows all my land, every inch of my fucking land!'

'OK,' Dermot said. He seemed quite unperturbed. 'This is your land. This is a map of the vineyard.'

Gus made a clumsy movement. 'There. Up there.'

'Where?'

'Up bloody there! Up on the bloody mountain!'

Marcus touched the map. 'Here?'

'No!' Gus bellowed. 'There! Further up!'

'Here?'

'Yes, yes. On the slopes of the bloody mountain. Where I said.'

Dermot said over his shoulder, his finger on the map, 'What of it?'

Gus made a jabbing gesture. 'You go. You go at first bloody light.'

'Why, Grandpa?'

Gus was overtaken by a fit of coughing. Sebastian was astonished to see Dermot produce a wad of tissues from his pocket and hand them without comment to his grandfather. When Gus could speak again, he said, 'That's where he's been ploughing. It's where he's going to plant the new bloody vines. He thinks I don't know. He thinks I can't stop it.'

Dermot looked at his father. 'What? Who's he talking about?'

Sebastian relaxed against the door-jamb. He smiled at his sons.

'Jake,' he said. 'Dad means Jake.'

———

Monica was very vivacious during dinner. Thinking the boys might be too conventional in their culinary tastes for paella, she had made one of her chicken and rice dishes, and told her grandsons that if they didn't like red pepper, they could pick out the strips of it and just eat the chicken.

'The Spanish *love* pimentos,' she said with animation. 'They put them in *everything* except chocolate cake.'

Marcus said, 'Mum buys chocolate with chilli in it.'

'Oh!' Monica said. 'How very with it! Then you are perfectly used—'

'Shut bloody up,' Gus said. He had a large glass of wine at his elbow.

'Hey,' Dermot said to him. 'You shouldn't talk to her like that.'

Gus looked pleasedly at him.

'Who's going to stop me?'

'I am,' Dermot said.

'Hah! You and whose army?'

Dermot said, 'If you speak to Granny like that again, we'll all go somewhere else and leave you to have dinner on your own.'

Gus muttered something.

'What?' Monica said.

'Ignore him,' Sebastian said.

Monica burst into tears. She began to pat her turquoise kaftan as if in search of a pocket where there might be tissues.

'Mum . . .'

'No!' Monica said between sniffs, batting Sebastian's hand away. 'No! It's fine! I'm fine.'

Dermot said easily to his grandfather, 'Now look what you've done.'

Marcus said, 'Is that wine?'

'Of course it is,' Sebastian said. 'It's what we make here, remember?'

Marcus held his glass out. 'Can I have some?'

'No,' Sebastian said.

'Yes!' Gus shouted. 'Bloody yes! Give the boy some wine!'

'Watered then,' Sebastian said. 'More water than wine.'

Monica, still sniffing, got up.

'I think I'll just—'

'Mum!'

She flapped a hand. 'I'm fine, darling. But I think perhaps I'll just—'

Dermot said to his grandfather, 'How about you say sorry.'

Sebastian stared at his son. 'What? He's never said sorry about anything, ever.'

Dermot shrugged. 'No time like the present, then. He could start now.'

Monica was still hovering. 'Marcus, darling, have you got what you'd like?'

Marcus was drinking in gulps. He paused, long enough to say, 'I'd like more wine next time.'

'I'm waiting,' Dermot said to his grandfather.

Gus shot a glance at Monica and grabbed his wine glass. He lifted it towards her. Then he drank deeply.

'Sorry,' he said loudly.

Dermot said remorselessly, 'Well, that's a start. But not a very good one.'

'Fucking cheek.'

Dermot said, 'If you want us to go up the mountain tomorrow, you'll have to do something for us in return. Not being rude to Granny, for starters.'

'Oh,' Monica said in confusion. 'Oh, darling. Darling Dermot. This – this is all too much.'

Sebastian reached for her hand and pulled her back down into her chair.

'This is delicious, Mum.'

'Is it? Oh, I don't know. I've been making it forever, you know. Nobody has to eat it, just to be polite.'

'We love it. We're eating it because we really like it.'

Marcus held out his glass. He said, 'Can I have some more wine?'

Sebastian picked up the bottle. 'Please,' he said.

Dermot was laughing. 'Honestly, Dad. First you tell him

he can't have any, then you're perfectly happy to give him a second glass if he asks politely.'

Gus leaned forward. He jabbed a forefinger in Sebastian's direction.

'What were you thinking?'

Sebastian stopped filling Marcus's glass.

'Sorry, Dad? What was I thinking?'

'Yes,' Gus said. 'Bloody yes. What were you thinking in not bringing these boys here before?'

———

On her way to the office, Katie rang Bella's number. She had rehearsed the message she would leave – casual, noncommittal, definitely not aggrieved or accusatory – but to her amazement Bella actually answered her phone.

'Katie,' Bella said, sounding as if they were in touch every day. 'Good morning on this pretty day!'

'I didn't expect you to pick up,' Katie said truthfully.

'Why not?' Bella said. 'I'm always here.'

'But I thought you were about to go to Spain.'

'I am,' Bella said, more tightly. 'At least for now.'

It sounded as if she was restraining herself from adding, *Because you don't want to, so I'm being sacrificed.*

'We so appreciate you going, Bella,' Katie said, with all the warmth she could muster. 'We really do. It's – it's wonderful of you.'

'Actually,' Bella said, 'I think it's pretty wonderful of me too. I don't really like that bit of Spain.' There were grunts in the background. Bella said, in explanation, 'That's just Jake. He doesn't like me talking about Spain except in glowing terms.'

Katie kept her voice neutral. 'Jake? Is Jake there?'

'Oh yes. He's been here since Thursday night. Mouse is thrilled, of course, to have Daddy to take her in an aeroplane.'

'I can imagine,' Katie said politely. 'I wonder, could I speak to him?'

'Of course you can. But why didn't you ring him direct?'

Katie said untruthfully, 'I didn't know he was back.'

'Oh, he's back all right. Met the new tenants and everything.' She lowered her voice coyly. 'Between you and me, I think he just wanted to make sure that Mouse and I really get on that plane.'

'Oh.'

'I'll fetch him,' Bella said. 'You can hear how empty the flat is, all these echoes. Poor little Mouse. At least she's been in Spain very recently, so we can talk about her bed in Granny's house and she remembers it. Or at least, she remembers Granny's necklaces!'

'Katie!' Jake said loudly, coming on the line. 'How *are* you?'

Katie tried not to sound frosty. 'I'm fine. But what about you? Why didn't you tell me you were coming back to England?'

Jake said breezily, 'Oh, Seb knew.'

'But you didn't think to tell *me*? Even a quick text?'

'Katie . . .'

'And if Sebastian hadn't chanced to ring Spain, he'd never have known either. What's going on?'

'Nothing,' Jake said. 'It's not ideal at the moment, to be honest. Dad's in a perpetual rage about not being able to drive and as usual, he's taking it out on Mum. But it'll settle. They'll get used to it and it'll all calm down.'

'It might not, though,' Katie said.

There was a short silence the other end, and then Jake said sharply, 'So you're prepared to drop everything and come out to Spain to deal with it, are you? You'll live with the parents in a single room in the house you grew up in and cope with all of that instead of going on with your important London life, will you?'

Katie felt a tide of shame and rage rising confusingly within her. She gripped her phone.

'Look,' Jake went on, more calmly. 'I don't want to cut either you or Seb out of anything. Not deliberately, anyway. But if I'm going to put up with living there – and putting up with it is mostly what it is – I've got to be allowed some leeway, some autonomy to do my own thing, run the business my way. I can't tell you and Seb every time I break a fingernail. You've got to trust me, Katie. You both have. If neither of you are prepared to drop your London lives to ride to the rescue of Mum and Dad, you've got to let me ride in my own way. OK?'

Katie let her held breath leak slowly out of her lungs.

'OK.'

'You don't sound very convinced.'

'Oh,' she said uncertainly, 'I am. Mostly.'

Jake said, 'What is it? Girls OK?'

Katie took a breath. She had promised herself, and Marta, and Nic, that not a mention of Marta's current troubles would escape her lips.

'Fine,' she said. 'In so far as teenage girls can ever be. You just wait.'

He laughed. Katie thought that his laugh sounded as if he didn't believe that Mouse would ever be afflicted with any run-of-the-mill adolescent problems.

'When are you going back?' she asked.

'Monday,' Jake said. 'Three suitcases and one baby. Taking a baby anywhere these days is like taking a Victorian bride to India. You would not believe how much stuff Mouse seems to need.' He paused. 'And most of it has to be fitted into one room. Our room, Katie, the old guest room. Could you live like that?'

CHAPTER TWELVE

It was getting colder on the dawn terrace now, and the light took much longer to break over the landscape. Monica had always made herself decent before she went out with her mug of tea – brushed hair, earrings with her high-necked white cotton nightgown – but now she added a boiled-wool Austrian jacket that had belonged to her mother, and a pair of fluffy slippers which Bella had given her the previous Christmas. It was, she told herself, only tactful to wear them, even though they were hardly what she would have chosen herself. Too mauve. Too fluffy. But it was manners to wear them in the presence of the donor and in any case, they were warm.

Being on the terrace alone with her tea was undeniably a comfort. It was the one comforting, or even comfortable, ritual that happened on a regular basis, this morning hour on the terrace, bracing herself for the demands and dramas – God, there were such dramas! – of every day since Gus had had his stroke. She couldn't really allow herself to realize how profoundly life had changed, nor how precarious it all felt to her. It was commonplace now for her to have bad nights, not just bad because she couldn't sleep, but bad because they seemed to be haunted by fears that were really, she knew, terrors. Fears about the uncertainties of the future, fears about Gus's complete obstinacy and his rages and her inability, it seemed, to get through to him, to rescue even a shred of what they had once had. She didn't miss him so much, she thought, as feel a desperation at what he had become. And the children! Sometimes, standing there on the terrace in her fluffy slippers and Austrian jacket, she couldn't imagine what the children should, or even could, do about them both. She strained her gaze to see the dear, familiar Rock of Gibraltar rearing out of the night-time mist far below her. Poor, poor children. What a dreadful thing she and Gus had done to them, even if they had never meant to.

And now here one of them was, asleep in the bedroom behind her. Her oldest child, her withdrawn, serious Sebastian, who seemed almost lively in the unexpected company of his own sons. She smiled, despite herself, in the dawn light. Those dear grandsons had been wonderful with Gus, standing up to him as he secretly adored them to do, ticking him off, impervious to his language. She was horrified that she had actually wept last night. Wept! In public! What was she thinking of? Sebastian had been adorable – they all had, actually – and wouldn't let her flee inside as she had wanted to, tried to. Of course, if you don't sleep properly you get very jangled up, and a bit silly, but all the same, Sebastian and his sons had been particularly sweet to her. That tall, skinny Dermot with his terrible haircut – privately, the word Monica used to describe his haircut was 'uneducated' – had been wonderful. He had even made Gus apologize to her! Of course Gus didn't mean it, and would be rude to her again whenever he was frustrated, which seemed to be all the time, but never mind, he'd actually said the word 'sorry'. Gus! Who, as Sebastian had pointed out, had never apologized to anyone for anything in his life.

There was a creak behind her. One of the shutters of the guest bedroom had been pushed back.

'Mum,' Sebastian said.

Monica trotted across the terrace in her fluffy slippers.

'Good morning, darling.'

Sebastian looked at her mug, yawning. He said, 'Is that tea?'

'It certainly is. English Breakfast. In the old days, I always had it sent from Piccadilly.'

Sebastian's hair was rumpled from sleep. He was bare-chested and wearing only pyjama trousers. Monica surveyed him.

'I shouldn't really either notice or comment, darling, but you seem to me to be in very good shape.'

Sebastian smiled at her.

'Good old Mum.'

'You and the boys saved my life last night,' Monica said. 'The boys were wonderful. I can't remember when anybody last stood up for me like that.'

Sebastian leaned on the sill of the window.

'Mum?'

'Yes, darling?'

'What's going on with the vineyard?'

'Oh,' Monica said airily, 'just some bee in Dad's bonnet as usual.'

Sebastian said soberly, 'I don't think so.' He paused, scratching off some peeling flakes of paint. Then he said, 'What is Jake planning?'

'I have no idea.'

'Yes, you do, Mum. Dad wants the boys to go up and look at the extra land that's been ploughed for the new vines. And even I know that you plant new vines in the autumn when the earth is warm. So whatever Jake is planning, it's imminent. What is it?'

Monica said unhappily, 'I have no idea. Really I don't.'

'So Jake has told you nothing?'

Monica didn't answer. She looked down into her tea mug.

'Look,' Sebastian said, leaning towards her over the sill, 'I know how you feel about Jake. And it's fine by me, promise. After all, he grew up here, went to school here, this is his place. It's really good of him to drop everything and come back, but doesn't something make you wonder why? I mean, why was it so easy for him to abandon London just like that?'

Monica said in a whisper, 'I was just so thankful that he could.'

Sebastian reached out to touch her arm.

'Of course you were. But I'm just saying, what isn't he telling us? These new vines and the secrecy round them. What's all that about?'

Monica said sadly, 'Dad is convinced they won't grow. He says the earth here is only right for Tempranillo.' She shot a look at Sebastian. 'There's going to be such a battle.'

Sebastian took his hand back.

'I know.'

'I dread it,' Monica said. Her voice was unsteady. 'I simply dread it. In fact—' She stopped and then she said in a rush, 'I'm not sure I can bear much more, not after—' She stopped again, abruptly, and flung her head back as if to stop tears spilling down her face.

'After what?' Sebastian prompted.

Very quietly, Monica said to the sky, 'After Jake asked me to lend him some money.'

———

'Look,' Daisy said. She was holding her phone out imperiously. 'Look at that.'

Katie was absorbed in an email on her own phone. She said absently, 'What, darling?'

Daisy shook her phone.

'Those boys. Those cousins of ours who seem to be in Spain. Look at these pictures!'

Katie focused. 'What pictures?'

'These,' Daisy said, shaking her phone again. 'Dermot on the terrace in Spain. Dermot with José Manuel on a tractor. Marcus with a huge glass of wine. Marcus grinning. Everybody grinning all the time, it looks to me.'

Katie took Daisy's phone and scrolled through the pictures.

'Wow,' she said, smiling. 'It looks terrific. Wonderful. They're clearly having a great time.'

'Clearly,' Daisy said with emphasis. She took her phone back. 'Lovely photos of a lovely place. Of *course* it's lovely.'

'It is,' Katie agreed. 'Even if it's also very complicated.'

Daisy sighed theatrically.

'You don't get it, do you?'

Katie looked at her.

'What don't I get?'

'Jeez,' Daisy said in exasperation. '*Honestly*. Mum, why are those boys there?'

Katie gestured vaguely. 'They've gone with their father.'

'And why haven't *we* gone? Why are those boys there and we never are? Why haven't you taken us to Spain?'

'But you did go, when you were little.'

'But not now! Not *recently*!'

'Daisy,' Katie said. 'You didn't want to. In fact, you refused.'

'I didn't. I never did.'

Katie held up a hand.

'Excuse me, Daisy, but you did. You said to me that living in Spain was your grandparents' choice and nothing to do with you.'

Daisy said sulkily, 'I didn't mean it.'

'Perhaps not. Perhaps not in hindsight. But it sounded as if you meant it when you said it. And we respect your opinion, Dad and I. When you say you don't want to do something, we have to believe you.'

Daisy said, in a rather altered voice, 'Are they OK?'

'Who?'

Daisy fidgeted.

'Granny and Grandpa.'

'No,' Katie said, 'they aren't. Grandpa had a stroke.'

'I know that.'

'And it has turned their life upside down. He can't drive any more, for one thing, and he's used to being independent. Granny would say arbitrary. She'd say he's used to being random and arbitrary.'

Daisy leaned on the kitchen table.

'Poor her.'

Katie put her own phone in her pocket.

'I'm interested that you say poor her and not poor him.'

Daisy didn't look at her mother. She said, 'It's very hard to be the person who has to live with someone who's suffered something.'

'Why do you say that?'

'You know why,' Daisy said. 'We've all got to make allow-ances for Marta now and tiptoe round Marta, but what about us? What about Florence and me? What about you and Dad? And now there's Grandpa. What about Granny?'

Katie held her arms out. 'Come here.'

'No,' Daisy said, 'I don't want a hug. I don't want anything like that. I just want you to know I know.'

'Darling . . .'

Daisy looked away. 'You think I don't care about how hard it is for you. Of course I care. I can't always show it, but I care. And now I care about Granny, stuck in Spain.'

Katie waited, almost holding her breath. Daisy was still leaning against the table but she was plainly working up to saying something important. Then she straightened up and looked at her mother.

'Mum,' Daisy said with real earnestness. 'Why can't Granny come here?'

———

Sebastian texted Anna to say that although the boys would be returning on the agreed flight, he was going to stay in Spain another night or two. The former Sebastian would have gone into lengthy explanations about needing to see Jake before he left as if he was compelled to ward off Anna's inevitable objections, but the new and liberated Sebastian didn't seem to be urged on by the same old demons. The former Sebastian, he reflected, would probably have rung Anna, too, rather than sending a text, and would then have been deeply cast down by the brusqueness of her reaction, and her almost inevitable digs at Monica. But now, even if the extraordinary shift in the balance of power gave him an advantage over Anna that he'd never had in all their time together, he was able – yes, he told himself, really truly able – to choose the way he communicated without agonizing over the consequences.

Anna texted back almost – this was not a word Sebastian would have used of her ever before – submissively. She didn't ask explicitly why Sebastian was staying on in Spain, nor did she comment on the merry photographs the boys had sent back of their weekend. She merely confirmed that she would be at the airport to meet the boys' returning flight on Monday evening, and hoped – this was also astonishingly uncharacteristic – that Sebastian had had a good weekend and that the whole situation hadn't been too stressful.

Sebastian stared at his phone screen. 'Stressful' was so very much not in Anna's vocabulary. 'Stressful', in Anna's book, described lives that were nothing like as well organized or purposeful as Anna's own. Perhaps she was attempting a little empathy. Or perhaps she was even trying to apologize for years of tyranny, for making Sebastian feel eternally apologetic and inadequate. He had looked at himself in the shaving mirror that morning and wondered, quite genuinely, what on earth Monica had meant when she had paid him the compliment of being in good shape. Was he? He bent forward and peered at himself in the mirror. He bared his teeth. Not quite even, but all his own. He squinted down his front, to his bare feet, planted on the Spanish tiles of the bathroom floor. Wow, he thought to himself in a dawning state of wonder, am I a kind of – of sex object to some? To *Anna*, even? He regarded himself in the mirror again. Do not be idiotic, he told himself sternly. Getting on with your sons, and stumbling towards some kind of real partnership with your wife shouldn't go to your stupid head. Pull yourself together, Sebastian. Even if you keep on grinning.

The boys pleaded to be allowed to stay in Spain. It was half term after all, they said, and there was nothing to get back for. Anyway, Grandpa wanted them to stay, he'd said so several times and forcefully.

'No,' Sebastian said.

Marcus was almost whining. 'Why not?'

'If you must know, it's because I need to talk to Uncle Jake. On my own.'

'But we needn't be there when you talk to him.'

'No.'

'Please, Dad. It's so cool here.'

'When I say no, I mean it. Mum is meeting your flight as arranged this evening.'

'What's the real reason?' Dermot asked.

'I told you,' Sebastian said. 'I told you that I needed to speak to Jake.'

Dermot folded his arms. 'I'm waiting,' he said, in the tone he used to his grandfather.

'Cheeky little—'

Dermot unfolded his arms to hold a hand up.

'Don't say it, Dad. Just don't say it. And don't treat us like annoying little kids. You brought us here so we could see it for ourselves, as adults, so it's no good pretending we have suddenly reverted again. Why don't you want us here when you talk to Uncle Jake?'

Sebastian said reluctantly, 'Because there might be a row.'

'Cool!' Marcus said.

'D'you want to say heavy stuff to Uncle Jake? D'you think he'll fight back?'

Sebastian sighed.

'I don't know. I can't tell. But I need to have nothing to distract me when I talk to him. And he needs no distraction either.'

'Meaning?'

'Meaning that if you are here, you provide an automatic excuse for a party.'

'There,' Dermot said. 'That wasn't so very hard, was it? Tell us what's really going on, and we accept it. Treat us like kids and we get all suspicious.'

'There's a protective paternal factor too.'

Marcus looked up at the mountainside where they had spent most of the previous day.

'Not if we're going to inherit all this.'

'Are you?'

'We might,' Marcus said. 'It produces bloody good wine.'

Sebastian was laughing.

'You've spent too much time with your grandfather.'

'He did all this, you know,' Dermot said. 'It was just rubbly old land before. He's made the vineyard. He's grown the grapes and produced the wine and won the awards. He's *done* this, all by himself, Dad.' He looked sternly at his father. 'And I think that is pretty impressive.'

—

'I can't really talk just now,' Monica said to Katie on the telephone. 'Jake and Bella and Mouse arrived an hour ago, and Sebastian's taken your father up to the village and there's generally rather a lot going on.'

'I'm in the office, Mum—'

'Oh,' Monica interrupted gaily. 'You *always* seem to be in the office!'

'—so I won't be long. I just wanted to put an idea to you.'

'I must say,' Monica said, in the same bright, false tone, 'that if there are *any* upsides to Dad's having had a stroke, the boys coming out here so often is definitely one. You have no idea how wonderful Sebastian's boys are.'

'Of course I do,' Katie said. 'I know them. I see them in London. I've watched them grow up.'

'They are marvellous. Especially Dermot with Dad. He didn't seem to mind *what* he said.'

'Mum,' Katie said, 'could I make a suggestion to you?'

Monica was plainly directing something else in the room. She said, after a series of half-intelligible interchanges, 'It's Mouse, Katie. She remembered about my pearls. It's the Poppits she loves.'

'Maybe this really isn't a very good time to talk.'

'Yes, it is,' Monica said indignantly. 'You said you'd be quick and I must be, too. What did you want to ask me?'

Katie said carefully, 'Well, it was something Daisy suggested. And Nic.'

'What an honour,' Monica said. 'Daisy *and* Nic.'

'Do you want to hear it, or don't you?'

'Of course I want to hear it!'

'We wondered,' Katie said, 'Daisy and Nic and I, whether you would like to come to stay for a while. For a rest, a change of scene. That sort of thing.'

There was silence at the other end of the line.

'Mum?'

Monica said, in a different and almost strangled tone, 'Thank you, Katie. But - but I couldn't.'

'Why not?'

'I – I couldn't leave here. And Dad.'

'Mum—'

'No!' Monica said vehemently.

'But Jake and Bella are there to look after Dad.'

'Do you hear me, Katie? No. The answer is no. It's very sweet of you all to think of it but I can't.'

Katie said slowly, 'Are you saying you can't because you don't want to?'

'Yes,' Monica said. 'Yes. That's it. I just – I just can't.'

———

Jake was surveying the office. He spoke to his brother in a voice that bordered on accusation.

'You've been in here.'

'No,' Sebastian said, 'I haven't. I haven't been near the business end of things.'

'Then who has? Who's made all this mess? Just when I'd started to sort it all out.'

Sebastian folded his arms and leaned against the door-jamb.

'Dad, I'd guess.'

Jake said, 'Dad couldn't find his way out of a paper bag these days.'

'Oh,' Sebastian said easily, 'I think he could. I think he's better every day. He's got more of a grip on things than you give him credit for.'

Jake put his hands in his pockets.

'He's an arch meddler, if that's what you mean.'

'I don't really,' Sebastian said. 'I mean that even if he never regains all his mental faculties, he's going to recover quite a lot of them, even most of them, just as the hospital said he would.'

Jake eyed him. 'What are you saying?'

'I'm saying,' Sebastian said pleasantly, 'that you might not have the autonomy to run the vineyard all your own way after all. It's Dad's place, Dad's set-up and Dad has, like all independent businessmen if you can call him that, run it all *his* own way for over twenty-five years. So you might have done the knight in shining armour thing at the beginning, but that, splendid though it was at the time, doesn't look so clear-cut and simple now. The bottom line is, you can't simply just cut Dad out and do as you please.'

Jake moved past his brother and sat down in Gus's broken office chair in front of the computer. He moved the mouse and brought up the home page screenshot of the vineyard, overlaid with the words, in ochre capital letters, 'Beacham's Bodega'. Sebastian regarded the back of his brother's head.

'Can I ask you something, Jake?'

Jake made an irritable gesture with his left hand.

'Not now, Seb. I've got to check all this.'

Sebastian didn't move.

'Well, I think I'll ask you anyway. Could you talk me through the new planting?'

There was a fractional pause before Jake said, without looking at him, ''Course.'

'Could you tell me what you plan to plant up there? More Tempranillo?'

Jake gave a faint snort.

'God, no.'

'It's just that it seems a bit far from the river for Tempranillo.'

'It is. We're going to diversify a bit.'

'With Dad's blessing?'

Jake said, 'When did Dad ever give his blessing to any idea that wasn't his own in the first place?'

'So,' Sebastian said, 'the answer to my question is no. You are implementing this scheme behind his back?'

Jake swivelled round.

'Look,' he said angrily, 'you haven't any right to ask these questions. You and Katie were absolutely thankful to let me ride to the rescue, so you can't, now that things have calmed down a bit, suddenly object to the way I want to run this place. Nor can Dad. You want me to take over? Fine, I'll do it. But you can't then have your cake and eat it. If I'm going to run this place, I run it my way. OK?'

'Not really,' Sebastian said. 'Because things change. They change all the time. To start with, Dad is getting better.'

Jake turned back.

'That's a different matter. And a different fight.'

'But we are all affected.'

'No, we're not! It's much more of a revolution for me. Bella and I have completely given up our life in London.'

'Why?'

Jake was suddenly still in front of the computer.

'What did you say?'

Sebastian unfolded his arms. He inspected his fingernails.

'I said, "Why?" Why could you abandon your life in London just like that?'

'I do not *believe* this!' Jake turned round to face his brother. 'How dare you? How bloody *dare* you?'

'Honestly,' Sebastian said, 'I don't know how I dare. I don't know what's happened to me, but something has. In the old days, I'd have accepted everything you said, and not dared to question you about anything. But I seem – and it may only be temporary – to be able to ask tough questions and not be utterly cast down when I get a tough reply. So I'll ask you again, what are you planning to plant without Dad's sanction in the newly ploughed land, and why could you leave London as immediately as you could?'

'Get out!' Jake shouted.

'Really? Is that your only reply to my questions?'

Jake swung back again. He hunched over the computer as if it demanded immediate attention. He said to Sebastian with finality, 'It is for now.'

———

Gus was mostly silent over supper. He hardly looked up from his plate or his glass and when Sebastian asked him something anodyne, he shouted angrily, 'It isn't the same without those boys.'

Monica said at once, 'I so miss them!'

Bella said to no one in particular, 'I don't know them at all. I mean, I've *met* them, but that's all really.'

'Oh!' Monica said. 'They're wonderful. They really are.' She looked across the table at Sebastian. '*Such* a credit to you and Anna.'

Sebastian gave a clumsy half-bow.

Bella turned to Jake. 'We never really saw them in London.'

Jake didn't look at his brother. He said clearly, 'Anna didn't encourage visits from Sebastian's family.'

'I may be speaking out of turn,' Sebastian said, 'but I rather think things will be different in the future.' He glanced at his father. 'They loved it here.'

Gus grunted.

Monica said, 'They didn't want to leave, bless them. Marcus said to me, "Granny, you know going back isn't *our* idea." Too sweet.'

'And now look at us,' Jake said. 'Family gathering round the supper table and hardly a picture of conviviality, is it?'

Bella looked at him.

'What's got into you, Jakey?'

'Nothing.'

Bella addressed the table at large. 'It was hard leaving London and all our friends.'

'Of course,' Monica said.

Sebastian looked at his sister-in-law. He said, 'I'm sure it was.'

'I mean,' Bella said, 'if it hadn't been for Granny's pearls, I'm not sure we'd ever have made it!'

'So pleased,' Monica said, 'to have been of use for something.'

Sebastian regarded her.

'You matter, Mum. You really do.'

Monica made a fluttering gesture with her hands. 'Oh, I don't know. I feel I'm just a giant problem, a perpetual nuisance.'

'Hah!' Gus exclaimed.

Monica looked at her empty plate.

'Katie . . .' she said.

Sebastian leaned forward.

'What, Mum?'

Monica continued reluctantly, fiddling with the stem of her wine glass. 'Katie said both Daisy and Nic had suggested I go and stay there for a bit. Of course I said no.'

Bella and Jake exchanged glances. Jake turned to his mother.

'Why did you say no?'

Monica spread her hands. 'Well, of course I can't. I can't leave here. Katie said did that mean I didn't *want* to but the thing is really that I can't. I can't be away from – from Dad.'

Gus roused himself. He picked up his wine glass and squinted at Monica through it.

'Why not?' he said.

CHAPTER THIRTEEN

Marta appeared compliant. She had stopped the surreptitious eating of crisps and chocolate if the contents of her waste-paper basket were anything to go by, and even if she hardly spoke at mealtimes, at least she attended them. She was now, she announced shortly after her first visit to Dr Mak, a vegan, which precluded most sweets anyway, since a large proportion of them contained gelatin. So she was eating better, and obediently attending her weekly sessions with Dr Mak and seemed to be more settled at school, which had, in its turn, been actively aware all along of the problems in Year Nine and had simply been waiting for a parent like Nic to notice for themselves and then demand immediate action.

Marta didn't change her habits of dress, however. She still wore, outside her school uniform, leggings and sweatshirts, and she still gripped the cuffs of her sleeves so that her hands were hidden almost to her knuckles. When it wasn't tied back for school, her hair still swung forward across her face, especially as her head was perpetually bent forward. She appeared to be in constant touch with friends and these days almost never seemed to go to or from school on her own. The difficulty of assessing how she was doing, or gaining even a shred of reassurance on her progress, was that she wouldn't speak.

Her sisters' reactions to Marta's situation were marked. Daisy opted to be out most of the time, banging about the house when she was infrequently at home, but spending most of her time – she indicated but declined to specify – with friends. She did her homework in friends' houses, ate out with them and only appeared to come home in order to exchange one set of black drapery for another. Having asked her mother if Monica had accepted the invitation to come and stay, and been told that the invitation had been refused, Daisy plainly considered that her family duty was done. She might sleep at home and use home's hot water and laundry service whilst charging her mobile, but apart from that, she made it very plain that she would prefer to spend time with the family she had chosen – her friends – rather than the one she had been saddled with at birth.

Florence was the opposite. Florence's reaction to Marta's wretchedness was to exhibit an exaggerated form of dependency. She started sucking her thumb again and began sitting on either parent's knee whenever they occupied a chair. She rang Katie, especially, for long and involved conversations about nothing in particular, and took to sleeping with her bed full of cuddly toys, a grey plush seal she had never taken any notice of before clasped in her arms. She left her bedroom door wide open at night, and insisted that the landing light be left on, even though, with the new and very public position of her bed, it fell directly onto her face.

'And you are suggesting,' Katie said to Nic, 'adding my mother, who doesn't even like me much, to the mix?'

Nic paused in unbuttoning his shirt prior to taking it off.

'Yes,' he said. 'And she does like you. We've had this conversation a thousand times.'

Katie was taking her makeup off in front of the bathroom mirror.

'Let's compromise,' she said. 'Let's just agree that I don't mean to Mum what my brothers mean.'

Nic took his shirt off and aimed it at the laundry basket.

'Bingo,' he said, and then, 'You mean quite as much to Monica. Just differently, because you are both women. Katie, I really don't think I have the energy to have this conversation yet again.'

She stared at him.

'But you're the one who asked her to come here!'

He said patiently, 'And Daisy. Daisy did, too. But as she has refused, this whole conversation is redundant.'

Katie looked back at the mirror. 'Sorry.'

'Accepted,' Nic said. 'Actually, I'm ready to scrap with anyone. I snarled at two perfectly innocent members of staff today for no reason except everything that's going on here.'

'Marta.'

'Yes,' Nic said. 'Marta.'

Katie looked at his reflection in the mirror.

'Do you think—'

'I don't know. Honestly, I do not know. And I'm scared to ask her.'

'Me too,' Katie said. 'Think of that. Scared of our own

thirteen-year-old daughter. Perhaps – perhaps we're actually scared of all of them.'

Nic pulled his socks off, one by one, and dropped them on the bathroom floor.

He said tiredly, 'Maybe that's what's the matter. Monica is scared of you.'

Katie turned.

'Do you think so?'

'Quite honestly,' Nic said, 'I don't know what I think about anything just now. I feel as if I've been hit by a truck.'

Katie dropped the used cotton-wool pads in the bin by the basin. She said, 'Sebastian should be back by now.'

'Oh?'

'From Spain,' Katie said. 'He decided to send the boys back and stay on himself for a couple of nights.'

Nic crossed to the row of chrome hooks on the wall and chose a bathrobe. Tying the belt, he said, without much interest, 'Why?'

'Something to do with getting things straight with Jake. About the vineyard, I think.' She examined herself more closely in the mirror. 'I look a hundred.'

Nic took no notice. He said, 'Daisy said the boys had had a great time. She wanted – no, demanded – to know why she hadn't been to Spain herself recently.'

'She said the same to me. When she said why didn't Mum come here.'

'Katie,' Nic said. 'Could I hold you?'

She glanced at him.

'Why?'

'I'd – just like to. I want to. It's been a very long time.'

'What has?'

'Since I held you. Since you let me hold you.'

Katie moved stiffly against him and put her arms round his neck.

He said, 'You're so tense. I can feel every nerve in your body is twanging.'

'Of course. With all that's going on, what else do you expect?'

He pulled her closer and laid his cheek against hers.

'All this,' he said. 'Everything at home and then work as well.'

Katie felt an irresistible lump rising up in her throat.

'Work!' she said. 'Thank God for it. It's the only thing at the moment that keeps me sane. And now – well, now I'm afraid I'm going to cry.'

———

Anna had laid supper for all four of them, and roasted a chicken. The boys were still full of enthusiasm for their weekend in Spain, and held forth in a way they had never, either of them, exhibited before, about the place and the landscape and the vineyard and their grandfather's achievements. Sebastian took his remaining bottles of beer out of the fridge and poured himself one without comment from Anna. He held the glass in a deliberately prominent manner to see if she would say something, and she didn't. She asked him to carve the chicken and didn't, as she usually did, then disparage the quality of his carving. She wasn't exactly docile, he thought, but she was certainly, wonderfully, less abrasive.

When the boys had left the kitchen, Anna asked Sebastian, most unexpectedly, whether the weekend in Spain had been as satisfactory for him as it clearly had been for their sons.

Sebastian was instinctively wary.

'Why d'you ask?'

Anna was washing up. She said, 'Well, it's more interesting than talking about Profclean, which is, I suppose, the alternative.'

Sebastian hitched himself onto a corner of the table, holding his second glass of beer. He said, as if it hardly mattered, 'I imagine that's all gone without a serious hitch?'

Anna left the roasting tin on the dishrack and pulled off her washing-up gloves.

'It has. The usual staff upsets but nothing I couldn't fix.'

Sebastian said, meaning it, 'Thank you.'

Anna clipped her rubber gloves into the clothes peg that hung by the sink for the purpose.

'Don't thank me. It's my business as well. I have just as much of an interest in it as you do.'

Goodness, Sebastian thought. Heavens. Usually Anna did the Profclean books with the air of someone doing a deeply unjustified favour for a most ungrateful recipient. Out loud, he said again, 'Well, thank you. Really.'

Anna didn't look at him.

'Coffee?'

Sebastian lifted his beer glass.

'No thanks. I've got this.' He looked down into his drink for a moment or two and then he said, 'I confronted Jake. Or at least I tried to. About his plans for the vineyard and also about the reasons for his being able to leave London so abruptly to sort Spain.'

Anna took a chair out from the kitchen table and sat down. She put her chin in her hands.

'And?'

Sebastian made a face.

'Not satisfactory. Or at least, not completely satisfactory. He has plans for new planting that Dad opposes and he managed to avoid telling me why he left London.'

Anna didn't move. She said, staring straight ahead with her unnervingly direct gaze, 'What about your father? How is he?'

Sebastian made a rocking movement with his free hand.

'You know Dad. He's getting better and sharper and of course he has now sacked all the therapists who Mum says were wonderful and patient and effective. He'll never be allowed to drive again, and he hates that, but I don't put it past him to drive illegally on the quiet, either. I left it to him and Jake to battle it out about the new planting. Interestingly, the boys were both on Dad's side. They said he knows his own land better than anyone.'

Anna nodded. 'And what about Jake and Bella's moving to Spain?'

Sebastian got off the table.

'Less good,' he said. 'I couldn't get a straight answer. I asked him at least twice, very directly, and he managed not to answer me somehow. He isn't exactly slippery, but he's elusive.'

Anna took her hands away from her face and laid them flat on the kitchen table. She said firmly, 'He *is* slippery.'

'Oh,' Sebastian said, 'come on. Not slippery exactly.'

'Yes,' Anna said firmly. 'In fact, a bit of a wide boy. A cheat.'

'No!'

She raised her gaze to look at him.

'It isn't *your* fault if you have a dishonest brother.'

'But I feel bound to defend him *as* his brother.'

'Well,' Anna said briskly, 'that's as may be. Only having one irreproachable sister, I wouldn't know. But I don't like the look of this situation in Spain.'

Sebastian felt a clutch of an old and familiar fear.

'Are – are you regretting allowing the boys to come with me?'

Anna's gaze didn't waver.

'No. Not at all. They loved it. And it might be theirs one day, or partly, but Jake mustn't be allowed to assume control and possession. That place belongs to *all* of you. Three children, six grandchildren.'

'Yes,' Sebastian said, 'I know.'

Anna stood up. She arranged her fingertips carefully on the table.

'I will ring Bella,' she announced.

Sebastian was startled.

'But you hardly know her! You never speak to her.'

Anna regarded him levelly. 'I'll find a reason to ring.'

'But why? Why would you ring Bella of all people?'

She smiled at him.

'To get a clue as to why they left London. Even if she won't tell me in so many words, I'll probably be able to guess something from what she *doesn't* say.' She looked at his beer glass. 'I got another dozen of those in while you were away. Would you like one?'

———

Carmen and Pepie had both told Pilar, very volubly, how impossible Monica was being about the shop. They were cooking what they usually cooked, they said, and keeping the shop both clean and well stocked, but all Monica did was to find fault with them. She came into the shop most days, Carmen said, and they had begun to hope that it would always be at times when there were very few customers, because she scared them off.

'We'd be scared too,' Pepie said, 'if we didn't know her so well! She looks like thunder and all she does is complain about our mistakes.'

'Which don't,' Carmen said, 'exist in the first place. We do exactly as she said, in the beginning.'

Pilar was washing the kitchen floor. She had made her sister and niece sit on the table so she could mop under their feet. Her own status in the household had risen recently, what with finding Lucia and the hospital visits, and she wasn't going to allow her family to diminish it again in any way. She took her time, rinsing the mop in its plastic bucket, before she said, 'Mr Gus is not the same.'

'We know that!'

Pilar mopped under the table in long, swooping movements.

'I mean,' she said, 'he is not the same to the señora.'

Carmen and Pepie exchanged glances.

'We know that, too.'

Pilar paused, leaning on her mop to squeeze it drier.

'It was suggested that the señora goes to stay with Katie in London. Mr Gus at once said, "Go. Why don't you?" and that of course hurt the señora's feelings.'

Carmen snapped her fingers.

'Of course she should go!'

Pilar began on the tiles in front of the sink.

'I know.'

'Well, tell her!'

'It is better if she realizes for herself.'

Pepie said, 'How long will that take? We are going mad in the shop.'

Pilar stopped a moment with her back to her sister and niece. She said sharply, 'Are you losing custom?'

They laughed. 'Of course we are!'

Pilar turned round. She wasn't smiling.

'Then I will speak to the señora.'

———

Terry was waiting in Katie's office. He was sitting in her chair with his feet, clad in stylish brown suede loafers, on her desk, frowning at his phone. He didn't move when she came in, but merely said, 'Aren't you perpetually amazed by the public antics of the rich and famous?'

Katie put an armful of files down on her desk and shrugged off the handles of her shoulder bag.

'Yes,' she said and then, 'What have I done?'

Terry took his feet very slowly off her desk and smiled at her. 'Nothing.'

'Then . . .'

'Why am I here?'

Katie crossed the room to the coat rack in one corner. 'Yes.'

'Suppose I just took a fancy to see you?'

Katie hung up her coat and turned to face her desk.

'Then – well, usually – you would summon me to see you. Not just walk in while I'm out at court, and give me a fright.'

'Have I?'

'Yes, you have,' Katie said. 'That's why I asked what I'd done wrong.'

'Nothing,' Terry said. 'I said so already. You've done nothing wrong. In fact, you are something of a star in the firm's firmament. I thought maybe you needed reminding.'

Katie stayed where she was, by the coat rack. Terry put his phone in his shirt pocket and lounged back in her chair.

'It's rough at the moment. Isn't it?' he said.

Katie said unhelpfully, 'I don't know what you mean.'

Terry laughed. He picked up a pen on her desk, inspected it and threw it down again.

'Come on, Katie,' he said. 'Parent troubles? Children troubles?'

Katie put her hands in her jacket pockets. She demanded, 'How do you know?'

'Doesn't matter.'

'It does – it *does*. Who told you?'

He pointed at her. 'Gotcha. Told me what?'

'Terry, please don't play games with me.'

'I'm not. I don't want to. But I'm not as work-obsessed as I appear. I notice stuff; I hear stuff. And I wanted to reassure you that when your personal world is falling apart, your work world assumes major importance. In fact, I would say that it becomes something of a refuge, something to be valued as the one thing in life that doesn't seem to be unmanageable and uncontrollable. Am I right?'

Katie looked at the ceiling.

'Yes,' she said, in a voice she hardly recognized as her own.

Terry got to his feet, without hurry.

'Thought so,' he said.

Still staring at the ceiling, Katie said with difficulty, 'Thank you.'

'Nothing to thank me for. I came to find you to tell you

that you are doing a grand job in difficult personal circumstances. And that although I hope the personal stuff gets easier, I am well aware of the value of your work life to you while it doesn't.'

'Suppose,' Katie said to the ceiling, 'suppose that whatever is going on in my home life actually doesn't get better?'

'It'll change. Things always change with time and those changes mean you are dealing with different circumstances. But even those changes won't affect work. Work goes on and as long as you work the way you're working, I am a very happy bunny. I'm leaving now. Have your chair back.'

Katie tipped her head down so that she could see him. He was standing in the doorway and held up a hand.

'Not a word,' Terry said. 'Not one. Nothing to say. Kravchuk's second son has just thrown up in first class on a plane his father doesn't own. Slumming it, plainly, poor kid. Some other passenger filmed him. OK?'

———

Bella was watching her mother-in-law drink her early-morning tea on the terrace. She had opened the shutters a stealthy crack or two, enough to see Monica's outline, but not enough to wake Mouse who, having had a wakeful night, was now deep in slumber, sprawled on her back with her slippered feet outside the kicked-back bedclothes. Bella yawned. It was going to be a long, hard day, as it always was when Mouse had had a broken night.

Monica, she noticed, was wearing her Christmas slippers. She was also wearing one of her white cotton Spanish nightdresses and a peculiar formal cardigan thing in olive green. If Bella could have seen her from the front, she knew that her mother-in-law would also be wearing earrings. Monica put on earrings the moment she woke up, before she brushed her teeth. She had told Bella that when she was younger she had loved hoop earrings, but now she mostly preferred pearls. Bella guessed that she'd be wearing her pearl earrings this morning. She leaned on the windowsill and very unobtrusively cleared her throat.

Monica turned at once. Bella opened the shutters a little wider and put her finger to her lips.

'Shh. Mouse is still asleep.'

Monica tiptoed elaborately across the terrace in her fluffy slippers.

'Isn't that rather wonderful? Still asleep at nearly eight o'clock.'

'We had a bad night,' Bella whispered. 'Lots of crying and not sleeping. Poor Mousie. She wore herself out.'

Monica regarded her.

'And you too, from the look of you.'

Bella tossed her hair back.

'Oh, me! I'm just the mummy.'

Monica gestured at her mug. 'Tea?'

Bella nodded. 'Lovely.'

Monica indicated the kitchen. 'See you there then.'

Bella said, 'I should stay with Mouse.'

'Should you? Why?'

'I don't want her waking and not finding me here.'

'Bella,' Monica said. 'You're her mother. Not her slave. We'll drink tea out here on the terrace and if she wakes up, you'll hear her.'

Bella pouted slightly.

'Bringing up children isn't the same as it was in your day.'

'Clearly not.'

'In fact,' Bella said, gathering courage, 'a lot of things are very different. Like our attitude to men.'

'Oh?' Monica said dangerously.

'Yes,' Bella said. She was standing straighter now and had swept her hair to one side and was holding a length of it in her left hand. 'Yes. I mean I wouldn't dream of letting Jake treat me the way Gus treats you. I wouldn't stand for it.'

Monica glared at her. 'Really.'

Bella grasped her hair more firmly.

'If I wanted to go to London,' Bella began. 'To see my daughter – to see Mouse, say – and my granddaughters, I wouldn't let the welfare of a rude old man like Gus stand in my way.'

Monica said faintly, 'He's had a stroke.'

'But he's still rude. He's a rude old man. And he's dreadful to you, really dreadful. I don't know why you put up with it.'

Monica said nothing. She looked down into her tea mug and then across the terrace at the view. Bella watched her. Then she said, 'Go. Just go. Why don't you?' She allowed a beat to fall and then she added, 'I would.'

———

Florence was sitting at the kitchen table solemnly eating her customary boiled egg, when the landline rang. Katie, tapping out an email reply, didn't even look up.

'Answer that, would you?'

Florence looked at Marta. 'You do it.'

Marta indicated the piece of toast in her mouth. She made

an indistinct noise. Florence went back to peeling minute fragments of shell off her egg. 'I can't either.'

'Honestly,' Katie said, plunging past them to retrieve the handset. 'How hard can it be?' She clapped the phone to her ear. 'Mum! Goodness, Mum, this early. No, of course it isn't early in Spain. What? No, not at all. Really. It's very nice to hear you. It's just that the mornings are always a bit of a dash.'

Daisy drifted into the room, complete with impeccable eye makeup and black lace mittens.

Florence said, 'Oh wow, so you *slept* here?'

Daisy yawned. Her forearms, above the mittens, were milk white below the fluted sleeves of her dress.

'I *always* sleep here.'

'No, you don't.'

'Stop it, girls,' Katie said into the telephone. 'Sorry, Mum. What? What were you saying?'

Daisy said to Marta, 'Nothing wrong with your appetite, I see.'

Marta said nothing. She bent her head so that her hair swung forward. The second half of her toast disappeared behind the curtain of her hair. Daisy sat down on the opposite side of the table to her sisters and eyed Florence's toast.

'Look at all that butter.'

Florence licked her egg spoon.

'I like butter.'

Daisy switched her gaze to her other sister.

'You can't have butter, though, can you, Marta. It's made from animal protein. So you have to eat that disgusting soy spread.'

'It's not disgusting,' Florence said. 'It's just weird.'

'Why doesn't she tell me herself?'

'Because,' Florence said, 'she's not talking. Are you, Marta? It makes living here pretty boring.'

'Of course,' Katie said into the telephone. 'No, we'd love it. All of us.'

Florence swivelled round.

'What?' she hissed.

Katie put her free hand over her other ear and bent her head forward as if concentrating.

'Not at all, Mum. It'd be lovely.'

Nic appeared in the doorway. He gestured at Katie and mouthed, 'Who?'

'Granny,' Florence said importantly. 'From Spain.'

Daisy sat up.

'Granny!'

Florence went back to her egg. 'Yes. Hey, stop that, that was my last soldier.'

His mouth full of Florence's toast, Nic said, 'Maybe she's changed her mind about coming.'

'I wanted her to come,' Daisy said as if opposing a general wish. 'I *suggested* she came.' She looked at her sister. 'Marta? Marta, what do you think?'

'Leave her,' Nic said quickly. 'Just leave her.'

Daisy leaned across the table towards her sister. 'What about us, Marta? What about us having to live with you? What about *our* mental health?'

'Stop it!' Nic said to her, louder this time.

Katie took the phone away from her ear. She said, to the room at large, 'Granny's coming.'

'Great!' Daisy said.

Florence pushed her egg cup away. She said, to no one in particular, 'You don't sound very pleased.'

Katie looked at Nic. 'I think – I think I'm startled. That's all. I wonder what changed her mind?'

Nic stood behind Marta and put his hands lightly on her shoulders.

'It doesn't matter why, does it? It's just very good that she's agreed to come at all.' He bent over Marta so that his mouth was almost touching her ear. 'Isn't it, sweetie?'

Marta said nothing. They were all looking at her, four pairs of eyes trained on her bent head.

'If you don't want to speak,' Nic said gently, 'then don't. Just nod your head to show that you're glad Granny's coming.'

They waited. Marta didn't move. After a second or two, Florence pushed her chair back with a clatter and stood up. She looked from one parent to another.

'Who's going to come with me while I brush my teeth?'

CHAPTER FOURTEEN

Jake deliberately chose a back-street bar in Ronda. It was the kind of place that in his childhood would have had workmen standing at its zinc-topped bar on winter mornings, downing shots of coffee and brandy before going off to plough fields or build railway bridges. He ordered a double espresso and, as an afterthought, a measure of Soberano, which was handed to him in a small thick tumbler. He carried the cup and the glass over to the darkest corner of the bar, away from the high-up television set which seemed to be showing all of Real Madrid's victory goals on a perpetual loop.

The bank manager had said no. He had said it very courteously and he had acknowledged that Gus had been a valued customer of the bank for almost thirty years, but all the same, the bank could not lend Jake any money. They could not now, the bank manager said politely, nor could they ever. Was Jake aware that Gus had already borrowed against the value of the vineyard?

Jake had gaped at him.

'But the vineyard keeps winning awards for its wines. Plus it sells all round the world.'

The bank manager waited. He wore a perfectly ironed white

shirt and a creaseless suit of some slightly shiny material. He was, Jake thought, in his thirties, and managing the Ronda branch of Spain's oldest bank was obviously a gratifying promotion.

'Señor Beacham.'

'Yes?'

'Señor Beacham, I am aware of the distinction of your father's vineyard. That is one of the reasons the bank agreed to re-mortgage the property when your father approached us. In addition, your father has been a Spanish resident and taxpayer since 1993. That was the year he registered with the authorities and received his NIE.'

'His *what*?'

'His *Número de Identidad de Extranjero*.'

Jake said faintly, 'I had no idea.'

'No.'

Jake looked at the bank manager's clothes. Perhaps it had been a mistake to drive to the meeting in the jeans and polo shirt he wore around the vineyard. Maybe it looked a bit disrespectful, however good and fluent his Spanish was. He said, slightly defiantly, 'I grew up there, you know. I was at school locally from the age of twelve.'

The bank manager inclined his head. 'That accounts for your excellent Spanish, then. I come from further north, near Madrid.'

'I can tell,' Jake said. 'Are you saying,' he went on, 'that even though my father had a stroke and I am now running the vineyard, and even though that vineyard is worth between three and a half and four million euros, that because I haven't been primarily resident in Spain for a minimum of three years, you are unable, or refusing, to lend me a single cent?'

The bank manager looked back at him levelly.

'Unable, señor.'

'For pity's sake!'

'I should make it plain to you, perhaps, that your father has been a valued customer of the bank's for over two decades now. We are Spain's oldest bank and although we are very up to the minute as far as technology goes, we still try to extend the old courtesies to our long-standing clients. By 1998, your father wasn't obliged to report his tax affairs to the authorities in the UK. He was a Spanish resident by then, and paid his taxes here. He has done that for twenty-five years.'

'And never told any of his children about it!'

The bank manager looked studiedly at the surface of his desk.

'Jesus,' Jake said with energy, 'Jesus. Can you *believe* it?'

'It is – very unfortunate. But not rare.'

Jake got up and rammed his fists into his jeans pockets. He looked accusingly at the bank manager.

'And I suppose you'll refuse to tell me how much of the estate he re-mortgaged, and why?'

'Not at all, as regards the latter point. If you will wait just a moment while I check the records . . .'

Jake leaned forwards, towards the screen the bank manager was now checking. He said, furiously, 'You bureaucrats are the bane of enterprising spirit everywhere. Do you know that? Are you aware of the damage you do to progress all over the world?'

'Your father,' the bank manager said, referring imperturbably to his screen, 'applied to my predecessor here six years ago in order to set up a shop for your mother to run a delicatessen, I think, and a retail outlet for the wines of the estate.'

'And how much did he borrow?'

'I am afraid I couldn't tell you that.'

'Of course you couldn't,' Jake said triumphantly. 'You can't do anything that doesn't tick a regulation box, can you? Well, I shall find it out for myself. I'll find it somewhere in Dad's papers. I might even ask him outright and if he can't or won't tell me, I'll be able to guess by a process of elimination, won't I?'

The bank manager rose to his feet and held his hand out.

'Thank you for coming, Señor Beacham.'

Jake ignored his proffered hand and marched to the door. He said, with his back turned to the room, 'It was an absolute waste of time, Señor Alvarez. Mine and yours. Good morning.'

Outside in the car, he looked at his phone to see what calls he had missed. There were none. And only one text from José Manuel back at the vineyard.

'The new vines have come,' José Manuel had written in Spanish. 'Delivered 9 a.m. They don't look wonderful.'

———

'Can I talk to you?' Dermot said.

Anna looked up from her computer. Dermot had had a fresh undercut and it only served to emphasize the size of his ears.

'Of course,' she said. 'I didn't hear you. Where's Marcus?'

Dermot gestured.

'Dunno,' he said. 'Maybe out. Or working.' He looked at Anna's computer screen. 'What are you doing?'

'Accounts,' Anna said pleasantly. 'Well, VAT for the business actually. What did you want to talk to me about?'

Dermot dropped into the nearest armchair. He balanced the side of one trainered foot on the knee of his other leg. He said shortly, 'Spain.'

'Ah.'

'Don't say it like that, Mum. Spain's great. And it's important.'

Anna swivelled herself round in her chair so that she could see Dermot properly.

'I wasn't saying it like anything, Dermot.'

He frowned, but not at her.

'Don't pretend, Mum.'

'I'm not.'

'The thing is,' Dermot said much more loudly, 'that Spain matters to us, Marcus and Dad and me, and it matters a lot to Grandpa who's really created it, so if you want to be part of something that's really important to all of us, you'll have to change your attitude.'

Anna said stiffly, 'There's nothing wrong with my attitude.'

Dermot snorted.

'Really? So you're fine with Granny, are you?'

Anna looked down at her hands.

'It takes two to tango, Dermot.'

'Marc and I got on fine with her. She's lovely.'

'A pair of handsome and enthusiastic grandsons is a very different matter from an unsuitable daughter-in-law.'

Dermot took his foot off his knee.

'Why unsuitable?'

'Not conventional enough,' Anna said. 'Not biddable and sweetly pretty.'

Dermot lifted his other foot and inspected his trainer close up. Then he said, 'Dad seemed really at ease there. He was fine.'

'Perhaps,' Anna said. 'It's new, this confidence of his. Perhaps things are better between Granny and Dad after Grandpa's stroke.'

'Maybe.'

Anna glanced at him sharply.

'What's that supposed to mean?'

Dermot lowered his foot to the floor.

'Nothing.'

'Dermot . . .'

'The thing is, Mum,' Dermot said with sudden energy, 'Grandpa has built something pretty amazing in Spain. And if you go on being sniffy about it, you're the one who'll lose out. Because we won't change. We liked it and if you can't like it too, then that's your loss. Not ours. OK?'

Anna looked down at her hands again. She nodded slightly. She said in a half-whisper, 'I do want to be part of it.'

Dermot began to get up. He paused halfway and pulled his phone out of his pocket.

'Good,' he said, and then showed her his phone. 'You can start building some bridges with Granny then.'

Anna looked up at him.

'Why? What do you mean?'

'Daisy says Granny's coming to stay with them next week. She's agreed to come.' He turned towards the door. 'Perfect opportunity, hey, Mum?'

———

When Mouse was born, Jake had gone online at once, and bought a cloth baby carrier which he and Bella could wear as a backpack. Bella, fearful about the lack of head support in the carrier, had decreed that it shouldn't be used, but somehow, it had made its way to Spain and the combination of greater strength in Mouse's neck and the bright warm autumn days made it a less objectionable proposition. In fact, Bella discovered, Mouse liked being carried about in her sunhat and often sang tunelessly to herself on her mother's back. Bella also discovered that taking Mouse around in this manner gave her the ideal alibi for finding out more about the business and how it worked. After a few days' walking near the house, Bella began to explore the estate, Mouse on her back, who was greeted enthusiastically by the men from the village who worked there. They also became the perfect audience for Bella's deliberately academic Spanish, laughing uproariously when she failed to understand what they were saying. Bella laughed too.

'*Soy una idiota,*' she said, over and over, and to Mouse, '*La momia es tonta.*'

She discovered, although Jake had not mentioned it, that the new vines had been delivered. There must, she calculated, have been hundreds of them, poor wilting things, which José Manuel had ordered to be regularly watered at sunset. She could ask José Manuel quite openly and straightforwardly about them, and from him she learned that Señor Jake had directed them to be planted in the newly turned earth up the mountainside.

'Really?' she said, shading her eyes and squinting up towards the north-east. 'Up there?'

José Manuel gave a shrug.

'That's my orders.'

'But,' Bella said innocently, 'how will you water them, so far from the river?'

José Manuel shrugged again.

'Search me.'

Bella and Mouse went up the mountain to inspect the recently ploughed earth. It looked very dry. Very exposed. Turning slowly in a complete circle, Bella said to Mouse, 'Would you plant vines up here? Especially the kind of vine that likes to be much further north than here? What do you think, Mousie?'

It was very still on the hillside, not hot but nearly so, and there were eagles gliding overhead on the warm thermals of air. The vineyard, Jake had told her, was on a migration path, so the birds were spectacular. As a boy, he said, he had regularly seen griffon vultures, and blackcaps and white wagtails were common, too.

'We ought,' Bella said to her daughter, 'to concentrate more on birds. In fact, we should concentrate more on everything here because to be honest, I don't know how long it will last.'

She looked down at her feet. She had worn sandals when she first arrived, but the roughness of the terrain had forced a switch to gym shoes.

'Look at Mummy's shoes,' she said to Mouse. 'You wouldn't believe they started life pale pink, would you?'

Behind her shoulder, sated with sun and air, Mouse yawned gustily.

'Right,' Bella said to her, 'home we go for our morning nap. I think we won't talk to Daddy today, will we? What do you think? Shall we wait till Granny's gone next week, and talk to him then?'

———

Sebastian had never, as his sister pointed out, been to Katie's offices. They were modern and minimalist behind a conventional and elegant Georgian façade, so that one stepped through the late eighteenth-century panelled door straight into a twenty-first-century foyer, worthy of an upmarket hotel. The receptionist, Sebastian thought, was a clone of every current convention of female desirability, young and slender with poker-straight glossy hair and flawlessly shaded eyelids.

Sebastian told her that he was here to see his sister. She smiled up at him with a display of astonishingly white and even teeth and said she would tell Miss Beacham at once and would he like to wait over there? Sebastian looked nervously at the low deep sofas she indicated, upholstered, apparently, in pale beige suede.

'There?'

The receptionist laughed.

'That's what they're for. Sitting on.'

'Not if you've ever lived with small boys.'

She laughed again and said, 'My mum would agree with you.'

It was odd, but rather fascinating, to hear Katie spoken to on the phone so professionally. Sebastian lowered himself gingerly onto one of the suede sofas and thought how incongruous his battered deck shoes looked on the smooth pale floor. Incongruous, certainly, but not out of place, not embarrassing or unsuitable. He wondered at that feeling, at the release of not, somehow, being oppressed by an habitual sensation of deficiency in sleek surroundings like these. Anna had seen him off at the front door like some kind of Stepford wife, docilely holding up his jacket for him to shrug on and almost – but not quite – saying she hoped he'd have a nice day.

'Seb,' Katie said.

She stepped out of the central glass lift, and came across the blond floor to kiss him. He stood up, stiffly. 'These sofas are so low.'

'I know,' she said. 'They're hopeless. Interior designer choice. Lovely to look at, useless in practice.'

He regarded her at arm's length.

'You – don't look wonderful.'

She put up a hand and tucked her hair behind one ear. Very quietly she said, 'I don't feel it. Actually.'

Sebastian glanced towards the receptionist, who was studiedly concentrating on something else. He said loudly, 'I've never seen your office.'

Katie turned towards the receptionist.

'Thank you, Dani.'

The girl looked up, and flashed another of her dazzling smiles.

'No problem.'

In the lift, sliding silently upwards, Katie said, 'She's a real find, Dani. She can read and write and answer the phone and look people in the eye. And she's only nineteen. Terry trawled the local schools to find her and then he paid for her to go on a reception training course and have her teeth fixed.'

Sebastian didn't look at her.

'What does she earn?'

'Above average for a receptionist. Twenty-seven thousand a year and she lives at home in Epping.'

Sebastian said, 'I pay my cleaners eight pounds fifty an hour. Cleaners are classically among the worst paid workers in the UK.'

The lift stopped. Katie stood against the open lift door and indicated her office.

'What does Profclean charge its clients?'

Sebastian obediently stepped out of the lift.

'We pride ourselves on not charging fifteen pounds an hour, like our rivals. So fourteen pounds.'

'So five pounds fifty profit for Profclean?'

'No,' Sebastian said. 'Because of transport and vehicles and cleaning materials. Wow, Katie, this is spectacular!'

'Yes,' she said, as if it were nothing to do with her. 'Great views.'

He went across to the main window. 'Do you want to tell me what the matter is?'

'Not much,' Katie said.

'OK then. Shall I tell you about Spain instead?'

'Please.'

He looked at her.

'Aren't you going to close the door? And offer me something?'

'Like what?'

'Tea. Water. Doesn't matter what. Katie, we're sister and brother.'

She moved slowly to close the door and then she leaned on it. She said, wearily, 'I know.'

'Well, then.'

'What would you like?'

Sebastian said firmly, 'A cup of tea and a glass of tap water, please.'

She said, still leaning against the door, 'I'm really glad you came. And I'm really pleased to see you.'

'OK.'

'How was Spain?'

He hesitated, then said, 'Awful and wonderful. The boys were fantastic. They loved it. Dad loved them.'

Katie didn't move. She said, 'I got such stick from Daisy. That she wasn't there too, to join in the fun.'

'She can go any time. With the boys. They're busting to go again.'

Katie looked at the ceiling.

'She was jealous. Of the boys loving it. She's always refused to go.'

'I know.'

Katie turned her head to look at him. She said, 'What about everything else? What about Mum and Dad and Jake?'

Sebastian came away from the window and dropped into Katie's client's chair. He said shortly, 'Awful.'

'In what way?'

'Dad at his most intractable and unpleasant, Mum at her most idiotic, Jake really irritating and ratty.'

Katie stood upright.

'Jake *ratty*?'

Sebastian glanced up.

'He was very self-righteous about having saved the day – unlike us, of course – and then refused to tell me why he'd been able to drop everything in London and ride to the rescue of Mum and Dad.'

Katie moved across to her own desk chair.

'Did you ask him outright?'

'Of course I did,' Sebastian said patiently. 'And he refused to answer.'

She looked at him directly.

'Oh God, Seb. What is going on? Is he some kind of wide boy?'

'Anna thinks so.'

'Does she?'

Sebastian smiled. 'She put it rather more forcefully than that.'

Katie put her hands briefly over her face. Then she said, in a brisker tone, 'What are we going to do about it all?'

Sebastian put his elbows on his knees. 'I think Mum is coming next week.'

'She is.'

'And something has happened at home. A change of heart.'

Katie sat more upright. 'Whose?'

'Anna's.'

'*Anna's?*'

'Yes,' Sebastian said. 'She has decided, she says, to take the boys out to Spain. They are dead keen to go again and she told me that she regrets her past attitude to the place, and would like to start making amends. So she's proposing to take them after school on a Friday night and come back forty-eight hours later.'

Katie stared at her brother.

'Wow.'

'I know.'

'How long have you been married?'

Sebastian shrugged. 'Almost twenty years.'

'Twenty years,' Katie said, 'of Anna steadfastly refusing to have anything to do with Spain.'

'I know,' Sebastian said again.

'Is it because Mum will be here in London?'

He grinned.

'I thought of that. But I think something else has happened.'

'What?'

'Don't know,' Sebastian said. 'And I don't really care. I'm just thankful for whatever it is. Katie . . .'

'Yes?'

'Are you dreading having Mum to stay?'

She sighed and fiddled with a pen on her desk.

'Not really.'

'What is it then?'

She ducked her head. 'Nothing.'

He got up and came over to her desk. Then he bent over until his face was quite close to hers. He said softly, 'Tell me.'

'I can't.'

'Is it,' he said, persisting, 'something to do with one of the children?'

———

Monica had forgotten, she told herself, how cold the autumns were in England. She had brought the boiled-wool cardigan with her but all the same, she made an elaborate fuss about the temperature, wrapping the cardigan tightly around her, and hunching her shoulders. Daisy, who had moved out of her bedroom for her grandmother, and was now sharing quarrelsomely with Florence, was extremely sorry for Monica, and made a great show of muffling her feet in a mohair blanket.

'It must be awful for you, poor Granny. Would you like a hot-water bottle? I know we've got one somewhere. Mum gives it to us for period pains. Marta and me, that is.'

Monica was genuinely grateful for the mohair blanket and the solicitude. She thought Daisy was extremely pretty and wore too much makeup. She also thought Florence was improperly opinionated for someone of her age and that there was something amiss, that she couldn't quite put her finger on, about Marta. It was all uneasy, really, staying with Katie, uneasy and unfamiliar, and the first few nights she had quite shocked herself by violently missing her familiar room and bed, in Spain. She had lain there, in Daisy's comfortable and astonishingly wide bed – is this what modern teenagers demanded these days, a *double* bed? – and told herself firmly that what she was suffering from was nothing more than acute homesickness, of which she should be nothing but ashamed at her age. Early-morning tea was brought to her by Nic, who wasn't to know of her own solitary Spanish ritual, any more than he could be expected to realize that she liked less milk in her tea than he gave her, and that the mug he brought her was too thick. Her early-morning tea mug in Spain – if she had thought of it, she would have brought it with her – was bone china and fluted, and she missed its delicacy. Just as she missed the silence of the Spanish nights and the darkness of the skies and the size of the stars.

Florence had asked – well, demanded, more accurately – if she missed Gus.

'Of course I do, darling,' she said automatically. She was sitting up in bed, in the boiled-wool cardigan, with her tea mug in her hands.

Florence was poking about – not having asked first, Monica thought – among her grandmother's trinkets and cosmetics on Daisy's bureau. She held up an eyebrow comb.

'Mum says he's a rude old pig these days. What's this?'

'It's an eyebrow comb, darling.'

'Wow,' Florence said. 'D'you really comb your *eyebrows*?'

Monica forced a smile. 'Sometimes.'

'Why?'

'Well, when you get older, your eyebrows sometimes get wilder. Less – less smooth. They don't lie flat so well. So you have to—'

'*Comb* them?'

'Well, yes.'

'Like – *hair*?'

'A bit,' Monica said. 'Why don't you put that down now?'

Still holding the comb, Florence hitched herself onto the side of Monica's bed.

'D'you suppose *all* grannies have these?'

'Well, no, darling, not all grannies—'

'Let's go back to Grandpa,' Florence said, interrupting. 'Is he rude to you, I mean you specially?'

'Of course not.'

'Mum says he is.'

'He's been,' Monica said carefully, 'extremely ill. Very ill indeed.'

'Did he nearly die?'

'It was more like a violent shock to the system. The kind of shock that means you might never be the same again.'

Florence was twiddling the eyebrow comb back and forth in her fingers.

'Daisy says she's tired of making allowances for people who've had shocks.'

Monica suddenly felt tears pricking unbidden behind her eyelids. She fumbled for a handkerchief in her cardigan sleeve and almost spilt her tea.

'Careful,' Florence said, watching her.

'Take my tea, would you, darling?' Monica said unsteadily.

Florence took the tea mug in silence, watching her grand-mother all the while.

'Are you crying?'

'No.'

Florence leaned forward.

'I think you are a bit. What are you sad about?'

Monica found her handkerchief and blew her nose. 'Nothing, darling.'

'Or everything,' Florence said.

'Please don't talk like that.'

'It's the only way I know how to talk, you know.'

Monica tucked her handkerchief back into her sleeve. She held out a hand.

'May I have my tea back, Florence?'

Slowly, Florence handed her the mug. She said, soberly, 'I don't think you are OK.'

'Yes I am, darling, I'm fine.'

Florence got off the bed and laid the eyebrow comb back on Daisy's bureau. She said, 'I'd better get dressed for school.'

'Good idea.'

At the door, Florence said, holding the handle, 'When I grow up, I'm going to be a lawyer, like Mum. Or a lollipop lady. What were you?'

Monica stiffened slightly.

'Nothing, Florence. I mean, I didn't have a professional job like Mummy does. I looked after Grandpa and Uncle Sebastian and Mummy and Uncle Jake and I helped Grandpa with his business and then I ran the shop.'

'Were you a housewife?'

'No,' Monica said, trying not to sound indignant. 'It said

on my passport "Married Woman". That's what I was. A married woman.'

Florence kept her hand on the door but turned to face her grandmother. 'Weird,' she said.

'Is it? Why is it weird?'

Florence opened the door and revealed the landing beyond.

'Being married isn't a *career*,' she said. 'It's just a – a condition. Like having curly hair. Or specs. Oh look. Marta's door's open. Marta's door is actually *open*!'

Monica looked where Florence was pointing.

'Oh! So it is.'

Florence turned back. She said, kindly, 'Don't worry about being weird. Heaps of people are. I mean, Marta is, for one.'

CHAPTER FIFTEEN

Jake told Pilar that Anna could have Monica's room for the weekend, and the boys could share the back bedroom as they had before. He added, nonchalantly, making coffee in the old Italian double pot all the while, that there was no need to trouble Bella with any of these domestic arrangements but just to go ahead, assisted by Carmen or Pepie or Lucia or whoever was around, with making up the beds.

'Fine,' Pilar said. 'OK.'

She was sweeping the kitchen floor as she did every morning, sweeping the dust out onto the terrace and then sweeping the terrace dirt, out through the balustrade into the rough land below it. Jake, now that she saw him every day, and had got to know his wife and child, was subsiding into something of a disappointment to her, and she was surprised to find how much she was missing Monica. She had thought, when Carmen and Pepie had come to her to complain about Monica, that she would be thankful to see the back of her for a while, but she had only been gone for a few days when Pilar discovered, rather to her surprise, that this frequently difficult and demanding person actually represented something important, beloved even, in Pilar's life.

'You have seen her almost every day since you were nine-teen,' Carmen said, in response to an unwarranted explosion of Pilar's temper. 'Of course you miss her! She's like another mother to you.'

'And another child,' Pilar said crossly.

Of course she would make up Monica's bed for Anna, with the best sheets, and put a vase of the little pink-tinged white autumn snowflakes that Monica was so fond of by the bed. But she would also, she thought privately, clear all Monica's pots and china trays and looped necklaces off the dressing table and lock them in the cherry wood chest that Monica had bought in Ronda more than twenty years ago. It was a carved chest made some time in the nineteenth century and it had a long and curly iron key which Pilar could drop into the pocket of her flowered overall. It would give her both pleasure and a strong sense of emotional direction to make Monica's bedroom as pretty and as imper-sonal as she possibly could. After all, it was to be briefly the room of someone Pilar had almost never met, even if she dusted her framed wedding photograph each week. Monica herself would completely understand the nuances of Pilar's attitude.

Bella offered to help make up the beds. She stood in the doorway of Monica's room, Mouse in her arms, and suggested that they put the clean sheets on together.

'It is so much easier,' Bella said, 'with two.'

Pilar, snapping the sheets out of their folds, said shortly that there was no need, she was fine on her own, she was used to it.

Bella stooped to lower Mouse onto her stout legs.

'I'm sure you are. I was just offering.'

'Thank you,' Pilar said, briskly tucking and smoothing. 'But I am nearly done. *Oye, cariña,*' to Mouse. '*Princesa.*'

Bella said, 'She's really settled. She loves living here.'

Pilar banged the pillows.

'It's a beautiful place.'

'And everyone is so friendly.' Bella looked at Mouse. 'Aren't they, Mousie? Don't we have lovely chats round and about?'

Mouse toddled across to the dressing table and raised her arms, grunting questioningly, to be lifted up.

'She wants the necklaces,' Bella said fondly.

Pilar bent to put her hands under Mouse's armpits in order to lift her onto the dressing-table stool. She said to her, 'There's the mirror. But no beads. I've hidden all the beads, all Granny's beads.'

Mouse regarded herself with satisfaction in the mirror, preening a little.

'Look at that,' Bella said proudly. And then, to Pilar, 'Very wise, if I may say so.'

'It is the señora's room.'

'Oh I know. It must mean such a lot to both of you. Could I ask you something?'

Pilar stayed where she was, supporting Mouse on Monica's dressing-table stool. She looked down at Mouse's red-gold curls, so unlike any of the children in her family, who all grew the thick black straight hair that she had herself.

'About what?' she asked.

Bella was watching Pilar's reflection in the dressing-table glass. She said, with every appearance of carelessness, 'Well, for example, about the vines?'

Pilar laughed. She bent down and wound one of Mouse's curls round her finger.

'If your granny was here, she'd tell you that I know nothing about what goes on outside and I never have. It's nothing to do with me. Nothing at all.' She dropped a kiss on Mouse's head. 'We women have enough to do inside the house, after all. Don't we, *preciosa?*'

———

Anna told herself that although she didn't feel exactly nervous about going to Spain, she definitely felt apprehensive. She wasn't afraid of the effect of Gus's stroke per se, nor of seeing her brother- and sister-in-law, nor of actually being in the place she had made plain for so long was definitely enemy territory. But when she added up all those elements, infused with her own attitude hitherto, the prospect was not exactly comfortable. It might have been better, she reflected, if she had cultivated more of a relationship with Katie over the years, but it was no good wishing for that now. Katie made it plain – didn't she? – that there was no time or space in her life for anything that wasn't family or work, and that situation had suited Anna very well throughout her marriage to Sebastian. Sebastian. It was worth considering Sebastian himself, too, these days. Anna couldn't quite work out what had happened, but she was not only looking at Sebastian rather differently but also, disconcertingly, with an awe that amounted almost to anxiety. Anna had never, in all their time together, regarded her husband with anything much more than an exasperated acknowledgement of his better points – loyalty, supportiveness, kindness, biddableness – and now, abruptly and alarmingly, something had shifted in quite a profound way. Now, Sebastian appeared to her, and obviously to himself, as someone very much more significant. Assertive, even. He was even standing taller. And straighter. A fellow choir member, a woman Anna had always regarded as a bit of a goose despite her clear soprano singing voice, had said something admiring about Sebastian at the last rehearsal, which had rather shocked Anna. It had been shocking because it had revealed how the outside world perceived him. 'That husband of yours,' the soprano woman had said casually to Anna, inspecting her luxuriant hair in her hand mirror before choir practice, 'he's quite a dish, isn't he?'

And now the dish appeared to have pulled off something of a family coup, too. He had taken their sons to Spain and the sons had adored it and come home full of it. They had even managed to make Katie's Daisy, hitherto the acme of cool party girl in her sons' eyes, jealous. What is more, Dermot had made it very clear to his mother that if she made any future difficulty about Spain, she would be on her own in dealing with it. Anna had capitulated in her own way over that, seizing the initiative as well as the opportunity to take the boys out to see what Dermot now unabashedly referred to as 'our inheritance'. The other matter, Monica, could be quietly shelved for now. Even if Dermot was relentlessly determined that his mother shouldn't elude what he saw as her responsibilities.

'You can postpone seeing Granny,' he'd said to Anna, his mouth full of cereal, 'but don't think I'm not watching. And waiting. Me and Marc both.'

Anna had sent Monica flowers when she arrived in London, and even as she despatched the order, she knew she had got it wrong. It wasn't just that they were the wrong flowers – a sensible pot of white chrysanthemums

– but it was inappropriate to send them anyway. Monica sent her a note that made the wrongness of the gesture manifest.

'How sweet of you,' Monica wrote, on a postcard of a London bus. 'Such a kind thought. Thank you, Anna. See you soon!'

Anna tore the postcard in two and put it in the kitchen bin where it would rapidly become covered in banana skins and teabags. She checked the fridge. There were four bottles of beer left, and an unopened bottle of Grüner Veltliner. The local off licence had recommended it as the wine of the moment and Anna had found herself, having enquired about it, buying a bottle. She shut the fridge again with a bang. This new anxiety she felt was disconcerting at best and alarming at worst. What had happened to her old certainties, to the old Anna who had effortlessly known best about everything? She closed her eyes and leaned her forehead against the smooth, unyielding surface of the fridge door. It was hard to acknowledge, but she didn't miss the old Anna. In fact, she was rather ashamed of her. It wasn't admirable, or clever, to know best about everything all the time; it just, in the end, made you lonely. And loneliness, Anna now thought, was the worst fate of all.

———

Jake had taken Mouse into Ronda to buy her first proper shoes. They were sandals, stoutly made and supportive to Mouse's feet, and he had told Bella quite forcefully and in front of his father that this was exclusively a father and daughter expedition. Bella appeared to accept the situation, merely pouring her father-in-law more coffee and remarking to him that she was sure he had been just the same when Katie was little, and just as possessive.

Gus was reading his day-old copy of the *Daily Telegraph*.

'No,' he said briefly.

'But weren't you as besotted to have a daughter as Jake is?'

Gus didn't look up.

'No,' he said again.

'Fathers,' Jake said loudly, cutting Mouse's toast into strips, 'weren't overly fatherly in my day. The culture didn't permit it.'

'So,' Bella said, refilling her own cup, 'your generation of men has to compensate.'

Jake said nothing. He sat down close to Mouse and tried to feed her the toast as a distraction. Mouse protested at being treated like a baby and in the ensuing din, Gus got up and limped noisily out of the room, taking his newspaper with him.

Bella took a swallow of her coffee. 'No wonder your mother went to London.'

'We,' Jake said to his daughter, 'will first go to the shoe shop Papa used to go to when he wasn't much older than you.'

Bella looked at the ceiling.

'Why can't I come?'

'Just you and me,' Jake said to Mouse. 'Just the way it used to be with Granny and Papa.'

'In the old days. The *olden* days. While I am stuck here with your father.'

Jake put Mouse's last crust into his own mouth.

'Ignore him,' he said to Bella, bending to lift Mouse out of her high chair.

'Oh,' Bella said with emphasis, 'I will. I'll go and practise my Spanish on the shop girls.'

———

Mouse came back from Ronda with her plump little feet encased in blue leather. The new sandals made a slapping sound on the floors as Mouse stamped about and she created a tremendous fuss at bedtime about having her new shoes removed, only mollified by having them put in the cot next to her, right up by her face. Jake was highly gratified by this display of attachment and refused to let Bella extract them from the cot once Mouse was asleep, or wipe them with disinfectant-impregnated disposable cloths.

In the end, Jake marched Bella firmly out onto the terrace, holding her by the arm.

'Leave the shoes there. Just *leave* them. I know you're jealous that I've given her something she loves so much, but you'll just have to bear that and choke down on it.'

Bella rubbed her arm where he had gripped it. 'You hurt me.'

'No, I didn't.'

'You hurt my feelings.'

'That's quite another matter.'

Bella shivered a little. 'Jakey . . .'

'What?'

'I don't like it when you're cross with me.'

He groaned. 'Oh, Bella. What now?'

'Did you hear what I said?'

He sighed. 'I'm not cross, Bella. I just want you to like it here.'

'Oh,' she said, 'I do. Or mostly I do.'

'But you're nervous about Anna and the boys coming. Is that it?'

Bella pouted.

'I don't really know Anna.'

'None of us do. It's for two nights only.'

Bella moved to lean on the balustrade and look at the lights far below in the velvety Spanish night.

'Jakey . . .'

'What now?'

'What are we going to tell her?'

'About what?'

Bella went on looking down at the lights.

'About why we're here. What we agreed.'

He came to lean on the balustrade beside her.

'There's no need to tell her anything,' he said quietly. 'It won't come up.'

'But suppose it does?'

'Bella, it won't. Why should it? The boys have made her come, after all. She wouldn't otherwise, she wouldn't come near the place. She and Mum do not get on, to put it mildly. As you know.'

'But,' Bella said, persisting, 'what am I supposed to do, if Anna asks me? I mean, what do I say?'

Jake sighed again.

'Don't do this, Bella.'

'Don't do what?'

'Don't give me this passive-aggressive shtick. Don't force me into a corner.'

'But,' Bella said, staring into the darkness, 'it wasn't me fleeing the bills in London. It wasn't me running away from creditors.'

'Stop it!'

'It wasn't me,' Bella pressed, 'who needed to try and make a fresh start.' Then she added softly, 'But it *is* me who had Mouse.' She let a moment pass, and then she said, in a more conciliatory tone, 'She loves her shoes. *Loves* them.'

'Yes.'

'Isn't it a beautiful night?' Bella said.

'It is.'

'There's one thing you can say for Spain: fantastic springs and autumns.'

Jake didn't look at her. 'Yes.'

She glanced towards the house.

'Doesn't it look lovely, lit up like this?'

'Lovely.'

'Jakey,' she said, 'shall I get you a brandy?'

———

Monica was impressed. She was impressed by the way Nic emptied the dishwasher without being asked, and noticed when there was no more washing powder. She had told herself previously that since he hadn't married Katie – or possibly, now she considered it, that Katie hadn't married him – he wasn't to be taken seriously as a proper person, a real and significant man, but when she saw him in daily, ordinary action as a father, she had to revise her opinion. He didn't seem to feel that his manhood was diminished by Katie's out-earning him. That was very surprising. Nor did he seem to feel compromised by domestic life. He brought Monica's morning tea and tried to cajole the girls into eating something for breakfast, and then he disappeared to teach his classes as if switching roles came as naturally to him as, when she thought about it, it had to the women of Monica's experience, all her life.

He was also quite comfortable with his daughters. In Monica's view, both Daisy and Florence needed a little quelling for different reasons, a little discipline in matters of emotional intelligence. It would, Monica could see, be perfectly possible to point this out to Nic, over a glass of wine sometime, and she could picture the reasonableness of the ensuing conversation, and the way she could make her opinion felt without immediately having that opinion taken as personal criticism. Because that's what Katie would do. Monica was miserably convinced of it. Katie would, the moment Monica said anything that wasn't blatantly admiring of the girls, flare up in their – and her own – defence.

That was really the problem about staying with Katie. That and the cold, and the persistent homesickness. Heaven knew, she wasn't homesick for *Gus*. When she rang him, as she regularly and conscientiously did, he was remarkably uncommunicative about his daily life. He had, she ascertained, dismissed all his therapists now, and spent his days in the office going over and over the chaos of his business papers. Privately, she thanked goodness for Jake, for the fact that he had, heaven knew how, been able to swoop to their rescue. It was miraculous. Any other reflections were dangerous and led nowhere. Of that she was convinced.

But none of it helped the present situation. Gus was Gus and Jake would somehow rescue the vineyard. Of course he would. But there was still Katie. And Marta, if she was honest, and she was trying very hard to be honest with herself. Sleeping in Daisy's bed was all very well, but it was temporary. Pairing up the socks and doing the ironing – she hadn't ironed for years, because of Pilar – and venturing out to the local supermarket to buy more yoghurts or toilet paper was probably the right response to living in a busy family, but it couldn't go on. It couldn't go on because, Monica told herself, it was ignoring the elephant in the room. And the elephant was her relationship with Katie. And, in a different way, with the enigmatic, elusive Marta. And it was no good – in fact, it would have been downright improper – trying to involve Nic in either. There were times, she had to admit to herself, when he came into her bedroom with her early-morning tea, that she had been sorely tempted to pat the bed beside her as an invitation to him to sit down, while she asked him what she could do to make things easier with Katie. In fact, she had indulged herself with a little fantasy imagining of such a scene, while knowing in her realistic heart of hearts that a fantasy it was, and a fantasy it must remain.

——

If Anna had felt any dismay at the prospect of visiting the vineyard, she gave no sign of it. Trimly and appropriately dressed in fawn trousers which precisely matched her fawn jersey, she allowed her sons to drag her about the house while they pointed out its charms and the spectacular view from the terrace. Dermot even laid a proprietorial hand on the huge palm tree.

'Granny was really worried that it had got whatever palm trees like this are prone to. But she's saved it, she really has.'

Anna was very admiring. Not once did she roll her eyes in Bella's direction, or indicate in any way that she was a victim of the adolescent fervour of her sons. She went where they indicated that she should go, and pronounced it all wonderful.

'Really, Mum?' Marcus asked. He was holding Mouse in his arms, as Mouse had made it plain she wanted to be held.

'Really. It's wonderful.'

Marcus said, looking at his baby cousin, 'We think so. Don't we, Mouse?'

Dermot ushered her into Monica's bedroom. He said, almost reverently, 'You're sleeping here.'

Anna hesitated on the threshold.

'Are you sure? Won't Granny mind?'

'She said you were to sleep here.'

'Did she? Really?'

Dermot nodded. 'Really.'

Anna looked round the room.

'It's – very nice.'

'Isn't it. And there's the bathroom. Local tiles hung the local way.'

'Lovely,' Anna said. 'Blue and green.'

'That's Moorish. Moorish colours. Especially the jade green. You must let down the mosquito net, even at this time of year. Granny would insist.'

'Of course,' Anna said.

Bella appeared from the corridor.

'I seem to have lost my daughter to your son.'

Anna smiled at her.

'He loves babies, always has. Thank you for the flowers beside the bed. A lovely touch.'

'Actually,' Bella said, 'that was Pilar.'

'Oh,' Anna said. 'Pilar.'

Bella glanced at Dermot. 'She really rules the roost here. Doesn't she!'

Dermot looked hard at his mother.

'She's wonderful too, Pilar.'

'You know,' Bella said, 'you can be wonderful *and* rule the roost.'

Anna smiled again.

'Of course you can.'

Dermot's gaze didn't waver from his mother's face. He said, 'I want to show you the vineyard. And you need to see Grandpa.'

'Now? Straight away?'

'Yes,' Dermot said. 'Now.'

Anna's smile became apologetic. 'I'm so sorry,' she said to Bella. 'But you see how it is.'

'Of course.'

Anna looked round Monica's bedroom as if memorizing it. 'It really is an honour, to be sleeping here.'

Bella folded her arms. 'Such a lovely view,' she said. 'Spectacular, even. We've got the same from our room, next door.'

———

Gus was in the office. He spent most of the day in there, checking the same columns of figures, picking up the same wads of papers and putting them down again, unable to remember precisely how to operate the computer, and furious at anyone, especially Jake, who tried to help him. Twice a day, José Manuel stopped what he was doing among the fermentation tanks and the great French oak barrels and came to lead his old boss out into the sunlight. Sometimes they spoke, but mostly Gus shuffled beside his *enólogo* in silence, his hand in the crook of José Manuel's arm, the rope soles of his old espadrilles stumping unevenly along the ground. They inspected the machines that cleaned the bottles and the empty linked crates that held the grapes after harvesting, and the great crusher that pressed the grapes, thousands of kilos each hour. They toured the fermentation room where a huge protected cork oak tree grew out of the floor and through the ceiling, and the underground space where the cleaned bottles were filled and corked and labelled. When they got to the cellars, and were in the presence of the huge oak barrels themselves, José Manuel would say quietly, in English, as if trying not to wake something of great significance, 'The cellar, for sleep the wine,' and they would both stand there in reverential silence, as if in a mighty presence.

José Manuel did not take Gus up the mountainside where Jake had instructed him to plough. Nor did he take him to look at the rows of new vines which had still not been planted and which required daily watering. There was neither need nor point. This vineyard had been founded on natural, local and organic principles, and so, in José Manuel's mind, it would remain. Chickens, geese to eat the local snails, an ancient breed of sheep, and vultures wheeling overhead all played their part in keeping nature in balance and producing the wine for which the vineyard had become famous, both the red Tempranillo and the white Petit Verdot. This was the way that the muscatel that Gus had introduced almost a decade ago, and which José Manuel was planning to submit for a Bacchus award in Madrid in the following February, had organically evolved. In fact, José Manuel was looking forward to explaining to the judging panel that maybe one of the reasons the wine tasted so impressive was that the sediment from the barrels was extracted, dried out, and then applied as fertilizer to the earth where the vines grew anew.

'Nothing,' he planned to say, 'is wasted. And the cycle of natural organic growth and death is complete.'

Dermot crouched down in the cramped space beside Gus's office chair. He said, cheerfully, 'Grandpa.'

Gus seemed to have trouble focusing. Then his face gradually became illuminated.

'Ah,' he said. 'Ah,' and spread his arms out.

Anna watched while her son manoeuvred himself awkwardly into the old man's embrace. Dermot said with difficulty, 'I've brought Mum.'

'Who?'

'Mum. Anna. You remember?'

Gus didn't look her way.

'Where's the other one?'

'Marcus? He got hijacked by Mouse. He's around. He'll be here later.'

Anna cleared her throat. 'Hello, Gus.'

He swivelled slowly in her direction, fixing his gaze on her midriff.

'What's your name?'

'Anna. I'm Sebastian's wife.'

Gus grimaced. 'I know,' he said. 'I know that. Where's he?'

'In London, Grandpa,' Dermot said. 'I brought Mum this time. And Marcus.'

Gus stared at Dermot urgently.

'I need to see Sebastian.'

Dermot adjusted his crouching position. 'Not this time, Grandpa. Next time. He'll come next time.'

Gus tried to twist round again.

'You,' he said.

'Anna, you mean?'

'Yes,' he said. 'Of course Anna. You, Anna.' He flapped a hand. 'Nice boys.'

'Yes. At least, I think so.'

'Sit down.'

'I can't,' she said. 'I can't see anywhere to sit.'

Gus said to Dermot, 'Get your mother a chair.'

He grinned at his grandfather.

'I can't. There isn't any space. And too much mess, anyway.'

Gus gripped his chair arms. 'Help me.'

'What?'

'Help me up. We're going out.'

Anna leaned forward to put a hand under Gus's armpit.

'Where are we going?' she said.

He turned, very slowly, and regarded her.

'Out,' he repeated. 'You, me and the boy.'

———

The house, Monica thought, was empty. Katie was still at work, Nic was at his college, Florence was at an after-school club and Daisy was involved in one of those strange ill-defined gatherings which involved, as far as Monica could see, an infinite amount of arranging for no apparent outcome. Katie said it was called 'hanging out'. Perhaps that was what Marta was doing, too, silent Marta in her huge sweatshirts, who kept her room so tidy and was vegan.

'She doesn't,' Florence explained helpfully, 'eat anything that has a face. Only plants. It's a belief system.'

She was also, Monica thought privately, battling with adolescence. She looked very much as Monica had looked at the same age, dark-haired and stoop-shouldered as if to deny the burgeoning signs of womanhood. There had been, Monica remembered clearly, no helpful teen bras in her day, nothing to span that yawning gap between being a flat-chested child and a full-breasted woman. Poor Marta. Poor Marta sandwiched between these noisy, outgoing sisters, silent in the face of the wretchedness of being half-fledged at thirteen, neither one thing nor another. At least, as far as Monica could see, she didn't have spots.

It was disconcerting to be in the house alone. It wasn't the first time and it wouldn't be the last, but it made Monica realize that in Spain she was never alone. There was Pilar in the house and the girls in the shop and the men in the vineyard. Always someone, and even if you couldn't see them, you could hear them. Jabber, jabber, jabber. The Spanish talked *all* the time, and even if she had complained about this incessant torrent of language, now that it wasn't here, she missed it. She looked at her watch. It was twenty past five. Only that. It was probably over an hour and a half until everyone – anyone – came home.

Well, Monica thought, I should be purposeful. I have done the ironing and plumped the cushions and the next thing I should do is make myself a cup of tea. But first I must go to the loo. Not downstairs because I really don't somehow like it, but upstairs in the girls' bathroom, which I prefer as it has a window. She went up the stairs in a deliberate manner, and crossed the landing to the bathroom door, which was closed. Closed, Monica thought. How odd. Why should it be closed when the last person who used it was me, and I'm sure I left it open?

She pushed the door open. There was a gasp. Marta was standing in front of the basin, her sweatshirt sleeves pushed up and her horrified face reflected in the mirror above the basin.

'I locked the door!' Marta screeched.

Monica stepped inside. She said calmly, 'No, I don't think you did.'

Marta spun round. Her naked forearms were completely visible. She shouted, 'Go away. Go away!'

Monica regarded her. She looked her up and down, then she closed the door behind her, and leaned on it.

'I'm not going anywhere, darling.'

Marta tugged her sleeves down frantically.

'*Please*, Granny.'

'Suppose,' Monica said, 'you tell me what is going on?'

'No! No!'

'Then we've got a long evening ahead of us, haven't we? I'm your grandmother, darling, not an authority figure. I'm on your side, don't you see that? On *your* side.' A strange calm settled on her, as if the bathroom had suddenly been flooded with golden light. She smiled at Marta. 'Come on, darling. I'm waiting.'

CHAPTER SIXTEEN

Anna lay still and straight in Monica's bed and knew that sleep was so far away that it possibly might not descend all night. It was cool in Monica's room and quiet, and the soft folds of the mosquito net created a gauzy veil that she was aware of, even in the darkness. Yet somehow, even though none of Monica's personal possessions were at all evident, and there was nothing intimately hers on either the bedside table or the dressing table with its glimmering triple mirror, Anna felt a powerful sense of her mother-in-law's presence and personality, a feeling that even if Monica wasn't actually here, the room would never be anything other than strongly infused with her being. Anna looked up into the corona against the ceiling from which the mosquito net was suspended and wondered, despite a definite sense that she shouldn't, how many nights Monica, too, had lain there and stared upwards and known that sleep would deny her any release from her thoughts before dawn.

They were busy, busy thoughts, too. Some of them were uncomfortable, and Anna was aware of her mind squirming away from confronting them, flinching from admitting any disobliging behaviour on her own part. She was, after all, not used to being wrong. In fact, she had comfortably, even complacently, prided herself on being right about most things, just as she had been competent at doing most things as well, effortlessly superior for the most unassailable of reasons. Anna's younger sister had obliged all their childhood, by deferring to her older sibling, admiring her, imitating her, following their mother's meek lead in universal approval of, and devotion to, their father. When Anna thought about it now, some – or was it many? – of her father's attitudes and behaviour patterns were frankly reprehensible. He hadn't so much dominated his wife and daughters as been excessively autocratic. He had also been very unpleasant to Sebastian, now Anna came to think of it – outwardly courteous but privately sneering and contemptuous, ridiculing his prospective son-in-law as feeble, and unworthy of the wonderful Anna. Her mother and sister had wept copiously at her father's funeral, and her sister had even cast herself across the coffin. Anna had prided herself on not weeping – her father would have commended her for her restraint – but now she wondered why she hadn't. Gazing up into the cloudy darkness above Monica's bed, Anna wondered for the first time if she had in fact been released by her father's death, instead of, as she had always supposed, having merely behaved with a self-control that he would have applauded.

She wondered why she should think of such things now, right now when her head was buzzing with all the extraordinary events of this first day in Spain. Surely what had happened in Spain was more than enough food for thought – and rich, complicated food at that – without rummaging about in her memories to wonder if her father had actually been more tyrant than godhead? Anna put a hand to feel the starched cotton lace that edged her Spanish pillowcase, realizing that she needed to touch something, to reassure herself of the reality of lying in Monica's bed after the dramatic scenes earlier in the day. Had they actually happened? Of course they had. If she were to tiptoe along to Dermot and Marcus's room and wake them to ask for reassurance, they would stare at her as if she was mad.

'Of course Grandpa said that,' Dermot would say. 'Of course he did. You were there. So was Marc. What's the matter with you?'

They had been, Anna recalled, standing by the unplanted new vines, her father-in-law and her two sons, and her. They were there because Gus had wanted them to be, had in fact directed them to be. Gus had his hand in the crook of Dermot's elbow, and Marcus had been holding Mouse in his arms.

Gus had gestured at the vines, rows and rows of them in black plastic pots.

'See that?'

'Yes,' the boys said in chorus, 'more vines.'

'Godello vines,' Gus said. 'Grenache vines. They won't grow here. Hopeless.'

'I thought Uncle Jake—' Dermot began.

'Knows nothing,' Gus said. 'Bloody nothing. Didn't ask me, did he? Just did it. Ordered them behind my back.'

Marcus cleared his throat. 'I think José Manuel has ploughed some land ready.'

Gus snorted. 'Waste of effort. He knew it. Knew it all along.' He gestured at the vines. 'Anyway, I've sold them.'

The boys stared at him. They spoke in unison. 'You *what?*'

'Sold 'em,' Gus said, 'to a winemaker friend of mine in the

north. He's got some Godello already. They're going up on Friday. Lorry's coming.'

Neither boy looked at Anna, but they exchanged glances with each other.

'Grandpa . . .'

'What about Uncle Jake?'

Gus raised his chin a little.

'He can whistle.'

'But—'

'He took a gamble and he lost,' Gus said loudly. 'He lost because he's a pig-headed fool who knows nothing and won't be told.'

Anna said, 'But you'll pay him for buying the vines.'

Gus didn't look at her. He sounded almost triumphant. 'No.'

'But Grandpa, you must, you should.'

Gus looked at Marcus.

'No, I shouldn't. He tried to get one over on me and he failed. He failed big time.'

Dermot looked straight ahead, as if he was not actually touching his grandfather.

'Whatever he's done, Grandpa, you should give him the money for the vines.'

'No,' Gus said again. He was grinning and Anna had a sudden flash of what he must have looked like as a young man, the man Monica had thrown her lot in with. 'No,' Gus said again and more emphatically. 'Anyway, I never wanted him here. I never wanted him to run the place when I had to go into hospital.' He glanced at Mouse, her arms clamped round her cousin's neck. 'Not your fault your father's so useless. Not your fault at all.' He looked from one to another of his grandsons. 'It was your father I wanted to run the vineyard. It was Sebastian all along.'

Dermot gaped at him.

'Dad?'

Gus nodded. He flicked a glance at Anna.

'I asked him. I asked him in the hospital when I couldn't make myself very plain. He took his time but he's done it. He brought you boys out and now' – he jerked his head towards Anna – 'there's you too.'

'Are you saying,' Marcus said, 'that you want Dad to run the vineyard?'

Gus nodded. '*With* me.'

Marcus said, 'Does – does Dad know this?'

And Anna had been unable to restrain herself from crying out, 'No!' at the very moment that Dermot, quietly but firmly had said, 'Yes.'

'Yes,' Dermot said again. 'He knows, deep down.'

Anna's hands had flown up to her face, to cover her mouth. Her first instinct had been to speak sternly and dismissively to her elder son, as she always had, but her second, and more powerful, was to check herself. In any case, the boys were paying her no attention, they were even turning away from her, supporting their grandfather, holding the baby, talking earnestly about the future, about the vineyard – about the need, Dermot was saying, to include Katie's daughters in any planning. They seemed, Anna realized, to have forgotten her, forgotten that she had had any part in this conversation, that any plans for the future should surely include her. Shouldn't they? She stood where they had left her, hands still to her face until José Manuel appeared from a nearby building and stood beside her, smiling and looking at the vines.

'On Friday,' José Manuel said in his heavily accented English, 'all gone.' He waved a hand towards Jake's vines. 'In English, you say good riddance, no?' He laughed. '*¡Adiós y buen viaje!*'

And then there had been supper, at the long table in the kitchen with her boys sitting either side of their grandfather and Marcus filling his own glass, she thought, far too often and enthusiastically. Earlier she had tried to help Bella give Mouse a bath, but Bella had closed the bathroom door firmly after telling her to go and rest on Monica's bed until supper-time. Then she had tried to discuss the afternoon's revelations with the boys, but they were preoccupied with persuading their grandfather at least to inform Jake of his decision, and they made it plain to their mother that their focus was on other and more pressing matters, none of which did, or should, include her. So she took herself off for a solitary walk up the mountainside track, but was cheated even of that by the sudden descent of darkness. Sitting finally on the edge of Monica's bed in the circle of light shed by the lamp beside it, Anna felt more disconcerted than she thought she ever had in her life before. She was, she realized, in a situation where not only was she not in control, but she also wasn't even relevant. She remembered, abruptly, about Sebastian, and thought, to her horror, that she might cry.

She was very subdued indeed when she crept into the kitchen for supper. Nobody had lit any candles in the kitchen, and the overhead lamps shed a harsh and unforgiving light. Pilar had laid the table and left a hefty stew of pork and beans for them, which Anna felt Monica would never have countenanced. The room, despite its charm and the dresser laden with pretty pottery, looked grim and cheerless, accentuated by a sudden wind that had got up and rattled the glass doors to the terrace as if someone excluded was trying to get in.

The atmosphere was no less turbulent. Her boys, she realized, were almost guarding their grandfather from their uncle, who was, in any case, drunk. Drunk and furious, furious enough to shout at Bella and contradict her loudly in front of everyone present. Bella's reaction was to go very quiet, dangerously quiet, sitting unnaturally upright and eating her supper in small, neat mouthfuls without once looking at anyone else or trying to engage them in conversation. At one point, Anna leaned towards her across the table and said, in what she hoped was an anodyne tone, 'Did Mouse go down all right?' and Bella said tightly to her plate, 'Yes, thank you,' and that was that.

Jake said nothing after shouting at Bella, to anyone. He sat slumped in his usual place at the table, one hand possessively on a wine bottle, with which he constantly refilled his glass. Only the boys were animated, plying their grandfather with questions and occasionally, Anna noticed, turning to their uncle and endeavouring to include him in the conversation. He ignored them, sunk in his own angry reverie, and when Anna pushed her chair back and stood up, saying that it had been a long day and she thought she'd turn in, neither he nor Bella appeared to take any notice. Her sons glanced up at her.

'OK, Ma.'

'Sleep well, Mum.'

She looked directly at her father-in-law. 'Good night, Gus.'

He was almost smiling, she thought, sitting there between his grandsons. He gave her a kind of half-wave, even if he didn't speak, and then she went out of the bright, uncomfortable kitchen and down the dark corridor to Monica's room, where Pilar had let down the mosquito net and closed the shutters and left only one bedside lamp on.

And now, here she was, wakeful and wound up, staring up into the dim folds of the mosquito net. She had heard Jake and Bella come to bed next door, but there didn't seem to have been any conversation between them, certainly no shouting or quarrelling. In fact, the wind had dropped as abruptly as it had risen, and a night-time silence as thick as the darkness reigned in its place.

Anna turned on her side. She had been so confident before she reached Spain, so certain that she could handle whatever the weekend threw at her. But now look, she thought: there's nothing I can do. I'm helpless, out of my depth. Her hand crept up again to feel the lace edge of the pillowcase. Monica's pillowcase. Sorry, Anna said silently to the pillow, sorry. Even if I don't quite know who I'm saying sorry to. Or for what.

———

Monica hadn't been in an English pub for over twenty years. Twenty years ago, she thought, a pub was a pub, with sticky, swirly patterned carpets in the lounge bar, and an atmosphere thick with smoke and the smell of beer in the public one. But this place, where Nic and Katie had arranged to meet her, was a revelation. It was light and clean and modern and the bartenders had sharp haircuts and there was a niche behind the bar, almost like a shrine, where all the gin bottles were displayed, bottle after bottle of artisan gin, infused with raspberries or spices under a chalkboard which named them all and explained their provenance.

She stood there, clutching her handbag in both hands, uncertain of the etiquette in such a place. Should she sit down? Or approach the bar? And if she did the latter, what should she ask for? What, after all, was a modern cocktail? Behind the bar, marshalling tonic bottles, a young bartender beamed at her. He had a haircut like Dermot's, a pinstriped waistcoat over a T-shirt, and jeans. Monica thought he might be a very young twenty, despite the fact that he looked fourteen.

He said cheerfully, 'What can I get you?'

Monica approached the bar and laid her handbag on it.

'I have no idea.'

'Most customers,' the young bartender said, 'are very specific. They ask for a certain spirit and mixed in a certain way.'

Monica smiled at him.

'Then suggest something.'

'Like?'

'Like your other customers.'

He gestured at the gins.

'I could make you a martini. An espresso martini. Or a dirty martini. Or a straight-up martini. With a particular gin, of course.'

Monica said, almost roguishly, 'And if I just wanted red wine?'

He beamed at her again. 'Eight to choose from. By the glass.'

'Goodness,' Monica said.

'A small glass, which is a hundred and twenty-five millilitres, or a big one, which is twice that.'

Monica widened her eyes. 'That's a lot of a bottle.'

'Yes.'

Katie said, beside her, 'Mum.'

Monica turned.

'Katie. How nice. I was just wondering . . .'

Katie addressed the barman. 'A bottle of the Shiraz, please, and three glasses. Over there, by that table.' She said, not looking at Monica, 'Were you flirting?'

'No!'

'It looked like it.'

'Katie,' Monica said indignantly, 'I was just being polite. He's about Marcus's age.'

Katie ducked her head to rummage for something in her bag. 'Sorry,' she said, unapologetically. 'It's been a bit of a day.'

Monica said nothing. She looked sadly at Katie, at the dark circles under her eyes.

Katie said, 'Not a work thing, I mean. In fact, work is often a salvation. Let's go and sit down.'

She was in flat shoes, Monica noticed, and her hair was in a knot that Monica now knew was deliberately messy.

'Nic's on his way,' Katie said. 'He's just texted.' She shot Monica a quick look. 'Mum, I'm sorry I snapped. I didn't mean to.'

'That's quite all right.'

'You always say that.'

'I expect I do,' Monica said. 'What would you prefer me to say instead?'

Katie glared at her. '*Mum.*'

'I can't get it right, can I?' Monica was aware she was clutching her handbag with both hands again in a way she knew was typically old-ladyish. 'Whatever I say is wrong.'

'Hello,' Nic said. He was smiling. Before he took off his rucksack, he bent to kiss Katie and then Monica, and then he said, 'Did you order us something?'

Katie put her mac over the back of her chair. 'It's coming.'

Nic began to extract himself from his backpack. 'Don't tell me you two have got off on the wrong foot already?'

Katie said crossly, 'My fault. It's always my fault.'

The bartender arrived with a tray bearing an uncorked bottle and three glasses. Nic looked at it.

'Wonderful.'

'Shall I pour?' the bartender asked.

Katie took a chair opposite her mother and pushed a glass forward.

'Please.'

When he had gone, Nic lifted his glass towards Katie and Monica.

'Cheers.' He glanced at Monica. 'What would you say in Spanish?'

Monica lifted her own glass towards him.

'*Salud*,' she said.

'*Salud*, then. *Salud*, Katie.'

'What is there to celebrate?' Katie said, almost desperately. 'I mean, we all know why we're here, and it isn't to cheer anything. We're here because we can't talk at home.' She stopped, and took a gulp of her wine. Then she said once more, 'Sorry, Mum.'

Monica said, 'When I say it's perfectly all right, I mean it.'

Nic stretched an arm across the table and took hold of Katie's wrist.

'Katie.'

'What?'

'It isn't that Marta confided in your mum. Well, she did in the end, but she didn't mean to, she didn't want to, but she got cornered and Monica wouldn't let her go till she'd heard what she needed to hear.'

Monica set her glass down with elaborate care. 'She didn't want to tell me anything. She thought she was alone in the house. She was appalled when I walked in, horrified.' She leaned towards Katie. 'The only advantage I had was being her grandmother, not her mother. If it had been you, at Marta's age, I wouldn't have coped, I couldn't have. The other day, all I had was the little bit of distance created by the generational gap.'

Katie said in a whisper, 'Is it because I'm working?'

'No.'

'I can't not work,' Katie went on wildly. 'I love working, I'm good at it, I am—'

'Listen to your mother,' Nic said.

'It has nothing to do with you working. Nothing.' Monica took a sip of her drink. 'But she needs to change doctors.'

They both jerked upright.

'Does she?'

'That's what she said she wanted.'

'Is – is that one of the reasons she's still doing it?' Katie said hoarsely.

'I wonder,' Monica said, 'if there really are reasons. I mean, I wonder when you're that age, whether you need a reason to do anything.'

'We aren't having a philosophical discussion about adolescence. Actually,' Nic said. 'We're talking about *Marta*.'

Monica stared fixedly at her wine glass. 'I was just—'

Katie said in a low voice, 'Mum, you have got to understand

that we are beside ourselves with worry. We can't help but feel that we've done something wrong, that we're to blame somehow. We don't know what to do next, we go round and round in circles. And that little episode you had, that moment in the bathroom with Marta, was the first breakthrough, if you like, in ages.'

Monica's gaze didn't move.

'I know.'

'So,' Katie said, almost in a hiss, '*help* us.'

Monica cleared her throat. She raised her head and looked across the bar.

'I'm trying to.'

'I think,' Nic said, 'that we should neither of us say anything, and just let Monica talk.'

'OK.'

Nic looked at Monica.

'The floor's yours.'

Monica's gaze didn't waver. She said slowly, 'Teenage was a new thing when I was growing up. Before that, you were just waiting to be a grown-up, like my mother, waiting to be old enough to have a lipstick of your own and perhaps even a cigarette lighter. But three generations later and the pressures on adolescents are so different, so acute. And if you are introverted, like Marta, you really suffer. All the endless comparisons. All the demands of convention to look this specific way, do these particular things, please the group.' She said suddenly and more warmly, 'That's the worst. Pleasing the group.'

Katie opened her mouth and Nic immediately shot her a warning glance.

'Poor Marta,' Monica said, almost to herself, almost

oblivious now to Katie and Nic. 'Poor little Marta. There's nowhere to hide these days, nowhere to go until you feel ready to be yourself, whatever that is. Being yourself, I mean. So I suppose what she felt was a kind of despair, end of her tether, frantic almost.'

'Mum,' Katie burst out, 'we know all this. We've talked about all this till we're blue in the face. It isn't about *why*. It's about what we *do*. That's why we're asking you, why we're having this fucking drink. You found Martha cutting herself in the bathroom, you talked to her, for God's sake. So *help* us, can't you?'

'Katie,' Nic said helplessly.

Monica looked at her daughter.

'I'm getting there,' she said, 'really I am. But I have to get round to it in my own way. My own time. And it doesn't help to swear.'

Katie flung herself back in her chair.

'Ye gods.'

'It was me,' Monica said, 'who suggested she change doctors. I asked her if Dr Mak was helping and she said not really and I said well then, what about a change, what about seeing someone you really like and trust who understands you more? What about that?'

Nic leaned forward.

'And?'

'She agreed. Or at least, I think she did. She wants to go on, you see, she wants to go on with – with what she's doing, and I said why. Why did she?'

Katie was sitting upright again, her eyes fixed on her mother's face.

'She couldn't tell me,' Monica said, 'so I said was it exciting or secret or – I think I said sexy, though I never know what that means – or did it make her feel part of some hidden private little club. And she wouldn't answer me to begin with and then she said she thought it was a bit of everything. So I said suppose she could say all that to a doctor, suppose she could say everything she'd just said to me to a doctor and the doctor would be completely trustworthy and not tell anyone else, and she nodded. She didn't actually speak, but she nodded. And she wanted to pull her sleeves down, as if she was ashamed or feeling very private, or something. Even though I knew, she didn't want me to keep looking and seeing.'

Nic said gently, 'Come on now. Drink your drink.'

Monica turned her head to look at him.

'I don't really want to. It's lovely, it really is, but it seems a bit – a bit beside the point.'

'Oh, Mum,' Katie said. 'What should we do? What should we do to help her?'

Monica looked at her.

'I don't know. But at least she knows I know now. And I haven't freaked out, knowing. In fact . . .'

'What?'

'We've had another conversation.'

'Mum!'

'What about?'

Monica looked across the bar again.

'Me, actually,' she said.

CHAPTER SEVENTEEN

'Would you like to give Mouse her porridge?' Bella asked with great sweetness.

Anna glanced at Mouse, who was grasping her spoon with possessive determination.

'Well, that's a very kind offer, but wouldn't she rather do it herself?'

Bella blew on the porridge bowl.

'Mouse has a spoon, and I have a spoon, too. Don't I, Mousie? And then Mummy, or Auntie Anna, can make sure that *all* the porridge gets eaten, can't we?'

Anna said firmly, 'Just Anna. Not Auntie Anna. Not Auntie anything, actually.'

Bella bent over Mouse's high chair.

'We were only copying our cousins, weren't we? Auntie Bella and Uncle Jake is what the boys call us. Don't they? I think it's rather charming. Old-fashioned but charming. And they're charming boys. Aren't they, Mousie? Especially Marcus. Oh, look at that! Mousie, I think you're blushing!'

Anna looked at Mouse.

'No, she isn't.'

Bella put the porridge bowl down on Mouse's high-chair

tray. Then she handed Anna a spoon. She said, as if Anna hadn't spoken, and in a confiding tone, 'Sorry about last night.'

Mouse put her free hand out to ward off any interference, and stuck her own spoon into her porridge.

Anna said untruthfully, 'I didn't notice anything.'

Bella went across the kitchen to make coffee. With her back to Anna, she said, 'Jake slept on the sitting-room sofa. He often does that.'

Mouse gestured at Anna to keep her distance. She wore an expression of great purpose and there was a smear of porridge on one cheek.

Anna said politely, 'I heard nothing, you know.'

Bella busied herself with the cafetière and a canister of coffee.

'But I'm sure you've been wondering why we could just drop everything in England and come out here, haven't you?'

Anna fixed her eyes on Mouse and Mouse, spooning porridge inaccurately, stared resolutely back.

'Not really,' Anna said. 'I've always thought you must have had a good reason, and I very much doubt any wondering even entered Sebastian's head.'

Bella poured boiling water into the cafetière.

'Oh, we did have good reason,' she said meaningfully. 'Or, at least Jake did.'

Anna said nothing. She attempted to dip her spoon into Mouse's porridge and Mouse instantly seized it with her free hand, pushing it away.

'You do it yourself, then,' Anna said to Mouse.

Bella carried the coffee pot across to the table and went back to the dresser to unhook two mugs.

'You show Auntie Anna how you can eat a whole bowl of porridge all by yourself.'

'She is,' Anna said, 'most impressive.'

'So determined,' Bella said. 'Just like her grandfather. Of course, Jake dotes on her. Doesn't he, Mouse? Aren't you the apple of Papa's eye?'

Mouse's gaze didn't move from Anna's face. She put another spoonful of porridge, approximately, into her mouth.

'And Papa,' Bella said, pouring coffee, 'was very glad to come to Spain, wasn't he? Very glad indeed. New country, new start, far away from all the nasty old problems and creditors in London.'

There was a tiny pause. Then Anna said, still regarding Mouse, 'To be honest, Bella, I don't really want to know.'

Bella said quietly, 'Oh, I think you do.' She held out a mug of coffee. 'Your coffee, Anna. I think you meant to find out. Because Sebastian is too nice to try.'

'I don't really want any coffee.'

'Take it,' Bella said. 'Even if you don't drink it. I can read you like a book, Anna. You came to see what your boys were so turned on by, and also to see what the set-up was. And why Jake and I could just drop everything in London, and stay.'

Anna took the coffee mug and held it awkwardly.

'Even if I did wonder about just how Jake could abandon London and rescue his parents, I certainly didn't want to find out this way.'

'And what way is that?'

Anna put her porridge spoon down beside Mouse's bowl. She was aware that she was shaking slightly.

'In revenge, Bella,' she said, a little unsteadily. 'In revenge for Jake's treatment of you last night. That's what you're doing, you're getting your own back for his behaviour to you at supper last night.'

Bella said distantly, 'I don't know what you're talking about.'

Anna advanced on her. 'Yes, you do. I saw it all.'

Bella quickly slipped into a chair next to Mouse and picked up Anna's discarded spoon.

'Open wide, Mousie. Let Mummy help you with the last mouthful.'

Mouse pushed her mother's hand away even more vigorously than she had pushed Anna's.

'No,' Mouse said.

'That's her only word,' Bella said. 'I always say to Gus that it's the one thing she picked up from him. She's so like him, in her own special way.' She didn't look at Anna, only at her daughter. 'Well, you got what you came for. Your boys have got something worth inheriting, and Jake has probably made as much of a mess of this as he made of everything in London. So I imagine that you're feeling pretty satisfied, aren't you?'

———

Daisy had stopped fighting with Florence about Florence wanting to have her bedroom door wide open. It wasn't so much that she was finding sharing a bedroom with her little sister any less of a pain, but more that she no longer felt such an antipathy to her family, such a powerful wish to have nothing to do with them. There was no doubt, after all, that it was weirdly comforting to have her grandmother there, and there were even subtle changes in the atmosphere and behaviours in the house that made her feel that it wasn't quite as unbearable to be at home as it had been till just recently.

It was difficult to put her finger on the reasons for this change: Katie looked and seemed more exhausted and ratty than ever, and she, Daisy, didn't have her own bedroom, and Marta's bedroom door was still shut. But oddly – and Daisy couldn't quite identify what the difference was – Marta's door didn't look so utterly shut, so completely, conclusively closed against the outside world. It was still shut, but almost tentatively so, as if you could open it, if you dared, and go in, and talk to Marta. Granny did, after all, even if Marta didn't say much in reply to her. Granny went in and closed the door behind her and you could hear her voice, from Marta's room, talking and talking. There were no screams or door slamming when this happened, and after Granny came out, she always looked like someone who was in no kind of hurry, but just kind of satisfied, Daisy thought; contented, like someone who has put down a burden they'd been carrying for a very long time.

And then there was Dermot. Dermot, whom she'd always rather despised as a kid cousin, who was texting her from Spain and saying interesting grown-up things about how significant and important it all was, and how she should come out and see for herself. He said that it wasn't just about him and Marcus after all, it was about her and Marta and Florence and even Mouse, who might only be a baby, but she'd grow up after all, and she looked as if she'd grow up bilingual, so she'd have a particular emotional involvement.

'You need to come,' Dermot texted. 'You need to talk to your mum about coming.'

Katie was difficult to talk to, at the moment. She was worn out with one thing and another, and even if Daisy resented her parents' preoccupation with Marta, she simultaneously hesitated to make her own claims. It was altogether easier to seek out her grandmother in the kitchen and offer to make her tea.

'D'you know,' Monica said, 'I was just going to make myself one. And one of those fruit teas for Marta. She really likes them, even if I privately think they taste of boiled sweets without the sugar.'

Daisy said with elaborate nonchalance, 'I'll make it and bring it up if you like.'

Monica appeared entirely unfazed.

'Lovely, darling.'

Daisy opened a cupboard in search of teabags.

'I can hear you sometimes talking away in Marta's room. What are you talking about?'

Monica sat down at the kitchen table. She said, 'Me, really.'

Daisy turned.

'You?'

'Yes,' Monica said. 'Me as an adolescent. Mum as one. How it was. And how it is now. Some things are better and some worse, but it's never easy, that bit between childhood and adulthood. I just talk, really. In fact, it's rather a relief, to talk like that. I've never talked about it to anyone before. As a generation we weren't supposed to, we weren't encouraged to unburden ourselves; in fact, we were almost forbidden to. It wasn't considered decent, describing how one felt.'

Daisy stood there, an empty mug in her hand. She said, almost hesitantly, 'I've got friends . . .'

Monica looked up. She smiled.

'I know, darling. But Marta hasn't. Or at least, not reliable ones.'

'Has Mum?'

'Perhaps it's difficult for her to find time for them?'

Daisy put the mug down. She said, 'What about Dad? Is he Mum's friend?'

Monica said carefully, 'You'd hope so.'

Daisy said, persisting, 'Is Grandpa your friend?'

Monica looked down at the table, spreading her fingers so that the light caught the old diamonds in her engagement ring. 'Not – really.'

'Was he ever?'

'Long ago,' Monica said. 'Long before Mummy was born.'

Daisy sat down opposite her grandmother.

'And then what?' she asked.

'Well,' Monica said, still studying her ring, 'then I made the wrong choice. I made the conventional choice and I was wrong. I put Grandpa before Mummy and Sebastian. Mummy hated being sent away to school. I knew she did, and I didn't listen to her, I didn't listen to what I knew she felt.'

Daisy waited a moment.

'Have you told her?'

Monica sighed.

'No.'

'Why not?'

Monica raised her head at last.

'I really don't know.'

Daisy got up. She took the tea mug and went back to the open cupboard.

'I'd like to go to Spain, Granny.'

'Would you, darling?'

'Yes,' Daisy said, dropping teabags into mugs. 'Yes, I would. It sounds like Grandpa's done an amazing job, winning prizes for wine, making a vineyard from nothing. D'you want Lapsang or Earl Grey?'

——

Anna found a relatively quiet corner in Gibraltar airport from which to ring Sebastian. The boys had gone off to do their own thing and had made it plain to their mother that this was their territory now.

'So – see you at the gate, then,' Anna had said, hoping she didn't sound too forlorn as she said it, and then she had had an unsatisfactory cup of coffee at the bleak little airport bar and wondered what else she should do, to fill in the hour before they were due to board the plane. Around her, she observed with some distaste, people – men, mostly – were drinking gin and tonics, and when she inadvertently caught the eye of one of them, he tipped his glass towards her and winked. 'It's always gin o'clock,' he then said and guffawed.

Anna was amazed at the strength of her desire to ring Sebastian. It was a Sunday evening, so he would probably be at home, perhaps with his feet up and watching a replay of the afternoon's important football game. They had had an agreement – well, it had been Anna who suggested it and Sebastian had merely acquiesced – that there would be no regular updates on the weekend, that Anna wouldn't relay each hour as it passed, but merely tell Sebastian an edited version when she got back. He had smiled when she suggested this and agreed in the manner of someone humouring the mistaken determination of someone else – 'OK,' he'd said good-naturedly. 'If that's how you want to play it' – but it clearly went against what he thought would happen. And now here she was, abruptly fizzing with the desire to hear his voice, to tell him what it had been like, to have in return his particular sympathetic understanding of what had gone on.

She couldn't wait, she realized. She couldn't sit on that plane for two hours, boiling with memories of all the events of the weekend, and drive the boys home and then hear them explode with enthusiasm about their weekend to their father, before they at last went to bed and she could finally, in a measured, considered, Anna-like manner, give Sebastian an account of what had gone on in Spain. She had an awful feeling that she was about to cry, and some residual part of the old Anna most certainly did not want to cry down the phone line to Sebastian. So she took stock of her own state of mind in a manner very familiar to her, and waited until she was in full possession – she was sure she was – of her emotions and then she dialled the familiar landline number of the house in London.

Sebastian plainly hadn't looked to see the number of the incoming call. He answered the telephone with the wariness of someone expecting another nuisance intrusion.

'Hello?'

Anna couldn't speak. All the feelings she thought she had mastered flooded back into her heart and mind, and collected in a lump in her throat.

'Hello?' Sebastian said again, a little more tiredly.

'Oh,' Anna said in a rush. 'Oh . . .'

'Ye gods,' Sebastian said in quite a different voice. 'Heavens. Anna. Anna! Are you OK?'

The tears were falling now, cascading down Anna's face. Through them, she said unsteadily, 'Yes, I'm fine. We're all fine. It's not that, it's nothing to do with us, the boys loved it. But . . .'

'But what?' Sebastian demanded. 'Is it Dad?'

'No,' Anna sobbed. 'No. It isn't. Your father's fine. It was just – everything else, everything that happened. The place . . .'

'Anna,' Sebastian said steadily. 'At least the place is wonderful.'

She shrieked, 'No it isn't! I hated it! I hated everything about it! I can't wait to get home!'

'And I,' Sebastian said in the same level tone, 'can't wait to have you back. How are the boys?'

Anna began to cry again.

'They're great. They loved it.'

'Is that why you're crying? Because they loved it and you didn't?'

'No,' Anna said, abruptly sobered. 'I didn't mean that. Did I? I – well, I just wish you'd been there.'

'You didn't want me to be there,' Sebastian said levelly. 'Remember? You had information you wanted to get out of Bella and you wanted to do that on your own.'

Anna said in a whisper, 'It shouldn't have been me.'

'Well, no.'

'I thought I was doing the right thing. I thought I should get Bella to confide in me, I thought I could handle Jake, and your father, and everything, but I couldn't. I couldn't handle it and I didn't want to. I just wanted to be at home, doing the things I know how to do, that I'm good at doing. I don't in the least mind the boys being keen on Spain, I really don't. But I can't join them. I can't join in.' She paused and blotted her eyes with a tissue. Then she said, 'Can I ask you something?'

'Of course.'

'Sebastian,' Anna said, struggling with tears again, 'Sebastian, have you seen Luminata?'

'Who?' Sebastian said.

'You know,' Anna said, gripping her phone. 'You know who I mean. The Romanian girl. Lumi?'

'Why on earth should I have seen her?' Sebastian said in genuine bewilderment.

'I thought – I wondered – I just assumed . . .'

'Anna,' Sebastian said warmly. 'Don't be an idiot. Don't be utterly ridiculous. All Luminata did was get me thinking a bit. I haven't seen her in weeks, she's part of the cleaning team. Heavens, you know more about her than I do, you're the one who has most to do with Profclean.'

Anna leaned again the nearest wall.

'I just want to come home,' she said in a whisper.

'You'll be here in a few hours. Then you can tell me all the horrors of the weekend. My dreadful father and my hopeless brother.' He paused and then he said in a different and less hearty tone, 'And I have something to tell you about Katie. Poor Katie, in fact. Fly carefully, Anna. You and the boys.'

———

Katie was working in her usual sea of papers. It didn't seem to matter that so much was done online now, there still seemed to be an ocean of paper, almost an endless amount of the stuff, so that the floor round Katie's home computer was as littered as her desk.

'Mum,' Daisy said.

Katie was absorbed in something. She had her glasses on

and was peering at her screen, her fingers poised above the keyboard.

'Mum,' Daisy said again, and then in a more peremptory manner, '*Mum.*'

Katie didn't take her eyes off the screen.

'Mmm?'

'I need to talk to you,' Daisy said. 'I need to talk to you *now.*'

'In a minute.'

'No,' Daisy said, 'now.' She bent forward and obscured the screen with a black sleeve and a hand in a black lace mitten. Then she said warningly, 'I can always turn it off, you know.'

'Don't do that.'

'Well, listen to me,' Daisy said. '*Listen.*'

Katie sat back and folded her arms.

'What? I haven't got long.'

Daisy perched herself on the edge of the desk and looked down at her mother.

'You've got as long as I need you to have,' she said. 'This is important.'

Katie indicated the screen behind her daughter. 'So is that.'

'This is *family*,' Daisy said, 'your family. I've had several messages from Dermot.'

Katie took her glasses off. 'Oh.'

'Don't say "Oh" like that. Don't say it as if it's nothing to do with you. It's *my* future, Mum – mine and Marta's and Florence's.'

'What is?'

Daisy gave an exasperated sigh.

'Spain is, of course. Dermot's quite right. It's our inheritance, all six of us, and I should go out and see it, like he has.'

'I think that we've had this conversation.'

Daisy brandished her phone.

'But he's just been. And he's messaging me *all* the time. And with Granny here . . .'

'Why does having Granny here make any difference?'

'It sort of reminds me,' Daisy said. 'It makes me think about Spain and her life there and that I should see it for myself like Dermot has. And you should go again. Why haven't you gone again?'

Katie said lamely, 'Granny came here.'

'You didn't really want her to,' Daisy said. 'It was Dad and me who wanted her to come. But you didn't much. Did you?'

Katie glanced sideways.

'I did. I really did. It's just something in our relationship that's never gone quite right.'

Daisy waited a second. 'Granny's really sorry about that.'

Katie's head whipped round. 'What?'

'She said to me,' Daisy said carefully, 'that she knew she'd made the wrong choice about staying with Grandpa in Spain. She said she knew you hated being at boarding school and now she really regretted doing the conventional thing and choosing her husband over her children.'

Katie was staring at her daughter.

'She *said* that? She actually *said* that?'

'Yes. I don't see why it's so important.'

'It's hugely important.'

'So is my going to Spain.'

Katie gave a little yelp of laughter.

'Touché.'

'Mum,' Daisy pressed, 'when can I go?'

Katie said recklessly, 'Any time. Whenever you like. Whenever school and exams permit you to.'

'Really?'

'Really.'

Slowly, Daisy stood up.

'D'you want to get back to work?'

'Truthfully,' Katie said, 'not much, now. I'm a bit jangled up with other stuff.'

'Not Marta?'

Katie stared at her.

'Why do you bring up Marta?'

'Because,' Daisy said, chipping nail polish from her fingernails, 'it usually is Marta, isn't it? I mean, it has been for weeks, until Granny stepped in.'

'Granny,' Katie said wonderingly. 'Granny. And to think I never knew.'

'Never knew what?'

Katie looked up at her.

'I think maybe I never knew Granny and she never knew me.'

Daisy stopped chipping. She said, 'Do *you* know me?'

Katie laughed. 'Probably not.'

'Grandmothers are kind of easier for grandchildren to know. Aren't they?'

'Is that what you think?' Katie asked, twisting in her chair to look at her daughter.

Daisy had lounged towards the door, but now she paused on the threshold. 'I like Granny,' she said firmly.

'D'you know,' Katie said, and she was still laughing, 'd'you know that I might be beginning to like her, too.'

———

Jake wasn't picking up his phone. Monica had rung him at all odd times of day to try and speak to him, but had never succeeded. She had left several messages asking him to call her, but he never did, so she left a last – and for her, rather sharp – message about his being plainly too busy to ring his own mother, and tried to put the matter out of her mind. She didn't ring Gus much now, either. He never did anything more than grunt at her, in any case, so even though Pilar, to whom she spoke every day, assured her that Gus missed her acutely, there was no evidence of it. And, quite frankly, she wasn't much inclined to look for evidence. She was, she thought, as exasperated now by the thought of Spain as she had once felt a raw homesickness for it. Odd, that, when you thought about it. England was still as cold, her bedroom was still Daisy's, but there was a creeping, unmistakable sense of being needed in Katie's household that gave life and warmth to even the bleakest days. She not only had a purpose now but a sense of mattering, a feeling of pulling together all the discordant elements in that strong-minded family, and making something unified of them.

It wasn't, after all, just being able to find Marta a new doctor. It had been Marta's approach to it, Marta's insisting that her grandmother be part of the process, and realizing that somehow, heaven knew how, Marta was taking ownership of her self-harming, and being responsible for it, as long as her grandmother was with her. And then Marta's sisters had clamoured for her attention, too, and she had found herself much sought after, rather than ignored and surplus to requirements, and given a shop to run as a kind of patron- izing distraction. She supposed she would have to go back to Spain soon, and shoulder her responsibilities again, and make some kind of relationship with Gus, but she didn't look forward to it. Sometimes, now, when she thought about Spain and the vineyard and her bedroom and the canariensis palm whose welfare had been her obsessive concern, she wondered if she had indeed been off her head or whether, as Daisy had hinted, she had merely been trying to make something out of what was on offer and that wasn't actually very much.

Monica lay where her granddaughters now knew to find her, on Daisy's bed under a watermelon-pink mohair blanket that Florence had brought almost reverently from her own room as a special loan. It got dark quite early now, with that particularly English damp rawness of autumn dark, and Monica had taken to having a little rest about now, propped up on pillows, the bedside lamp on, the radio burbling peacefully away and a bone china mug – Marta had found it for her, at the back of a cupboard – of Earl Grey tea in her hands. It was the time of day when the girls sought her out – those girls about whom she now felt only protective and defensive – sometimes using their homework as an excuse, but mostly just drifting in, fiddling about with her earrings or pots of face cream, quite often with nothing of significance to say, but just – she knew this and it delighted her – to check on her established presence, and reassure themselves of it.

There was a knock on the door. Monica smiled. None of them usually knocked. Why should they? She cleared her throat. Which one would it be?

'Come in!' she called.

The door opened a little and revealed Katie. Monica sat up a little, startled.

'Darling!' she said. 'What are you doing home?'

Katie advanced into the room. She was in a work dress and the flat shoes she wore outside. She said, a little awkwardly, 'I wanted to see you.'

Monica patted the pink mohair blanket beside her knees. 'Come and sit down.'

Katie advanced almost hesitantly into the room, and sat where her mother indicated. She glanced at her mother and said, almost accusingly, 'You called me "darling".'

Monica laughed. She gestured with her tea mug.

'Did I? Don't I always?'

'No,' Katie said. 'No. You don't. It's – it's one of the things I wanted to talk to you about, actually. In fact, I think there's quite a lot to say.'

CHAPTER EIGHTEEN

After a few bad nights on the sitting-room sofa, Jake took himself off to sleep in the back bedroom. He saw no need to announce this removal formally to either Bella or his father, but simply transferred the plaid cotton bathrobe he had had since he was eighteen to a hook behind the door, and left his phone charger plugged in to a socket beside the twin bed he had chosen to sleep in. Nobody made any comment about his decision. Bella asked him how he had slept each morning, as if it were completely normal for him not to have shared her bed, and Pilar began to leave neat piles of laundry on the second bed in his chosen bedroom, boxer shorts and polo shirts, and then, he noticed, his battered old espadrilles with the trodden-down backs appeared, as did the quilted gilet he wore on chilly mornings. On the third morning, he was woken by Mouse, appearing at his bedside and demanding that he read her Peppa Pig. He reached across and fumbled to switch on the bedside lamp.

'It's five twenty-five, Mousie.'

She brandished the book.

'Now,' she said sternly.

Yawning, he heaved her up under the duvet with him.

'Did Mummy send you?'

Mouse ignored him, bending over the book and stabbing at the picture with her finger.

Jake yawned.

'That's George.'

Mouse made an exasperated sound as if she knew perfectly well that Peppa Pig's little brother was called George. Jake kissed the back of her neck.

'Did Mummy send you in to wake me, I wonder?'

Mouse picked up the book and pressed it against her father's face.

'Hey, stop it! I get the message. We'll read it. We'll read Peppa Pig going to the library and Peppa Pig learning to ride a bicycle.'

Mouse took the book away and regarded her father for a moment. Then she switched her gaze to the doorway, where her mother stood in her nightie with her hair down her back.

'How sweet,' Bella said. 'Father and daughter in bed together. Can I join you?'

Mouse and Jake opened their mouths simultaneously.

'No,' they said.

———

'I talked to my mother,' Katie said.

Terry watched her. She almost never came in to his office, but for some reason, she had come in now, without an obvious reason, and was standing there in front of his desk, clearly needing to talk.

'Oh yes,' Terry said noncommittally.

'I was telling her what you said to me a couple of years ago, about how you wanted to refocus the firm to stay ahead of the cyber game, and you said to me, "You're the lawyer, you know all about litigation, but we need to shift a little, we need to become more consultative, we need to explain to our clients how to manage risk in the modern world." Do you remember that?'

'Of course I do,' Terry said. 'And I would have said that you are a prime example of someone who has added value to what you already know about the law.'

'That's exactly what I told my mother. About adding value, I mean. I said to her, suppose we have a client who needs advice on how to manage a data breach, or social media in general. Or take one of our very rich clients, who hates publicity, but whose children innocently post pictures of themselves skiing, thereby giving away their location, never mind the fact that they have the luxury of being able to go skiing in the first place. I said to her, just imagine how you would feel if you were someone who was really anxious to avoid media attention.'

Terry cleared his throat. 'Exactly,' he said. 'Couldn't have put it better myself. And your point is?'

Katie looked at him as if she were seeing him properly for the first time.

'It was my *mother*. I've never told my mother about work. I've never talked to my *mother* like that. We talked about trolling and abuse and the dopamine rush enjoyed by seeing someone humiliated. And the anonymity. We talked a lot about anonymity.'

'Good,' Terry said. 'Very good. I'm glad you talked to your mother.'

'I just needed to tell someone,' Katie went on. 'It was such a relief to talk like that. And I'll need a few days off, to go to Spain. There are some things that need sorting in Spain.'

'Of course,' Terry said. 'Any time. You choose the days and just go.'

'Thank you.' Katie didn't move.

'Good,' Terry said again. '*Good*. Thank you for telling me. Can I ask you something?'

She smiled. She looked, he thought, like someone who'd had a refreshing night's sleep.

'Of course.'

'Have you said what you've just said to me, to Nic?'

She stared at him.

'Nic?'

He leaned back again and put his spectacles on, to indicate that the interview was over.

'Just a thought,' Terry said.

Back in her office, Katie dialled Jake's number. She waited for it to go to voicemail, but instead Jake answered after four rings.

'Katie?'

He sounded as if he were outdoors.

'Jake. Where are you?'

'Where d'you think? In the office as usual.'

'No, you're not,' she replied good-humouredly.

'What d'you mean?'

'You aren't in the office, Jake. You're outside. I can tell. What's going on?'

'Dad's in the office,' Jake said crossly. 'Dad's always in the office. I'm – I'm up the mountain.'

'Why?'

'Just needed to clear my head.'

'And,' Katie said. 'Has it?'

'What?'

'Cleared your head. Being up the mountain.'

'What's it to you? Why do you care?'

'Of course I care, I'm ringing to tell you that I'm coming out.'

'What?' Jake said, genuinely startled. 'Here?'

'Of course there. I'm coming on Wednesday.'

'But that's the day after tomorrow.'

'I know. I'm coming till Sunday night.'

'OK,' Jake said with sudden energy. 'You come. You come and snoop about like everyone else and tell me exactly what I've done wrong and who I've let down, and side with Dad and Bella and—'

'I'm coming,' Katie said, cutting across him, 'to see you.'

'Me!'

'Yes. You.'

'Why?'

'To build bridges,' Katie said. 'To find a way forward. To - well, to make peace.'

Jake said bitterly, 'Don't bother.'

'Why not? Because you think you're a lost cause?'

He gave a yelp of mirthless laughter. 'Everyone else does.'

'I don't,' Katie said. 'I really don't.'

'Being fake nice to me won't make anything any better.'

'It isn't fake.'

Jake grunted. Katie pictured him kicking at the stony earth beneath the high blue Spanish sky.

'See you Wednesday,' she said. 'By suppertime. Could you get Pilar to make up a bed for me?'

She put her phone down for a moment and flexed her

fingers. Then she picked it up again and pressed the buttons that would connect her to Nic.

———

Florence was in the kitchen eating crisps when Anna rang the doorbell. Crisps were permitted at weekends only and today was Tuesday. She went reluctantly to open the door – also forbidden, after dark – swallowing hard and painfully, and found, standing outside, the unfamiliar figure of her aunt.

'Hello,' Anna said. She was wearing a mac like Katie's, but it looked altogether different. Florence's hand flew to her mouth. 'Hello, Florence.'

Florence said hello with difficulty. Because weekday crisps were forbidden, she had crammed a huge handful into her mouth, and they were not disintegrating conveniently.

'I imagine,' Anna said, walking past Florence and into the kitchen with irritating composure, 'that you are eating something you shouldn't be. Aren't you?'

'No,' Florence said untruthfully and indistinctly. 'Just a – rather big mouthful.' She tried to smile. 'Actually.'

Anna made no move to unbutton her mac.

'Is your mother home?'

Florence swallowed a final mouthful with relief.

'Not yet. Granny's here, though.'

Anna smiled. She was quite pretty, Florence thought, even if a bit too neat, like a doll or a cartoon. Nice hair, though. Very shiny.

'And where's Granny?'

'Well,' Florence said, 'she's resting with my special blanket and Marta's with her.'

'Marta?'

'Yes.'

'Marta's why I came.'

Florence remembered her manners.

'Would you like some tea or something?'

'No thank you, Florence.'

'It's such a pity,' Florence answered reproachfully, 'that you don't want to see *me*.'

'I do want to see you.'

'But not as much as you want to see Marta.'

Anna let the strap of her bag slip down her arm and then she put her bag on the table. She didn't look at Florence.

'I don't think that you have been causing the same level of anxiety as Marta has.'

'But I *could*,' Florence said. 'How do you know about Marta anyway?'

'I don't actually think it's any of your business.'

'It's family business,' Florence said stubbornly, 'and I'm family. So it is my business.'

Anna gave her a sudden smile.

'I can't fault your logic, Florence. It was your uncle Sebastian who told me.'

'I just call him Sebastian.'

'So do I.'

They regarded one another for a moment. Then Anna said, in a more conciliatory tone, 'Perhaps I could see Granny – and Marta? Perhaps you would let me go upstairs and find them?'

Florence waited a moment and then she marched to the kitchen door and held it open.

'They're in Daisy's room,' she said grandly. 'Help yourself.'

'Hello, Dad,' Katie said.

Gus didn't turn. He raised his head and stared at the wall ahead of him, but he didn't turn.

'Who is it?'

Katie stepped into the office and put her right arm around his shoulder. He felt bony and spare. She kissed his left cheek.

'It's me, Dad. I've just got here.'

He put an unsteady hand to grasp hers on his shoulder. He said, a little shakily, 'Where's your mother?'

'She's in London, Dad. With Nic and the girls. I've come for four nights.'

'Why?'

'To see how things are. To try and get a bit of a handle on things here.'

'Things are fine,' Gus said with finality.

She slid her arm from around his shoulders and perched on the edge of his desk, so that she was looking down at him.

'I don't think they are. Actually.'

Gus said nothing more. He began to shuffle through the papers on his desk as if he were looking for something. Katie watched him. After a while, she said, 'What are you looking for?'

'An invoice,' Gus said angrily. 'I know it was here.'

Katie put her hand gently on her father's wrist.

'Stop it, Dad.'

He tried to bat her hand away.

'No, no.'

'Dad,' Katie said. 'You don't need the invoice. Sebastian has all the invoices on file already. He's got all the business details, sales and wages and everything. He's had them for months.'

'Not months!' Gus shouted.

'Well, a month anyhow.'

Gus glared at her. 'No, he hasn't. He hasn't got everything.' He banged the cluttered desk with his fist. '*I've* got all the details here.'

Katie folded her arms. 'I thought you wanted Sebastian to run the business.'

Gus went on rummaging.

'I do. *With* me.'

She looked up at the ceiling as if a thought had just struck her.

'Dad, suppose . . .'

'Suppose what?'

'Suppose Sebastian did the nuts and bolts of the business, and you did the wine.'

Gus paused.

'What do you mean, do the wine?' he asked suspiciously.

Katie looked down at him again.

'Well,' she said, as casually as she could, 'suppose you do what only you can do and supervise the blending and tasting and quality control. And Sebastian does the books. The figures and things. Paying José Manuel and the workers. Pilar and Carmen. While you ensure that the product, the wine from Beacham's Bodega, is as good as it's always been.'

Gus said nothing. Katie waited, not moving. Then he raised his eyes to the certificate framed in corks on the wall.

'Or better,' he said.

Katie waited. Then she said, as nonchalantly as she could, 'OK then. Or better.'

'This is the first year we haven't won a medal,' Gus said bitterly.

'That won't do, will it?'

'It'll be the *only* year, too, if I have anything to do with it.'

'That's more like it, Dad!'

He looked at her sideways.

'What is?'

'Fighting talk like that.'

He glanced away again.

'I miss your mother. I miss fighting with your mother.'

She gave a wry smile. 'I don't think *she* misses the fighting, though.'

He said, almost in a whisper, 'It's all I know how to do.'

'You'll have to learn some new tricks then, won't you, for when she comes back.' She stood up.

He looked up at her, almost pitifully. '*Is* she coming back?'

Katie resisted the impulse to put a hand on his shoulder again. 'Oh yes,' she said, 'she'll be back.'

'When?'

'I don't know. Soon.'

He was still looking up at her.

'Where are you going?'

She smiled again and moved towards the door. 'To see Jake.'

———

'Can I talk to you?' Nic asked.

Marta was at her desk in her bedroom.

She slid her phone under a Spanish grammar book, and swivelled on her chair.

''Course,' she said politely. 'What about?'

Nic lowered himself awkwardly onto a beanbag. 'Granny.'

Marta was suddenly alert.

'Granny!'

'Yes,' he said, 'Granny. What aren't I doing right with this thing?'

'I think you're too big for it. Isn't it comfortable?'

'Far from. Look away while I get up. If I can get up.'

Marta stared obligingly at the window. It was black outside already, black with an orange glow from London street lighting.

'Right,' Nic said, 'I'm OK now. On your bed, if that's all right.'

Marta inclined her head.

'She's not going, is she?' she said, with sudden desperation.

'Who?' Nic said. 'Granny? Well, she'll have to go back sometime, but that's what I wanted to talk to you about.'

Marta cried out, 'She can't go!'

'No, I know she can't. I know you don't want her to. None of you do. That's why I came up with my plan.'

'What plan?'

'I haven't told anyone about my plan yet. Not Mum, not Daisy, not Florence. I wanted to ask what you thought of it first. What if we convert the garage for Granny?'

Marta looked startled.

'The garage!'

'It isn't used for anything except storage, after all. And as it's next to the house, perhaps we could make it into a little flat for Granny. Maybe we could even build a room above while we're at it, so we'd have another bedroom and bathroom.'

Marta leaned forward. Her eyes were shining.

'Oh *yes*. Then she could live with us all the time.'

'Well, when she wasn't in Spain, she could. She could live partly there, partly here. So you like the idea?'

Marta nodded vigorously. Then, as if she'd suddenly remembered something, she stopped and swivelled away from her father so that all he could see was her hair swinging forward and almost obscuring her face.

'Marta,' Nic said. 'What is it?'

She muttered something.

'What?' he said. 'What? I couldn't hear you.'

Marta didn't move.

'Why did you ask me?' she said, more loudly, from behind her hair.

'For all sorts of reasons. But chiefly because you have a special relationship with Granny.' Nic's voice grew warmer. 'Yes, that's it. That's it, Marta. You are *special*.'

There was a pause and then Marta said, clearly, 'I don't want to be.'

'What d'you mean?' Nic asked in genuine astonishment. 'What d'you mean, you don't want to be special. Of *course* you're special!'

Marta didn't look at him. Instead, she raised her head a little and stared at the wall behind her desk. She said furiously, 'Don't you see? Don't you get it? I don't want to be special, I don't want to be different, I want you to treat me just like you treat Daisy and Florence. Don't you understand?' She raised a hand and flipped back a curtain of hair so that he could see her profile. Then she said, as if she were delivering a coup de grâce, 'At least *Granny* does.'

—

It took some time to find Jake. Katie was determined not to ask anyone where he was, so found herself touring the whole vineyard in search of him, practising her creaking Spanish with the workmen, and with José Manuel, and the girls in the shop (it looked denuded, she thought, and as if no one had an energetic and coherent plan for it any more) until she finally found her brother making an unnecessary log pile out of a casual stack of sawn-up fallen timber. He was working with the focused intensity of someone who knows perfectly well that what they are doing is merely a displacement activity. His gilet was off, and his shirt clung to his back with sweat. When Katie shouted his name, he took no notice at first, and then he stopped, his back still to her, and put one hand to his brow as if he was, for the moment at least, too breathless to speak.

Katie surveyed his log pile.

'Very neat,' she said. 'Very Swiss, in fact. Very unSpanish.'

'Needed doing,' Jake said, gasping a little.

'If you say so.'

Jake said nothing. He bent double suddenly as if his recent exertions had been superhuman, and when he straightened up, he said tiredly, 'Spit it out then.'

Katie perched gingerly on the log pile.

'What d'you mean?'

Jake shrugged.

'Tell me what a mess I've made of everything. Why don't you? Everyone else has.'

'I do have one question, actually.'

'Ha! Thought so!'

Katie looked straight at her brother.

'How much do you owe?'

He looked up at the trees.

'Clever,' Jake said. 'She's clever, my sister. One question, properly thought out, gets all the answers.'

'How much?' Katie pressed.

Jake grinned at her.

'Wouldn't you like to know? Wouldn't you like to know something I haven't told Bella and I haven't told Dad.'

'How much, Jake?'

He looked away.

'Not much.'

'A hundred thousand? A quarter of a million? Your flat in London?'

Jake clenched his jaw. 'That,' he said. 'But I owned it.'

'The flat?'

'And – and a bit more.'

'How much more?'

Jake shifted. 'Not – not more than a hundred and twenty. Hundred and fifty tops.'

'What you still owe?'

Jake nodded.

'Let me get this straight. You've lost the flat in London, and you still owe something, so that amounts to, what, nine hundred thousand or—'

'Call it a million,' Jake said angrily. 'Why don't you?'

'Because I'm here to try and find a way through,' Katie said calmly. 'That's all. I'm not after blaming anyone, Jake. I'm here to try and sort stuff out.'

'You and Sebastian—'

'Are on your *side*, Jake.'

'Huh.'

'We are. Whether you like it or not.'

'I *don't* like.'

Katie stood up and looked down the mountainside, away from Jake.

'Suppose we could find a way through and a real use for your gifts.'

He laughed sarcastically.

'What gifts?'

She glanced at him.

'You have a lot of gifts. Your way with people, your fluent Spanish, and actually, your devotion to your daughter.'

'She means the world to me.'

'I know. I know she does. Jake, don't you want to be the kind of father who is admired and respected for all the right reasons?'

He kicked a stone.

'S'pose so.'

Katie waited a moment. Then she said, in a more tentative tone, 'Shall we start again, from there, then?'

———

Bella turned from sorting out her wardrobe. She said, very sweetly, to Katie, 'Oh, you aren't sleeping in here. I know it's where you usually sleep, but it's one of our bedrooms now and Pilar has made up your mother's bed for you.'

Katie installed herself on Bella's bed and leaned back on her arms.

'I know.'

Bella was a little flustered.

'Then why . . .'

Katie smiled at her. 'I wanted to talk to you.'

'Me?'

303

'Yes, you,' Katie replied, sitting up a little.

Bella took several dresses on their hangers out of the wardrobe and held them protectively against her.

'Goodness me,' Bella said to the dresses. 'What on earth could I have done now?'

'Nothing,' Katie said.

'Nothing? Well that's a relief.'

Katie sat up straight and folded her hands in her lap.

'Bella,' she said. 'Could you help me?'

Bella held the hangers in one hand and smoothed down the dresses with the other.

'You're all the same, you Beachams. It's what you always say when you have dug yourselves into a hole and need a helping hand to get out of it. Please can you help, please can you do this, please can you do that, and all the while you, the helper, are being stitched up and taken advantage of until you're left without a leg to stand on. So the answer is no, Katie. No. I won't help you. I'm done with the Beachams, I'm done.'

'Of course,' Katie said.

'What do you mean? Didn't you *hear* me? Didn't you hear what I just said?'

Katie looked straight at her.

'Oh yes.'

'Well, how can you say "of course" when—'

'Bella,' Katie said patiently. 'Could I just put an idea to you and then you can shoot it down if you don't like it?'

'OK. I suppose.'

'I was in the shop today, and it looks sad. Really sad. Neglected and run-down. It would break Mum's heart to see it like that.'

Bella replaced the dresses on their rail in the wardrobe. She spoke with her back to Katie.

'I wouldn't know. I haven't been in. I used to run a shop, you know. In Notting Hill. I was running the shop when I met Jake. He came in one day and then lots of days after that.'

'I know you ran a shop. It was a delicatessen, wasn't it?'

Bella stepped away from the wardrobe. She said, almost proudly, 'Italian. Italian foods. I speak restaurant Italian, you know.'

'Did you own the shop?' Katie asked, almost carelessly.

Bella laughed.

'Heavens, no. I managed it. The owner was an Italian who lived in Turin or somewhere.'

'Bella?'

'Yes?'

'How would you feel about running a Spanish food shop? How would you feel about doing what you did in Notting Hill here, in Spain?'

CHAPTER NINETEEN

Jake stood outside the little house on its steep village street. The street itself was still too precipitous for cars, as it had been when his parents first bought the place as somewhere that would shelter them as they embarked on this great experimental adventure of making a life and a living in Spain. In 1993, Gus always said, as if he had somehow pulled a fast one over an innocent, he had paid only a handful of pesetas for an admittedly unrestored house in one of Spain's famous pueblos blancos. It was the arrival of the expats that had changed it, smartened it and cleaned it up; people like Gus and Monica who had wanted bathrooms, and gardens, and running water. The house that Jake was standing outside boasted its pretty Moorish canopied window on the ground floor, in 1993, but little else to recommend it. It was Monica who had insisted on installing a kitchen and a bathroom, and Monica who had created a patio garden at the back, out of the ramshackle space that had previously housed a goat and a pig and an earth closet.

It was unsurprising, therefore, that his parents had never sold the house. They must have had, understandably, a profound sentimental attachment to it, and as the vineyard prospered, the value of the little house, however much it rose with the modernization of the village, became less important. So Gus and Monica let it. They let it throughout Jake's childhood, all his growing up, latterly on a long lease to an elderly Danish hippy, who filled the house with the scent of joss sticks and furnished it from the bazaars of India, but who had at last given in to her increasing infirmities and gone back to Denmark. And now – well, now Sebastian and Katie were suggesting that Jake and Bella and Mouse should live there. At least, Katie was suggesting it. She had the grace and the diplomacy to put the proposal forward as if it was only an idea, as if Jake had some choice in the matter. Sebastian, it seemed to Jake, didn't bother. Sebastian had said much less tactfully that if Jake wanted to have any part in the vineyard's future, it was the village house or nothing. Just as he had said that Jake could use his Spanish and his charm as a salesman for the wine, on, it seemed to Jake, a laughably small salary, or he could fend for himself.

Katie had found him on her last morning in Spain slamming his way round the kitchen. She had stood in the doorway, holding a dressing gown of Monica's tightly across her front, and watched him.

'Morning, Jake.'

He was banging a coffee pot down on the gas burner, his hair rumpled and his plaid robe open over the boxer shorts he had slept in.

He said furiously, 'He didn't even *come* here.'

Katie chose a kitchen chair and sat down in it, still holding the front of the dressing gown as if it were a talisman.

'What?'

'Sebastian. He just rang me. He just did it over the telephone. The *telephone*. He told me, in so many words, that I could have a sales job on practically no money, or nothing, and the village house – which is *minute* – or nothing. That was it. *It.*'

Katie picked at some encrusted jam on the table surface.

'Oh.'

Jake swung round.

'Is that all you can say? "Oh"? After all I've done, all I've given up, the way I've looked after the parents—'

Katie held a hand up. 'Whoa. Wait.'

Jake kicked irritably at a non-existent stone on the floor.

'He's got a bloody nerve.'

Katie looked at the coffee pot. 'I'd love some coffee.'

'You'll get it. When it's ready. Honestly, I could—'

'Jake.'

'What?'

Katie looked up at her brother.

'Think about it, Jake. Think about the situation. Think about the people. Mum, Dad, us three, our partners, our children. And our personalities, our commitments. We've all got to give ground somewhere, we've all got to make compromises of some kind. Except possibly Mouse, but even she will, in time, as she gets older.'

Jake hunched over the coffee pot, his hands on the rail of the cooker. He said resentfully, 'He could have told me face to face.'

Katie got up to pour herself a glass of water. She took a long draught and then she said, 'Not really, if you think about it. We've all been coming out to Spain like yo-yos ever since Dad's stroke. Haven't we? Sebastian'll probably have to come out once a month anyway, in future, but if he was going to talk to you in person, either he'd have to come here – and Anna and the boys have just been – or you'd have to go to London. That kind of conversation is what the telephone is for.'

The coffee began to percolate loudly.

'Humiliation, you mean?'

Katie put her water glass down. She folded her arms.

'Face it, Jake.'

'Face what?'

'You *did* screw up.'

Both the coffee pot and the room fell abruptly silent. Jake didn't move. Katie tried not to look at him.

'So you think I should be grateful, do you?'

Katie cleared her throat. She moved across the kitchen and unhooked two mugs from the dresser. Then she carried them to the cooker and put them down beside her brother.

'No, Jake. I don't think you should be grateful. But I do think you should accept your situation.'

Jake picked up the coffee pot. He said contemptuously, 'A sales rep!'

Katie went back to her chair.

'Not necessarily. What about we call you sales director?'

'Semantics.'

'OK then. Sales rep. Plenty of people are brilliant at selling. Be one of them. Be the best.'

Jake handed her a mug of coffee. 'You're trying to humour me.'

'Not for long,' Katie said, putting both hands round her coffee mug. 'I haven't the patience for it.'

Jake took another chair at the table and sat down. He said sourly, 'Sales rep in a two-bedroom village house.'

Katie took a swallow of coffee. 'What about me?' she asked.

'You!'

'Yes. Me. All you can think about is your own situation and your sibling rivalry with Seb. But there are three of us, Jake, three of us, and we all have complications.'

He glanced at her.

'Do you?'

'Yes,' she said. 'Of course I do.'

'But I thought—'

She held up a hand again. 'Stop there. Stop right there.'

He gave her a wry grin.

'If you say so.'

'I do.' She took a breath. 'Jake,' she said, 'there's quite a lot to tell you. OK?'

———

It had taken her some time to tell him, he thought now, and despite himself, he'd been impressed by how unemotional she'd been, how few loaded adjectives she used even when she was talking about Marta. Marta! It gave Jake a lurch of inward panic to think that Marta's predicament might one day be Mouse's, too. It was not to be thought of, it really wasn't, just the idea of it had him gasping in panic. But Katie spoke of it with astonishing steadiness. She even apologized for seeming so absent from Gus's crisis and its aftermath and at that point, Bella and Mouse had come in, which provided a welcome excuse for a change of conversation but frustrated Jake out of saying some heartfelt things that he had wanted to say. Bella said archly that she wondered what new Beacham scheme they were hatching alone together in the kitchen like this, and Katie had stated calmly that she, Bella, would be told everything as soon as plans were finalized.

Bella had looked at Jake.

'What plans, Jakey?'

'The future,' Katie said, getting up. 'The future of all of us and for all of this.' She glanced down at Mouse. 'Hello, my about-to-be-bilingual niece.'

He looked up at the house now. Newly whitewashed walls and deep turquoise paintwork. Black iron grilles and balustrades. The Danish hippy had left a large, glossy-leaved plant outside the closed lower shutters, and surely the vine Monica had planted in the patio behind the house would by now have climbed the pergola to create densely satisfactory shade in summer. He turned his head. The view was as stunning as it had ever been. Sudden tears pricked abruptly behind his eyelids. There was his debt to the family. This huge sum. Katie had been very nice about it, he supposed, but she had made it clear that she and Sebastian were expecting that the business would be repaid. Jake, Sebastian had said over the telephone, would work off his debt, month by month, year by year. He and Katie would raise a loan in England and gradually the profits from the vineyard and Jake's efforts as a salesman would pay it off. It was a perilous situation, Katie had said. She and Sebastian were taking a huge risk for the sake of their parents and – more importantly – their children. The parents would not be told initially, but eventually of course they would be made aware, and if Jake raised the smallest objection, then Gus and Monica would be correspondingly informed.

It was up to Jake, Sebastian said. Everything was. The birds of his careless and self-indulgent life had finally come home to roost. He brushed at his tears irritably. He could hear Katie's voice in his head, suggesting, lightly, that self-pity was probably behind them. He sniffed hard and cleared his throat; then, resolutely, he put the key in the door. At least Bella hadn't seen the tears. Nor, more importantly, had Mouse.

———

'Right,' Monica said, settling herself. 'What did you want to tell me?'

Sebastian smiled at her.

'Nothing,' he said.

She looked round the coffee shop, as if the answer to her question might be apparent somewhere there.

'But why . . . ?'

'I just wanted to see you,' Sebastian said.

Monica looked immediately flustered.

'Did you?'

'Yes, Mum. I wanted to say that I don't think I've been exactly an exemplary son over the years, but I mean to be rather better in future.'

'Oh,' Monica said.

Sebastian gestured at her coffee cup.

'I mean, I should know, shouldn't I, that you don't like any kind of milky coffee and always order an Americano in the mornings and an espresso after lunch and then no coffee in the afternoon in case you don't sleep at night.'

'How do you know that?'

He smiled again.

'It doesn't matter how I know. It just matters that I didn't know till now, and I should have.'

Monica took her scarf off and folded it with unnecessary precision.

'I don't like the word "should".'

'Then I won't use it again.'

She put the scarf in her bag. Then, still without looking directly at him, she said, 'You look different.'

'Do I?'

'Yes.' She darted a glance at him. 'Taller. Better altogether. I think – I think your posture has improved.'

Sebastian laughed.

'You're the mother,' he said cheerfully. 'If anyone's going to notice these things, it should be you.'

'Don't make fun of me.'

'I'm not.'

She looked about her again then said, almost unsteadily, 'I don't seem to know what to do any more.'

'About me?'

She nodded.

'But things are better with Katie, aren't they?' he asked.

She looked up instantly.

'How d'you know that, too?'

'Katie told me. And she told me how great you're being with Marta. How, if it hadn't been for you, there probably wouldn't have been any kind of breakthrough.'

Monica seized her bag and began to rummage in it for a tissue. Sebastian took a perfectly laundered handkerchief out of his trouser pocket and held it out.

'Here, Mum.'

Monica seized it.

'It was nothing,' she said, blowing her nose the while.

'No, Mum. It was not nothing. Can I just say that we have all – all – done things that in retrospect we wish we hadn't, or had at least done differently?'

Monica blotted under her eyes with Sebastian's handkerchief. She nodded again.

'Would you see Anna?'

She swallowed. 'Of course.'

'I mean,' Sebastian said, 'I know you aren't exactly each other's type, I know you aren't what either of you would choose, but it would be very helpful to me and to the boys if you could come to some kind of agreement together.'

Monica smiled tightly. 'I said yes.'

He put a hand on hers. He was grinning.

'That's all I ask. I don't expect you to love each other. Loving is what I do, both of you.'

'Is that why you wanted to see me?' Monica asked. 'To persuade me to see Anna?'

He shook his head.

'Nope. I told you. I wanted to see you, Mum.'

She looked at him sideways. 'You know, I would have preferred that Anna had asked me herself.'

'She wanted to. But I wouldn't let her. I wanted to ask you *myself.*'

'Why?'

'Because,' he said imperturbably, 'I think we have a lot of ground to make up between us. And Anna is part of that ground. As much my fault as yours or hers.'

Monica looked unconvinced.

'You'll have to give me time, you know. I have a lot to adjust to.'

'As long as you like.'

She indicated her coffee. 'It's very nice. But why do they have to give you so much in this country? Why does it have to be a *bath* of coffee?'

He laughed and took his hand away.

'It's a relief when you say Mum things like that.'

'I suppose it's the American influence, giving you a huge helping.'

'Not like Spain.'

Monica looked suddenly vulnerable.

'No,' she said quietly. 'Not like Spain.'

Sebastian put his hands in his trouser pockets.

'Do you miss it?'

Monica bent her head.

'No,' she said. 'Yes.'

'Do you miss Dad?'

She seemed frozen to the spot. 'Same,' she said eventually.

'We've thought about that.' Sebastian's voice was gentle. 'Katie and I. We've talked about it.'

Monica couldn't speak. She knew he was still sitting there, across the table from her, but she was suddenly afraid to look up and meet his eye. She heard him say, 'Mum?' several times and only when he leaned forward again and asked if she was all right could she nod and whisper that yes, she was.

Now he was trying to take her hands. She couldn't somehow let go of the handkerchief so it was all rather clumsy, but he got hold of them and held them, even though she knew hers were shaking. His hands, however, were warm and confident. And large. How could she not have known how large her own son's hands were?

'Mum,' Sebastian said. 'How would you feel about living in two places?'

———

Katie lay in the bath with her eyes obediently closed. Florence had also ringed the bath with lit candles and left the room with much elaborate tiptoeing.

'Dad said you should have a bath, didn't he, so you'd better do it properly.'

'I'll try, darling.'

'After all,' Florence said, fluffing a towel with great ceremony, 'there's him and Granny and all of us to get supper.' She looked sternly at her mother. 'I think you should come down in your bathrobe, actually.'

It was obviously an instruction. Being the youngest child had given Florence a particular appetite for it, often accompanied by a raised and warning forefinger. When she was small, Katie remembered, she had liked to line up all the stuffed animals on her bed, and hector them for hours. Daisy had slept under a huge floppy goofy-looking bear that Nic had won at a fairground, and Marta had gone to bed with a small cloth rabbit to which she was still passionately attached. Katie had shown pictures of the girls to Pilar, in Spain the weekend before, who had stopped her energetic mopping of the tiled floors long enough to lean on her mop handle and look at the photographs on Katie's phone.

'She,' Pilar said, jabbing a finger at the picture of Marta, 'looks like the señora. Wouldn't your mother have looked like that, at that age?'

Pilar had flecks of grey in her hair now. She also had deep lines running from her nose to her chin and although as energetic as ever, gave off the distinct air of there being more need to draw on sheer willpower than there used to be. Clanging back the shutters in Katie's bedroom her first morning, she said without preamble, 'When will the señora be back?'

Katie, who had hardly slept, struggled to remember where she was.

'Good morning, Pilar.'

Pilar turned from the window.

'I don't mind keeping the house going until she comes back. *If* she comes back. But there is no point doing it for anyone else.'

Katie sat up slowly.

'Doesn't she ring you?' she asked.

'No.'

'I think she does,' Katie said with more force. 'I think she rings you every week.'

Pilar glared at her.

'She needs to *live* here again.'

'I'll tell her.'

'You do that. You tell her. You tell her the palm tree has died.'

'But it hasn't.'

Pilar was half out of the door. 'Your mother,' she said with vehemence. 'Your mother. She cares more about plants than she does about human beings.'

She slammed the door behind her with extraordinary force and Katie waited to hear sounds of the household stirring in consequence. But there was nothing. It was eerie, like being in a bewitched castle in a fairy tale. Katie reached for her phone and texted Daisy.

'Tell Granny that Pilar sends her love.' Then she added, 'Pilar fashion. With a lot of noise.'

It was only a week ago, she thought now in her scented bath, that I was in Spain, trying to sort Dad and Jake and Bella and realizing all the while that not only have the levers of power shifted, but that the future is at best unpredictable. Any new arrangements could be overturned by events without a second's warning.

She opened her eyes. Florence had left a new bar of soap in a china dish by the bath. It was a china dish that Monica had given Katie years before which she had never used but had, interestingly, never discarded either. She picked up the soap.

'Granny chose it,' Florence had said importantly. 'She bought it for you.'

Katie sniffed the soap. It was scented too, headily redolent of Katie's childhood, of Monica's dressing table, of the cut-glass bowl of face powder that had belonged to Monica's mother. Florence seemed hardly to have noticed her absence last weekend, and now Daisy was home – even Daisy – and putting music on and wanting to be part of the complicated business of making food for supper that they could all eat.

She sat up, soaping her arms. She suddenly felt an urgent need to be downstairs with them all, to be handed a glass of wine by Nic and raise it briefly towards her mother, to be part of the chaos and unity of a Friday night in her own kitchen. She glanced over at the hooks on the wall. Her bathrobe hung there, beside Nic's. She wouldn't put it on, she decided, she would wear his instead. That would convey to him, silently, all he needed to know.

———

'I like it,' Bella said.

Jake grunted. He leaned against the door-jamb leading out into the patio garden. The Danish hippy had made an outdoor table top by pressing shards of coloured glass into wet cement, now illuminated by a harsh overhead bulb adorned with a few withered vine leaves.

'I do,' Bella said. 'It's a sweet little house.'

'With the emphasis on the little.'

'Oh,' Bella said, 'I don't know. It's not *so* little. There's a bedroom for us and a bedroom for Mousie and we can walk to school. I like being in a village.'

Jake sighed. Bella went on, brightly, 'Mousie likes it anyway. Don't you, Mousie? All those nooks and crannies to explore. And no—' She stopped.

'What?'

'No grumpy old Grandpa.'

He glanced at Mouse. She was sitting on the kitchen floor, concentrating on fitting a plastic lemon squeezer together.

'So you'll run the shop?' he said to Bella.

'Of course!'

'I thought you didn't want to.'

'Well, Jakey, you thought wrong. As you do about lots of things.'

He looked at her. She wore a fluffy pale blue sweater that made his eyes itch just to look at, and her hair was tied back in a ponytail with a matching pale blue ribbon.

'Bella, I thought you hated Spain. I thought you wanted nothing to do with anything Spanish.'

She looked round the tiny sitting room.

'Is that an old bread oven?'

'Probably.'

'It's lovely, here. Charming. We can really make it our own.'

'So,' he said, his voice a mixture of bewilderment and relief, 'you like it? You really do?'

She nodded, bouncing her curls.

'I love it. We both do. Don't we, Mousie?'

Mouse flung the lemon squeezer across the kitchen floor. On her hands and knees, she began to make rapidly for the staircase.

'Look at that! Already!'

Jake said unhappily, 'We won't have much money.'

Bella followed Mouse to the staircase. 'Up you go! Careful now. We've never had any money.'

'Thank you.'

She turned from the bottom step of the stairs, her hand on the white plastered wall.

'I'm going to make a go of the shop.'

He looked at her. 'I'm sure you are.'

'I mean a real go. I'm going to make that shop into something very special.' She climbed the stairs. 'Not too far and fast, Mousie!' Then she glanced back at Jake. 'And I'll expect no less from you.'

'What does that mean?'

Bella laughed.

'What it's always meant, Jakey.'

He moved away from the doorframe.

'Bella, are you threatening me?'

She was still climbing upwards after Mouse.

'Certainly not,' she said lightly. 'But I would like to see you looking at the future as a challenge.'

'A challenge? What sort of challenge?'

She looked down at him for a moment. She was smiling. He had forgotten how pretty she was when she smiled.

'To start with,' Bella said, 'just to start with, you could prove them all wrong. Couldn't you?'

CHAPTER TWENTY

It was too cold now for Monica to take her early-morning tea out onto the terrace: too cold and too dark. It was also often windy, and the wind rattled the leaves of the palm tree in a spooky and unnatural fashion. In fact, Monica thought, southern Spain really wasn't designed for any weather except the heat of the summer sun. After all, the locals insisted on tiled floors and curtainless windows, both perfect for life in the blazing sun, but pretty hopeless from November to March. Not just hopeless either, but forlorn. As forlorn as the house had looked when she'd got back to it, despite Pilar's best efforts. It looked neglected and dejected, in a way that was hard to define but definitely there.

'I am going to start today,' Monica said to Pilar on her first morning back, 'by going into every room in the house and reminding it that it is *mine*.'

Pilar had put an artificial flower – an improbably blue daisy – into her coiled black hair. She didn't smile, nor change out of the flowered overall that Monica suspected she slept in, but she had replaced the strings of beads hanging on the dressing-table mirror, and put a small fat cactus, like a green thumb, beside the bed. Pilar said that her father had grown the cactus from seed, using his own special mixture of peat and perlite.

'It's very nice.'

'I don't think you like cacti,' Pilar said. 'But he grew it for you.'

'I really appreciate that.'

'And I have moved Mr Gus.'

Monica made a face at her. 'You never have!'

'I said to him, you never look at the view, you never look out of the window, so it is a great waste that you are in this bedroom.'

'And?'

Pilar smiled, showing her gold tooth, of which she was very proud.

'He is sleeping in the boys' bedroom. In the back. He likes that the boys slept there.'

Gus had not come down with the taxi from the village to meet her at the airport. She hadn't expected that he would, but all the same she was disappointed. Not just that he hadn't come but that he was clearly unchanged in his stubborn habits. She had expected that she would find him in the office, but he was sitting in the kitchen instead, reading the paper with his spectacles on. The spectacles needed cleaning. They always needed cleaning. He'd looked at her for a long moment, then he said, 'You're back.'

'Yes,' Monica said. 'For now. Till the flat's done.' She held a hand out. 'Your glasses are filthy.'

He leaned forward so that she could take them off his face. 'Are you going to live in London with Katie?'

Monica blew on one lens.

'I shall go back and forth. Time there, time here.'

'Phew,' Gus said.

Monica polished the lens with the hem of her sweater. Not looking at him, she asked, 'Did you miss me?'

Gus glanced away.

'Sort of.'

'You mean yes.'

'Yes.'

'To be honest,' Monica was now blowing on the other lens, 'I think I missed living here more than I missed you.' She looked around her. 'This room needs my attention. Whoever thought of putting the coffee pots there? And where are my copper pans?'

'Jake's gone to live in the village,' Gus said. 'With his wife and the baby. Nice baby.'

'I know. I'm pleased to think of a family living in that house again.'

'So it's just me,' Gus said. 'Just me, rattling about here on my own.'

Monica held his spectacles out to him.

'Katie and the girls and Nic'll be here for Christmas. And then Sebastian next year, regularly. And I expect the boys too, now and then. Maybe even Anna.'

Gus put his spectacles back on. 'You look well,' he said.

'I am,' Monica said. 'I have a life. I have purpose.'

'So do I,' Gus said.

She got up to open cupboard doors. 'Don't be childish.'

'I'm better,' Gus said.

'Ah, there's one copper saucepan. Honestly. Why is it there? Tell you what . . .'

'What?'

Monica straightened up, holding the saucepan.

'You might think you're better, but I'm getting at least one of those therapists back again.'

'No.'

She glared at him.

'*Yes.*'

He picked up the paper again.

'One therapist only, then,' he finally said. 'That girl with the pigtail. As long as I can have the dogs back.'

She went over to the glass doors to the terrace. 'My palm tree made it!'

He grunted.

Monica looked out at the terrace. 'It needs sweeping. All those dead leaves.'

Gus said from behind his paper, 'It's going to be a good vintage.'

'Is it?'

'Yes,' he said. 'One of the best.'

He was very familiar, sitting there in his old fisherman's jersey with his spectacles on and his feet, socked for winter, thrust into faded old espadrilles. And familiar was good in this case, she decided, good because it was positive. She went across the kitchen to hang the copper pan on the wall where it belonged.

'Well done,' she said to him. 'I'm proud of you.'